Montag Press 978-1-940233-04-8
Cover art © 2014 Charlie Franco
Cover design © 2014 Charlie Franco

Montag Press Team:
Project Editor – Janet Towle
Layout Designer – Badger McInnes
eBook Design - Camilet Cooray
Promotion Design & Layout - David Ball
Managing Director – Charlie Franco

A Montag Press Book
www.montagpress.com
Montag Press
536 E. 8th Street
Davis CA, 95616 USA

NICHOLAS MORINE

MONTAG

To all you poor bastards out there, living in fear.

1. THE WRECKAGE

The building nearly shook with the machine gun fire of bass drums, pounding out a death metal blast beat. Great, frenetic waves of bass vibration pulsed throughout the nightclub, driving into the teeming crowd – their fists raised up, pumping, breaking the acrid, smoky air.

The Wreckage was one of the smallest bars in one of the poorest cities of the Middle Eastern Union. The territory stretched wide across Old Europe and the African Continent, crawling over the corpse of the Russian Federation until crashing like a frozen wave against a depleted and lethal no-man's land that was the Far East, and the equally inhospitable south-facing Asian border.

Food riots were not uncommon. Climate change and pollution of all sorts pitted and scarred the Earth, weather patterns were unpredictable and entire environments and ecologies died, survived, or mutated. The law was not kind, nor particularly fair. Life was harsh, brutal, and often cut unnaturally short; especially if you didn't have *the money* – which nobody really did.

Here, though, the walls were covered with neon-coloured graffiti and prints of old punk rock and metal icons covered with cigarette burns and peeling at the corners. The antique wood pillars were covered with populist bricolage, living bulletin boards advertising shows, sexual services, drugs, personal effects – all in the vulgar language of underclass cant. The crowd was a grotesque mirage, a portrait of savage faces with predatorial eyes.

A young woman, perhaps twenty, was fiercely banging her head, long braids snapping against her knees. On the edge of the mosh-pit, a group of young punks were nodding their heads to the beat and smoking a joint. A cocaine-crazed woman with a shaved head and combat boots kicked at the stage, screaming alongside the lead vocalist. A low growl. One simple chant, growled from the core of the human body. Hate.

Khalil, bassist for Infidel, worked the thick strings of his four-stringed bass furiously, a steady stream of E notes with a few variations thrown in towards the end of the measure – the sweating, bestial crowd raising the devil's horns in cathartic release. Hassan Jarah, frontman and vocalist, tossed his long black hair, to the side and picked up a beer from on top of a nearby amplifier.

"That was *Resembling the Dead*, from our new album. Twenty dollars at the door, or ten bucks with a food bank donation. Thanks to all you motherfuckers for coming out tonight." At this, scattered cheers and an overenthusiastic and wholly drunk, "I love you, Hassan!" from somewhere within the now dispersing pit, cast in almost complete darkness now that the stage lights were the only ones left on.

"Up next is History of Violence, so enjoy your break and drink some more beers. Make sure to tip Heba, fuck knows she doesn't make enough to put up with this shit all night." A couple of laughs then the lights went dark; the band began the process of cleaning up their gig gear. Moving towards the bass amp, Khalil placed his bass in the stand and grabbed his bottle of beer.

Their drummer, Shawn, came out from behind his set and clapped Khalil hard on the shoulder, his hands hot and sweating. Shawn observed his friend; his firm jawline sporting a full beard and his long curls of hair the colour of midnight – Khalil cut an impressive figure.

Since emigrating to the MEU from South Africa, Shawn had found the large and muscular Khalil a valuable ally on what could prove to be violent and deadly streets. Since then they'd cultivated a friendship that only outlaws and fringe-folk can say they share.

"Amazing, man! We rocked! Did you see that pit? Wild!"

Shawn was the most extroverted member of Infidel, always excitable and ready to party.

"Not bad man, we were super tight. Want to help me pack up and then we can grab another beer or what?"

The drum kit belonged to the house, so Shawn had very little else to do. The promise of another round of beer was sufficient to ply his favour, and he quickly began shutting down the amps and unplugging cords like a man possessed. Music was Shawn's life – for Khalil, it was a way to pay the bills.

"Hey Shawn, how much did we make tonight – you know what the door is?"

The drummer ran a calloused hand through his close-cropped hair, brows knit together while he worked on the mixing board, adjusting it to History's preferred settings with his free hand.

"Hmm, yeah. I think we made about two hundred each. We woulda made some more money if the cops would lay off the raids in city center. Still, two hundred ain't that bad."

"Yeah, but I need this money. This is the only job I've got." Khalil was a little agitated; he'd already spent twenty dollars on a taxi here and another twenty on beer, with his rent due next week.

"I hear you Khalil. Look, if you can't cut rent, just come live with me and Heba for a coupla months. We can jam and get even better, maybe take on another band at the same time. Mainstream – make a bit more *money*, you know?"

Khalil nodded and sipped his beer, enjoying the somewhat bitter taste. He pulled a face, pursing broad, full lips. Taking a look around the club now, he saw so many free conversations in what was surely one of the last unlicensed venues left in the aging city – intimations of love and lust in the drunken shadows.

"Out for a smoke?" Shawn was finished with the equalizer and now his calloused fingers were fumbling at his pockets, searching for his lighter.

"Sure."

They proceeded offstage and along the edge of the common room toward the fire exit, propped ajar by a half-empty case of beer. Shawn took the time to shoot a glance at Heba as she leaned over the bar – wiping away the perspiration of a dozen bottles and making small talk with a man Shawn didn't recognize. That didn't bother Shawn; he wasn't the jealous type. She was his dusken, desert rose. Besides that, one can't afford to be jealous if your girlfriend is an attractive bartender in the rough part of town. He and Heba went deep and understood one another, as best he could tell. He wasn't worried.

The hinges squealed with neglect as the metal door swung backward, clanging dully against the rusted railing of the third-story emergency stairs. It was a somewhat breezy evening and a blast of cool air brushed past the two musicians as they took to the landing.

Khalil leaned back against the railing, running a hand through his long, curly black hair. A little over six feet tall, wearing a leather jacket, black denim, and a black t-shirt – he cut an impressive figure. He was imposing, though stocky and wide, old muscle still taut from lessons learned years ago. His countenance was typically grim, prone to brooding and rumination. Intense brown eyes complimented his olive complexion and thick beard.

Shawn handed Khalil a joint, then flourished his stainless steel lighter and sparked the dutiful little flame into existence. Khalil leaned in and lighted his, puffing a few times. The paper peeled back from the burning cherry, turning to ash and resembling flower petals. The petals soon broke free and fluttered downward on the wind. The taste of the flower was earthy, like soil.

"Thanks, man."

"No problem. Listen Khalil, how have you been lately? I know it's only been a week since you and Haifa broke it off..."

"It's not too bad. I don't know what to say about it, really. She didn't like my lifestyle, and she definitely didn't care for me doing *this*."

Khalil looked pointedly down at the smouldering joint he held pinched between thumb and forefinger.

Already he felt more relaxed, his mood markedly improved – a slight levity lifting him *up*.

Shawn laughed, then casually tilted the beer to his lips. He shook his head in slight disbelief.

"How did you manage to date her for almost two years then? Didn't she know about this scene the whole time? The booze, the weed, the music? It's risky and we all know it."

"Love is blind, Shawn."

"She knew. Not your fault, my man."

A brief touch of Shawn's hand on his shoulder. Khalil smiled briefly at his friend and met his eyes before looking down and taking another drag. He handed the joint back to the drummer.

The two rockers rocked back and forth idly, steam and smoke rising and unfurling from their lips. Khalil shifted and felt his leather jacket furl over the rail as he leaned against it, looking out into the street. Winter was making its initial push, the small arcs of snow bend downward, low, congealing tightly against pillars and sconces where the small mounds might gain traction against the blustering winds.

Miniature hurricanes roamed alley and street, stirred piles of light and fragile flakes upward into the gray-black sky. The snow was as irregular as the Laptev sea the town-city bordered – an outlying city in an outlying province of the MEU. The climate famous: one moment a gentle rain of tiny flakes, the next a near-whiteout.

The current conditions laid somewhere in between, the romantic sort of frozen rain; thick, ponderous flakes that melted as soon as they touched the skin.

Half a foot of snow had already built up on concrete, dotted with footsteps. Street lights flickered and died momentarily before finding renewal, casting swaying halogen circles onto the pure white snow below.

No cars took to the streets here; it was not the safest neighbourhood in the city. The law of urban sprawl had taken effect here for nearly a hundred years, an expansion outwards. There had been a wave of new, shiny, glossy subdivisions and strip malls on the outskirts, while decay and poverty were the veins shooting through the crumbling and criminal interior. A concentric circle. Peel back the layers, each revealing deeper, darker flaws of a filthy concrete mosaic.

Neon-coloured LED signs lit up behind dusty windows were about the only colour amidst battered brick and snow. It was the ripe shade of infection visible between rotting folds.

Still, as a lean looking crow and his mate hopped along, breaking the crests of still-pure snow beneath a mottled streetlight pecking for scraps of food – Khalil couldn't help but think of what life was like outside of the MEU, lands where liberty seemed to be more than fiction or fairy-tale. Shawn broke the silence, leaning over the emergency railing and looking down onto the street as Khalil was.

"Going to be a cold winter, bud."

"Don't I know it. I don't heat my place, I just toss on an extra sweater, or count on the fuckers around me to turn the heat on in their apartments."

Shawn laughed in earnest, understanding. A wry smile spread across his rough features.

"What you need is a good woman. Heba is all I need to keep me warm. Cheaper than oil, that's for damn sure."

The weed was working its peculiar magic, and Khalil couldn't help but chuckle. Even here, in the dirtiest and deadliest bar left in town – things somehow seemed brighter, the odds beatable.

From inside the club the noise of a few deep strikes of the bass drum could be heard.

Almost time to duck back inside for another drink and the rest of the show. Khalil raised his beer in brief salute to Shawn and re-entered the club, heading for the bar. The floors seemed stickier than usual tonight – probably because this was the first show in a few weeks.

Heba looked up through the fringe of hair that fell over her brow, lips pouting in a playful grin. Something about her posture was catlike, an unconscious grace. She was an attractive woman of about thirty who didn't look a day older than eighteen. She carried her medium-brown hair, tinged with streaks of sun-bleach, up in a modern twisted style, not quite an explosive topknot.

"Hey Heba, how's it goin'?"

He was feeling great now, very relaxed.

"Not bad. Tips have been above par, actually. No fights. So far, so good!"

"Awesome. Glad to hear it."

"Listen Khalil, about you and Haifa..."

Genuine concern here.

"Can you afford the rent on your own? I mean, without her?"

"Yeah, no problem. Got a new place. Cheaper, actually. We're back playing shows, right?"

He was a terrible liar, and would be lucky to make it to the end of next month before being evicted – for the third time. Heba knew better than to push it.

"Just want you to know, you can stay with us for a bit, while you look for work. If you need to."

His job prospects were certainly slim – he hadn't worked for a Corp for at least a decade and had no viable excuse. He was a heavy marijuana smoker and Corp-mandated drug tests would expose that within the first round of interviewing for any job from line cook to CEO. To be honest, he'd rather not even think about it. Khalil drank the remainder of his beer.

"Yeah, thanks Heba. We'll see how it goes. 'Nother beer, please."

The bass grew louder and the drums reached such a furious beat that all else was obliterated – a kaleidoscope of colour. Human bodies with faces upturned and fists raised high in the choking, oppressive air.

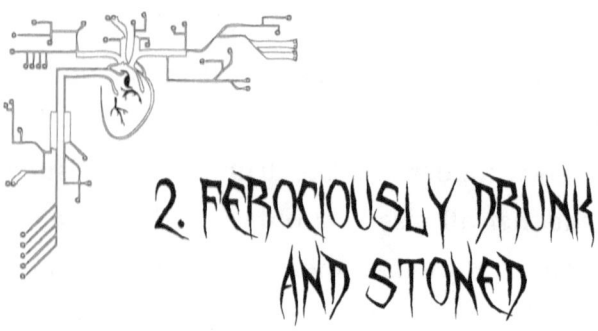

2. FEROCIOUSLY DRUNK AND STONED

It was cold as hell walking home, the snowstorm having picked up in the late hours of the night.

Unconsciously, Khalil kept his shoulders constantly shrugged, the leather jacket taut across his back. His apartment was only an hour's walk from the Wreckage, but at this hour it was best to take one's time, to avoid looking overly suspicious.

He'd left all his gear back at the bar – Infidel would also be playing tomorrow night. No need to haul hundreds of pounds of wires and ancient machinery around in a taxi until after then. In the meantime, Khalil quite enjoyed the feeling of breathing this fresh, black air.

The streetlights were ragged and only half-operable here by the waterfront and, with the right kind of eyes, it was sometimes possible to glimpse the stars. Otherwise, the sky was persistently gray, the sick ash pallor that haunts the faces of the terminally ill.

He was walking down Saturday Street when his toe stopped up short; he almost tripped and fell. He realized it was a woman wrapped in a cheap sleeping bag. As he regained his balance she began to stir restlessly, shaking a thin mantle of snow loose from her coverings.

"Sorry about that."

The woman began to stir in earnest, moaning as if struggling to wake from a nightmare. Khalil reached his hand out touch her shoulder. He'd spent many nights in the same position and did not bear the prejudices that others might regarding the homeless, especially with the liquor bolstering his sense of honour. This was the right thing to do.

She sat up, glassy eyed and disoriented.

"Who're you?"

"I gave you a kick by mistake walking along here and woke you up. Here, to apologize."

He fished in his jacket pocket until his fingers came up against warm glass. His extended arm offered a half-full bottle of homemade rum – the good stuff. All weariness faded from the woman's face; she suddenly appeared almost ten years younger than her mid-forties. Her face was angular and studious, the dull eyes of the drunken derelict were absent here. She took it from his hand and took a deep pull.

Wiping her lips clean, she said, "Thanks. You make that?"

"Naw, friend of mine."

"Cheaper and untracked. I like a smart man." A sweet smile, playful. He liked this girl.

"Khalil." He extended the same hand which had offered the flask. Her fingers were long, tapered, and lightly calloused.

"Katja."

"Sleep here often?"

"I bet you use that one on all the girls." She took another sip and handed the flask back to her good samaritan.

"Not really. You're my first." It was true; it's not like he tripped over a body every day.

She laughed and produced a battered pack of cigarettes.

"Smoke?"

"Fair trade. Sure."

He reached over and plucked a king-sized home-roll from the carton. Obvious the package was just being used as a container for illegal smokes.

"Cold night."

"Yeah." A definite tone of resistance. *Don't you dare ask me to come home with you.* An unspoken imperative. He respected that. It was nothing personal. She handed him an old-school Bic, brightly coloured yellow – easier to spot if dropped or misplaced in a haze. This girl was a real veteran.

"What's your story?" Khalil asked. "Don't fuck with me, I used to live in the hold-out on the corner of Venturi and Ascot and the bridge over the Gendpereau on nights the cops were hot. Been there." No bullshit; everyone who spurned the military service or the religious workhouses in favour of sleeping in the streets had a story to tell.

Snow began to fall again, flitting in and out of existence at the edge of the ellipse cast by the streetlight. He touched the flame of the lighter to the end of the hand-rolled smoke and sucked at it, enjoying the biting heat of of the tobacco filling his throat and lungs, pushing his mind sharply into relief. He took another long drag and felt more alert, almost conversational. She seemed to feel the same gravity between them; her eyes made a decision and she continued.

"Feel sick all the time. Dunno why. Can't shake it. Not my fault or anything; can't help it." She smiled weakly.

He felt like a reflection, but managed to maintain composure. The usual.

"Talk to anyone about it?"

They sat in silence for a few moments, the intermittent neon lights opposite casting a purple-yellow glow onto a layer of snow a dozen feet distant. A few footprints marking passage stood out in an uneven line on the far side of the road. No tire tracks.

"No, not really. Went to a few shrinks and got a few

scrips. Those things fucked me up even worse in some cases. Pot and booze now, and the booze makes me sick."

Khalil nodded, closing his eyes.

"What changed?"

"I was raised a certain way and I was told that hard work and honesty would pay off...I did everything I was told to! I did everything right!"

"You were betrayed."

Her eyes clenched shut. She wrestled with this truth. It wasn't his place to push it any further. She opened her eyes and nodded, pushing the tears back behind her wall. Khalil felt his own rush up and inward from his lungs, reacting to her. He pushed them back down firmly; he was dangerously out of practice. Empathy was weakness and betrayal. Conversational drunkenness and sloth – mental incapacitation – was encouraged on off time.

"You're not alone."

She had already regained her composure, barely-wet streaks the only evidence of a loss of self-control, soon to be forgotten, drowned under a sea of smoke and whiskey. Her eyes glazed over again and she regained her poise, straightening her back.

"I know. You're here. And you're not alone either. But how far does our fellowship really run? We're both drunk. Would you take me into your home?"

A fair question. It was obvious to him that she wasn't

asking about sex but rather about selflessness. The discomfort and unease of letting a stranger sleep under your roof. Promises were cheap. Lots of self-righteous slobs out there got off on taking the talk on the big ideas. Not many took a bum home.

"Yes, for a while. I would try to help you at least – and if things didn't work out, they didn't work out." A new admiration developing between them; her for him as a signal of hope, however small and inconsequential.

"Just don't steal my computer, or my bass. They're all I got."

She laughed at his small joke, a nervous sort of laughter that seemed more genuine for it.

"Thank you for indulging an old woman. I'm just on the run from a fella. He's good to me when he doesn't drink. These days he drinks a lot. I do have a few places to lay low, though tonight I just needed to do this. For myself, to prove I could, you know?"

He did.

"Thank you for teaching a young man a few things."

With that they parted ways, Khalil's quads protesting as he rose, stiff from his onstage antics and the onset of the freezing cold. He brushed the snow from his thighs and reached once more into his pocket, grasping what was left of his flask.

"One for the road. I play at the Wreck, and when I'm not playing, I'm *drinking* at the Wreck. If you ever need a few hours here and there in the dish pit or serving I could probably help. Need a place to stay, have that for a week or two, too. Night." He palmed the glass container into Katja's hands and walked away.

To him, a memory that tumbled almost immediately out of his mind. To her, a phantom, some alcoholic street Jesus.

He cursed himself for having given his rum away as his lonely walk went on. The soft snow pushed up over his boots and down back against his ankles, melting and chilling his feet. Idle thoughts formed in his head as he stretched out his right arm which contained a subdermal impant.

Khalil tapped at the flesh of his arm quickly and as accurately as possible after a dozen beers; he'd been fitted with a subdermal display – like everyone else in the fucking country – during his first year of Private Academy. In his case, a corporate orphanage. Entirely private sector. No regulations, no responsibility but to the private shareholders and military stakeholders. Hearts blacker than an overcast sky in the dead of night – no lights, no stars. Account bottom lines blacker still.

Khalil barked a laugh. There was a sardonic, self-pitying note buried in there that no amount of bravura could cover. It's all songs, sweat, and a camaraderie with the crowd, but the crowd can't be around all of the time, or even most of the time. He needed them, a cathartic catalyst, rising him to the highest high – an ubermensch for some brief moments in time. It helped him to forget, and forgetting was what was necessary to put one foot in front of the other, to break the soft crust of the snow, to leave a hole in your wake that would slowly be filled again.

The orphanage Khalil had called home as a young boy was owned and operated by Damocles Military Systems, an extremely wealthy and influential defense contractor. They handled most, if not all, of the dirty work that MEU Central Government wanted done. Of course, while it was technically a privately owned corporate entity, the installation was actually owned and operated by the VP Interior on the Central Executive. The subdermal tech lodged in the bassist's forearm was top-of-the-line, military grade – and that's why it cost him his entire life's savings to have a street surgeon break it, slice it, and install the mod chip.

From then on, Khalil carried a small balance, held a fake name and a false address – and he never showed up on the Grid. Ever.

His personal philosophy was one of self-sufficiency, tolerance for others so long as they did not mean him harm, and utter contempt for lies and hypocrisy. That's what made it so hard to live in the time and place that fate had thrust upon him. It wasn't self-pity so much as straight perception.

To his mind it was a grand play, and in this he agreed with Shakespeare's metaphor about the world being a stage. People, micromanaged by their flesh bosses as often as their electronic ones, were easy to predict, easier to manipulate.

Threaten a pawn with demotion to the city proper or even with a reprimand at their useless job – they'll fold, crying and cowering. Most of those types were so jacked-in to the latest episode of *Cooking Cook-Off* with Jaxon White or the latest phenom crime-thriller-reality-show-cop-propaganda *The Real Beat* that they'd completely forgotten that they have an implant.

Until they bought the wrong thing from a grey-market internet vendor or uttered the wrong phrase at the water cooler in some nondescript, monochromatic office somewhere, their lives ran on autopilot and they produced without complaint.

Humans as livestock, complete with electronic tag.

The thought sickened him.

Then Jim, or Timur, or Alla, or Lise disappears and nobody bothers to ask why or where, the elephant in the room watching for the slightest mention so that it might produce another disappearing act.

"Oh, that's strange – perhaps they took the family on vacation."

"I bet they moved out West. You know the economy is booming out there and maybe they could move up a ring in a new city with more opportunity!"

A symbiotic relationship, the invisible parasite growing fat alongside the victim. Khalil couldn't stomach that shit, saw through the illusion no matter how much liquor and smoke ran down his throat, and had to deal with the consequences.

"Sue definitely got promoted. I heard from the sales super. You know how great her numbers were!"

Khalil caught himself aping the excuses, playing out the scene in his mind's eye. He perceived the truth and once again couldn't contain his laughter. Gallows humour fit the bill – if you couldn't change the truth you could at least laugh at the absurdity that it presented, the sheer gall of the corrupt and oppressive force standing plainly in front of a room filled with cowards eager to bend and scrape for scraps.

The proof of the herd? Almost all subdermal implants were automatically fitted with a latent GPS system – unless you have clearance to opt out for "reasons of national security" or the like. This group included most officers (corporate, military, or law enforcement), and pretty much anyone making high six figures.

Oh, and anyone willing to have the subdermal hacked for the right price and the risk of arrest. You get caught with a chopped implant and you'll never see the light of day again. Common knowledge, even amongst ringdwellers.

You can run, but you can't hide. That's what they say, anyways.

And why would you? If Khalil were rich, or even employed, he would be able to afford a full-wall vidscreen and turn his critical faculty off each and every night, sublimating the torturous and unpredictable human condition beneath the perfect gloss that only reality television (now wholly half of all cultural programming being released) could provide. Khalil had to admit, he had a certain fondness for a few of the programs. You can't be "on" all of the time.

He raised his gaze from the sidewalk, taking a breather from his wrestling match with inner demons. Snowflakes were floating down lazily now, ponderously swimming upwards at times, catching the light for an instant before cutting away into the periphery, into total darkness.

Again, he lamented the loss of his rum. He could feel the painful fingers of sobriety starting to drum against his skull. The rum was decent for home-made. The Wreckage didn't serve the Corp stuff after hours – which would be illegal, highly enforceable as alcohol was a tracked commodity; every bottle taken from the server would register immediately. Some found it comforting, in fact, they left their viewscreens on at night as a "precaution against burglars." Those types of people – ringdwellers – ate, slept, and dreamed the illusion, blinded like gaping children by an edifice of projection, yet they themselves were without reflection. They did not produce, they did not imprint, they consumed and were imprinted. Khalil preferred the cold snow melting in his boots and light flakes of snow settling on his face, melting in his beard.

If you can't handle a little discomfort, you'll never be able to face death, or worse. Something his father had said to him – perhaps real, perhaps the false bravery of a father on the run. So he embraced the cold and wind-swept walks down dark streets, his only company the stars and slanted streetlights.

It was so refreshing to hear nothing but the slightest whisper of wind and the sibilant sound of snowflakes giving way beneath his boots – especially after hours of musical thunder and lightning. Not many people walked anywhere anymore – most took the filthy, grime encrusted bus here in the city or drove their family sedan throughout the rings. In a concrete world where the term "fresh air" was an oxymoron, not many people had much use for the outdoors.

Who could blame them? This place looked like *shit*.

After about an hour's walk from his encounter with Katja (he'd just managed to remember her name as he rounded the final turn towards home), Khalil was greeted by his apartment building, a dilapidated brick and mortar structure that had seen better days – craters scarring the facing of the building, particularly near the ground floor where a few bored punks and drunk vagrants often spent their evenings. A sign proclaiming **"Absolutely No Parties or Rowdy Behaviour"** in English, Russian, and Arabic hung prominently on an archway in the lobby above the tiny tin mailboxes.

Fumbling for his keys, he eventually cleared the lock and entered the lobby, shuddering slightly as the warmth from the building washed over him. Eight flights of concrete stairs greeted the musician, the eggshell paint peeling away in blotches. The dim light playing over the walls in the stairwell was reminiscent of the sword and sorcery fantasy locales in the older videogames Khalil was so fond of at Pixels, the dusty and weak bulbs flickering like torches set deep in stone-hewn sconces.

The rent for this building was unreasonably high given the questionable aesthetic design and structural soundness, but the landlord didn't ask any questions and didn't expect any dialogue other than a signed envelope passed through a mailslot in the basement come the first of each month. Human contact was expendable – the complicit patsy who ran this tenement was more than happy to collect anonymous cheques without having to see the desperate, unshaven faces of those who scrambled to collect it.

Numbers were neat and numbers were clean.

Persons and personalities on the other hand were jagged, incalculable elements that struck fear into the heart of the authoritarian – be they slumlord or military adjuncts or instructors, countless inscrutable faces that all bore the same stern, serious expression.

He felt like punching it in, every single time. A single fist smashing an inhuman face, forever.

There are places you shouldn't go, mentally – while drunk, especially. Like a ghost chained to Khalil's soul, memories rose within him.

He had been raised by a countless number of such faceless ghosts, a VISAGE attached and active on each and every Damocles employee. The VISAGE was a second skin, a fashionable cybernetic collar that projected a variety of facial features that were entirely forgettable. Persons wearing a VISAGE did not stand out in a crowd and could subsume their personal image and identities at will with the flick of a wrist or the twitch of a finger. In Khalil's experience, most personnel wearing the VISAGE never turned it off after having used it for a few years. He had been tortured by dozens of faces in his life, and none of them had been made of flesh and bone.

Perceptions left larger wounds than the truth, even though they didn't share a bed. His bed was calling him; sobriety was introducing a sour and heavy mood that was blunted only by his tiredness.

Khalil reached the door, slightly winded from the stairs and altogether unsure of what brought on this flood of thoughts. Drunk again! Stoned and soul-searching, trying to sort out the mess that was his life and starting with the very beginning. Forget about Haifa, forget about ten years spent searching for a better life and, somewhere, a hand to help pull him out of this muck.

Ten years of drugs, booze, and death metal – the only freedoms that poor fuckers like him had left, the only agency he felt he could still exercise without being dominated even further, below this dirt and filth, into the crust of this depleted Earth itself. He'd worked every day of his life after going off the grid, crap jobs for unscrupulous smut peddlers and racketeers who didn't mind hiring criminals. Dishwasher, unskilled labourer, bouncer at a dive gay bar called La Lune Violet – a resume not even a mother could love.

He could forget about the constant harassment from the small time loan sharks, the insects and vermin he shared a residence with, and the constant threat of being disenfranchised entirely. Homeless for the third time and thirty years old.

Eviction was an old threat, and had lost some of its bite, if not all of it. Once you face down a few demons, win or lose, the rest don't look as bad.

He mentally conjured an image of his mother, beautiful long brown hair and the kindest eyes. A ready smile, full of laughter.

His father's face, in comparison, from suntanned leather. Strong, resolute, and powerful – not power given by rank authority, but instead cultivated by charisma and personal integrity.

Laughter dies. Steel rusts. Those are lessons that one learns in increasing measure with the passing of years. The terrible irony is that memory – the only actual and meaningful preservation of that laughter and that steel – fades in step with the march of years. You don't get that time or those experiences back. You don't get to live them again. Memory is all you have.

Passing through the door and snatching another flask of rum from the top of a painted bookcase he took a long, hard, burning drink. His mistake.

He could never forget the faces of his parents, fuzzy and intangible, dangerously inconstant – threatening to be washed away forever by years of hard living. His own damn fault, and he wasn't stopping anytime soon.

He could never forget the crack of the whip across his legs, his back, his chest – long white lines on dark, dusky flesh; this irregular cartography stared Khalil in the face every morning. Staring back at him from a dirty mirror. Under the garish fluorescent light, flickering and humming with electricity, his scars screamed to him, never whispering.

He felt himself walking back under that covered bridge, walking to that depleted and rotting house, and smiling sickly at the ghost in the window. He unlocked the door in his mind and walked inside.

The Damocles installation was enormous; nine hundred acres of mountainous wilderness, overlooking a placid and beautiful lake fringed with the whitest snow. One hundred thousand orphans, give or take a few — all the recipients of the inherited sins of sedition and subversion. His parents were official Enemies of the State, and though Khalil and the rest were only children, they shared the taint of their parents' crimes.

He had been eight years old when his parents disappeared. He screeched with rage and fear until they took him, bound him with metal cords, and whipped him in the dark. The VISAGE appeared in front of his blurry, bloodshot eyes and tear-streaked face, coolly demanding answers to questions he didn't even understand.

This continued, as did his childish and shameful cries, for weeks; until, as they calmly insisted, Khalil Madi, eight years old, fell to silence.

3. THE POLITICS OF DUMPSTER DIVING

Khalil found the cold, sweating porcelain of the toilet bowl to be a constant friend during the early hours of the next morning, his heaving body slumped over the throne. He had been vomiting for hours, and the top of his skull felt like it was going to explode from within. Khalil envisioned a messy grey-purple pulp sprayed all over the peeling paisley wallpaper.

"I swear to fucking God I will *never* do this again," he groaned, a futile prayer to a God he didn't even believe in. Maybe that's why he always felt like shit the next day – he just needed Faith!

He'd left his television on all night in some effort to provide human company and consolation. Currently it was displaying some neatly drawn cartoon characters. A rabbit dressed up as a pirate was busy shooting his blunderbuss at some sort of gelatinous cube, the heavy lead pellets alternately carving lumps away from the jelly and puckering its surface. He preferred to avoid leaving the news channel on for too long.

Khalil laid his head down on the toilet seat and squinted his eyes shut, trying to block out the pain shooting through his head and chest. Just part of being a bad-ass. He smiled darkly to himself in the same manner that one does when opening the fridge to half-emptied condiments and day-old bread. It was the smile worn by men who can find humour in the dark as easily as in the light of day. He had to get up – just the fuckin' way it was and always would be.

After pulling on a pair of faded denim jeans, – Khalil ran a hand over the rough stubble coating his jaw. No time to shave today; he'd agreed to have coffee with Haifa and pick up a few things that he'd forgotten when moving out. Time enough for a quick shower though, just to wash the stench of alcohol and marijuana from his hair and skin. He tossed the jeans lightly on the bathroom floor and stepped into the bathtub. The water was hot and refreshing.

Haifa had told him that she couldn't handle any of it anymore – the drugs, the poverty, the music, the I-don't-give-a-fuck-what-anyone(including her)-thinks-attitude. There had been someone else. Aiden, Darren, Damien – something like that. Rich guy with abs and a silver spoon lodged so deeply down his throat it probably peeked out of his ass. Fuck him.

Khalil shook his head, trying to clear his thoughts and instead receiving a wave of pain and vertigo; his hand snapped at the shower bar reflexively to catch himself. After a few minutes spent letting the boiling water run down his aching neck and back, Khalil straightened and exited the shower, dripping.

Reusing a lime green towel from yesterday, he left the bathroom, leaving damp footprints on the carpet as he slunk back towards his mattress on the floor. Groaning slightly as he knelt back into bed, Khalil pulled the screen from its moorings and tilted it down toward him as he lay on his back. Rigged up on an hinged arm similar to lights in the dentist offices, he could manipulate the screen to any orientation he preferred. The display was so large that it filled his field of view.

The desktop sprang into existence, an array of icons and accompanying auras. With his right hand, Khalil swept the space in front of the monitor, brushing the untouched folders without auras to the mist-ensconced background. The brightest of the folders, radiating a dozen distinct colours, sprang into the foreground – projected in front of the screen in three dimensions.

Khalil had a somewhat tenuous connection to the net – he was leeching wireless access from a variety of neighbours with retail-boxed network security software. Today his connection appeared quite strong – a new tenant had moved into the ninth-floor apartment above him and had made the fatal mistake of retaining the default password on her router – *admin*. Of course, tenants moved out all the time for various reasons in a place like this, but the arrangement held in excellent standing for the time being.

Various newsfeeds sprung from the politics folder – Khalil's preferred aggregates from around the globe filling his vision with various 3D thumbnails, moving and displaying the gist of their stories in ten second montages. He gestured toward a roiling storm of black and red in the upper-right corner, and the thumbnail expanded to fill the entire screen.

A surgically enhanced (who *wasn't?*) blonde filled the screen, her bright red lips spread in an inviting smile, her eyes gazing straight into Khalil's. With a sweet and delicate voice, her smile faded as she began to report on the story.

"Tragedy has struck yet another Damocles Defense installation, seen here in State 37 of the Middle Eastern Union in the city of Hapsburg."

Here the vidscreen dissolved the image of the anchor and presented high-definition, three dimensional footage of the Damocles Defense building, ruptured in several places – the wounds belching flame and jet black smoke. The sound of the fire was amplified, stirring Khalil's headache and bringing with it a wave of dissociation and nausea.

"The domestic terrorists responsible for the attack were caught fleeing the installation and were quickly apprehended by local police forces."

The installation melted away to be replaced by a series of mugshots, the photographs visibly altered to any trained eye. The men and women, a half dozen in all, looked primitive, dull, and violent. Place this in contrast to the rather herculean labour they had just enacted. No deaths, simply destruction of military capital.

"No Damocles employees were injured, as military forces were able to evacuate the building in record time."

Another likely lie. Logically, on a typical workday, blasts of that magnitude would be sure to have killed anyone in the immediate area – brisk evacuation after the fact or no.

"The public shares of Damocles have tumbled nearly twenty percent since the attack, their vulnerability extended into the fiscal realm as investors shun this show of *weakness*."

A kernel of truth rationed out at the very end. Billions of imaginary dollars had disappeared from accounts, the largest tragedy this world could conceive. Bigger than death, rape, and torture. Hell, those things all produced money. That's why they were always in fashion.

With a snort of disgust, Khalil tapped the screen near the bottom-right corner and the image slid back into nothingness.

The air was cool and crisp as it met his face. The sky above was blue without a cloud in sight. Snow still clung to the ground, with only a few lonely patches of greyish-yellow grass poking through. There were several pigeons fighting over some dried up bit of food in the center court, warbling at each other. From the moment he exited the threshold of his apartment building, he became intensely aware of the CCTV cameras suspended on swivels on every telephone pole and nearly every roof. No wonder he didn't like being outside.

If you aren't doing anything wrong, you have nothing to be afraid of, right? The oldest canard in the censor's repertoire.

How often did they turn the cameras on themselves? A question unspeakable and perilous.

The walk to The Spartan was a fairly short one, down one long length of Hurpool street and onto Oxford – about fifteen to twenty minutes walk from the central-city tenement in which Khalil lived. The breeze seemed to lift his spirits somewhat, and the circulation of blood from the walk started to ease the pounding inside of his skull to a tolerable level.

Hurpool Street, sloping gently downward towards the harbour – this was, after all, still a port city – was in decent enough repair, coated in that new light beige cement mixture that had all but replaced the dull grey concrete of his childhood. Figures waiting for the bus took no notice of Khalil as he passed, though he was watching them. He felt you could learn a lot by watching them go about their day; people-watching was one of his favourite activities – he almost felt as if he knew someone just by observing them for a handful of moments. His doctors had called it a disorder. He knew better. He was fucked up but not for those reasons.

There was a small black child, her hair done up in cute pigtails, wearing a bright purple windbreaker. Her face was filled with joy as she dug at some unidentifiable thing in between the cracks within the bus shelter. She would be kind, energetic, and forthright. There was a stone-jawed businessman, his hair just-so, wearing a cheap tie from the nearby big-box store knotted deeply, contorted as artfully as if it were the finest silk from Saville Row. A polyester imitation that best suited his personality, tonelessly repeating corporate talking points to some complicit inferior. All flash, all style. No substance, no heart, no grit, no balls. Khalil smiled widely at him as he walked by, separated by the glass of the shelter.

As he approached the corner where the small cafe was located, Khalil saw a bright flourish of colour disappear around the mustard-yellow corner of the building. Growing nearer, he could hear muffle muttering. Khalil had an idea of who it might be, and turning the corner to look down the squat alley confirmed it.

"Festif! What the hell are you doing back here?" Khalil

said to the bundle of rags and stitches digging through a battered, forest-green dumpster.

"Lookin' for breakfast, what the fuck does it look like?" spat the old man, apparently just as owly as Khalil.

"Sorry, man. Look, did Haifa get here yet? I'm a little late; I was supposed to meet her here ten minutes ago."

Festif's eyes seemed to wax over slightly as he crouched low on his haunches, cradling a half-eaten bagel in a dir. He snaked his head to the left, thinking briefly.

"No, no, no. Can't say that I have to be honest. If I see her back here, I'll send her out your way, though, okay?" He paused. "Look, you have anything on you?"

Khalil smiled and shook his head. The old bastard never forgot to ask! Reaching inside his leather jacket, Khalil produced his stainless steel cigarette case and handed Festif a joint.

"Now you save that for later, okay? I don't have much left and I'm dead broke."

Festif nodded, not paying much attention, already putting flame to paper. Khalil would likely have joined him, but there were things to do first. Pinching the bridge of his nose and squinting against the still-strong headache, Khalil waved goodbye. Festif had already oc-cupied himself with one of the hard laminated pieces of paper sewn into his cloak – puffing on the joint intermit-tently in between reading quietly to himself, grumbling something barely audible.

Khalil had known Festif now for several years, four or five to be exact, having met him at a midnight poetry reading and art exhibition at The Duke. Despite his extremely eccentric dress code and apparent nervous tics – Festif frequently spoke to himself in the form of remembered prose and poetry – he was surrounded by other patrons who apparently were friends, or at least good acquaintances. Khalil had walked over to the table, beer in hand, and introduced himself.

The rest was history, personal and political.

Festif was a street philosopher; at least that's what he called himself. He claimed to hold a Ph.D in political philosophy and a Master's degree in literature from Delhi, but he also said that the best food was often found in dumpsters or garbage bags and that success was merely a state of mind.

He was rumoured to have a fortune, but had been living on the streets or on the couches of bohemian individuals for over two decades – since the Collapse, a global economic depression that saw the subsistence farmers and workers of the industrializing third-world refuse to continue working for exploitative wages. He had refused to work for a corporation from those days forward – and Corps were the only legal means of employ.

Festif and Khalil shared precisely this sort of kinship – a shared understanding of the malaise, the leeches on

the corpus of their culture. They were both anti-capital-
ists. They could smell the fear in the air, no matter how
much salt water brine rolled in from the harbour. They
both knew the truth of what had happened over the past
few decades.

Capitalism had staggered under such a fierce sucker
punch, so righteous and self-assured was He. The corps
didn't know what the fuck to do – how do you make a
materially impoverished and yet culturally thirsty people
in Africa work for pennies an hour? It was no longer suitably profitable to operate domestically; the stone could
give no more blood.

Threats of violence would gain no traction. The
people of the third world stared death in the face on a
very real and material basis. Where death was the rule
in countries, provinces, and villages on the bottom rung
of the global-capitalist ladder – it was the unpleasant exception in North America, and the prosperous portions
of the the MEU – Africa was still struggling with civil
war, starvation and pestilence. Great swathes of the irregular Southeastern-Pacific border with the Asian syn-
dicates were poverty-ridden with scant resources..

Surgeons, scientists, pharmacists worked especially
hard to keep the human spark going well beyond natural
obsolescence, much to the delight of the pharmaceutical, food, beverage, tourism, and marketing industries.
Live longer, consume more, demand everything.

If you don't make the cut...

People dying at ten, twelve, twenty, and thirty in the worst parts of the African continent could not be cowed by threats of violence any more – they had tasted a better world through technological apparitions, broadcast pictures of a world where sickness did not always result in years of poverty and a lingering death, words of a world where people spent the majority of their time in leisurely pursuit of hobbies, games, and culture – songs of a world where your life meant something more than hunger pangs, creeping disease, dust, dirt, and death.

These African rebels – men, women, children – and those who tread similar footsteps in poorer quarters of Khalil's own province – may have held the Western ideal much larger-than-life in contrast to the reality. They were willing to die for the chance at something better. They were even more desperate than he was. He was metaphysically hungry, a life underground. They were starving to death in plain view.

Festif understood that, too, Khalil felt. Festif was a revolutionary. His kind continued to eat what scraps were left over from the table of commerce instead of contracting with them. Africa had burned, seethed, and died. The Collapse was now remembered as simply another recession, a financial hiccup where what had been red was coerced once more into black in very civilized manner.

It's very easy to mobilize the passion of man and inflame his heart with revolutionary furor when he sees his wife beaten down by clubs or his daughter broken and maimed by a bombshell. It is much less easy to maintain a peasant's siege against the hand that feeds. The only employers to earn any semblance of daily bread from were the very same multinational monopolies that these hungry people sought to overthrow.

Their land and local ecology was unworkable, poisoned by rampant industrial waste and cut-rate manufacturing byproducts. They could not even grow their own staple foods in lieu of the prepackaged rations they purchased at inflated rates from the corp store. Infants, children, wives, and dark-eyed husbands withered and began to die of hunger. You can't eat ideas, and you can't nurse your infant from the breast of what is just and righteous. They gave in. Of course they did.

Anyone would, who had any love for the gift of life – cheap and filthy though it may be. It was either that, or starve. These bold (boardrooms across the nation used the terms *troublesome, uppity, and ungrateful*) Africans, reaching beyond their caste and colour for figments of the West, took a pay cut below mean subsistence and went back to work.

Khalil's overstimulated consciousness began to wind down to denouement from this nihilistic crescendo; it was not in his nature to stare too long at once into the abyss.

That is how red becomes black. There is no other way. Festif would repeat these lines at least once during any given conversation, as an axiom for how the world *is, was, and always would be.* In his mind, ancient philosophers like Plato and Aristotle were joined by later thinkers like Sartre, Barthes, Rousseau, and Nietzsche in the search for Truth or Beauty. Festif shook under the weight of his knowledge, the words burning in his mind and slipping from his lips in increasingly unguarded moments.

The Truth is, life is suffering. The Beauty is, life is finite.

4. COFFEE AND CIGARETTES

Khalil walked into his favourite coffee shop with a bit of hesitation, though he relaxed somewhat when a quick scan of the place showed he'd beaten Haifa there. He was cheerily greeted by the waitress behind the counter, though Khalil didn't recognize her. She must have been new. Long, dark hair and a pair of beautiful handmade earrings dangling. Lipstick a shade too light for her medium complexion. Still, rather nice looking.

Rather than stand about looking like some type of pale, still-wincing drunkard – no problems here, half of the clientele in the cafe appeared to be nursing some form of narcotic aftershock and drowning the nasty depressants with cup after cup of stimulant. He decided to take a seat in the corner booth.

The vinyl tabletop was decidedly retro and heavily stained with unknowable dyes, which seemed to fit with the premodern theme of the Spartan as a whole. A hundred coffee rings intersected beautifully on the cheap veneer of the table; he couldn't help but take a moment to simply observe this found collaborative art. Paradoxically banal and yet undeniably intriguing, Khalil always found himself entranced by these displays. The simple thought of: someone, sometime, sat here and thought the same way he was thinking now, creating this. No matter how small or insignificant, there was a time and a purpose and a thought here, normally washed away like crumbs from the table, etched here in something slightly more permanent. He stared at the darkest ring, decisive and indelible chocolate near the center of the table.

Was this the first stain – a theft of tacky vinyl virginity? Or was this the last and most recent cup-stroke (to account for its strength of hue)? Who made you? He had to wonder.

Did they undertake your creation in keeping with the faith of this aesthetic specimen intentionally, or was Mr. Smith simply having a god-damned terrible day at work?

This human ephemera captivated Khalil; he found himself becoming increasingly concerned with the notion of transience. After all, he didn't own a house, a car, a digital phone. He didn't have a fixed address (he'd lived with Haifa for about a year, the exception to the rule), and he associated primarily with other low-rent musicians or people "between jobs" with no career to speak of. Entropy and erosion would be especially hungry for him, and they would wipe him clean, like a crumb from the table, in about as much time after he died. This nihilistic train of thought, an ultimate reduction of all things in life into the dustbin of the ineffectual, was deeply disturbing to him. It was a persistent and sometimes ceaseless vision.

All art perishes, but if you observe it, capture it – even if for a moment – then at least it *lived*. That's enough justification for his fancies, particularly in an increasingly cold and calculating world.

Khalil broke from his thought-trance to see a heavy leather purse drop down into his field of vision, landing solidly on the window-side of the opposing bench-seat. Haifa. Despite his best efforts, he could feel a fluttering in his stomach and a bit of nausea broke the surface. The coffee wasn't helping.

She was beautiful in the classical sense, a small, delicate nose and large, expressive eyes set within a dun Persian complexion, her skin smooth and her body trim and near flawless. Her hair was short, cropped off to the side stylishly in a modern business look which was the only gripe Khalil ever internalized about her appearance – his preference for longer locks hard to overcome. Not that it mattered anymore.

He searched his gut for some sort of resolute facial expression. She'd been cold – near frosty. Deaf to his pleas – *It was a mistake! We love each other!* – for the first two weeks – a shameful affair where, in moments of weakness and quite frequently of drunkenness, he'd ended up begging her to come back. He'd cried for the first time in years, telling her that he could change – and that he *would* change (he never would, but Khalil had lied before, and felt this was worth lying about). Drunken howls did little to persuade her of his positive resolve to become a career man.

She was his only way out. He admitted to a love-hate relationship with the bleak landscape of his life. That was a very painful thing to admit. He felt like a fake, his nobility a ruse, a defense mechanism for a weaker man. If he ever made it to Two, he wondered, would he stop hanging out with Shawn and Heba and Elliott for fear of drawing attention? Perhaps his refusal to work for Two had been part of her decision. If it was, it looked like his guilt was pointless – he wasn't going anywhere.

She was beautiful, and way out of his league. She was also nothing like him.

Khalil raised his face from the tabletop as she was seating herself.

"Hey," he ventured, somewhat shyly, mustering a sickly smile.

"You look like hell." A statement of fact, no note of concern for his well-being actually present. If anything, a tone of superiority – real or imagined?

"Thanks. I work hard at it." His smile firmed up a bit.

Good, Khalil had his legs beneath him now.

"How have you been doing lately?" she asked pleasantly, looking over his shoulder at the approaching waitress.

Play this one cool.

Khalil knew there was no need to tell her the truth – she already knew how things were. No point talking about his poverty, sickness, and needs to Haifa, who had successfully avoided these issues during her few short years of university, with her social clubs and sharp outfits. Even now he couldn't help but admire her form; she was wearing a pantsuit, pressed neatly and fitted closely to her firm and athletic body.

He was taking too long to respond. She looked away from him and fidgeted awkwardly.

"Not bad. Played a show last night at the Wreck, and we've got two more coming up."

The waitress finally arrived tableside and cheerily asked the couple for their orders. Haifa ordered a latte. Khalil just wanted a cup of black coffee for his head, against the protests of his loud and discontented stomach. He made sure to smile for the waitress – she was cute, after all. Haifa didn't seem to notice.

He was the jealous one, remember?

"I brought your things," she began, unzipping the huge purse. Her hand ferreted out the offending items; she removed them one by one. A rolled up white dress shirt with a wrinkled red tie. A holdover from the one formal dance that she had successfully dragged him to. After a half-hour of awkward conversation at her friends' apartment before the gala, Khalit hit the cash bar hard. There's only so much pretentious pseudo-intellectual nattering a man can stomach!

A small, battered coffee grinder. Not for grinding coffee. The kief still clung, golden, to the inside of the plastic cap. It was placed in a clear shopping bag to reduce the chance of imparting any smell to her handbag. Next to the coffee grinder, a half-empty bottle of cheap scotch. Legit, corp-produced at least. Khalil would drink that tonight.

A few books, purchased from a collection of small, back-alley secondhand bookstores – the kinds of places filled with the spicy smell of pulp.

Sagging, obsolete altars to knowledge the world no longer cared to know.

Over time, simple cultural erosion could be seen like sands of an angry desert, wearing down the spines and the faces and the very organs of monolithic classics to a handful of universally accepted digital summaries. Abridgement seemed like castration to Khalil. He needed the whole dose, the whole shot, the entire crazy and disturbing picture called The Truth. Dostoevsky, Orwell, Barthes, Nietzsche, John Steinbeck, and even William Gibson. All neatly stacked and placed within another shopping bag to stifle that smoky, organic smell that he lived for and that she despised.

Lastly, a framed love poem. Not good enough. She'd even purchased the frame for it, calling it wonderful and throwing her arms around his neck as if he were the most important thing in the world to her, pressing the warmth of herself against him.

When they had sex that night it was more than passionate, her skin against his – she pressed back against him with an animal urgency. Khalil felt his headache flare up again for some reason, and he winced.

"Too much to drink last night." Once again, not a question, just a statement of fact – she's obviously not surprised to see him in this state. The waitress returned, delicately laying down both the chai latte and the black coffee, steaming. She smiled at them both before retreating.

"Yeah. Had a gig at the Wreck and it got a little out of hand." Here, a sly smile.

She looked unimpressed.

"Why do you even bother with that, Khalil? You can get a job under the table – there are plenty of people hiring illegals in this neighbourhood. Work out back somewhere, make some real money. Maybe Damen could get you a job."

This again. Well, if it was going to be the last time they spoke, may as well make it worth his while. Now that Khalil had all of his stuff back from her, at least.

"Look Haifa, I told you then and I'll tell you again. I don't want to work at that shit. I have something to give the world. I have something to offer beyond picking up staff cigarette butts and working a dish pit for a few dollars more than what I make doing something that I love. If you want money, and you do, then go run off to loverboy Damen. I bet his shoes cost more than my Gibson."

Ah, hitting home now! Khalil experienced a flush of excitement and anger as he saw her countenance darken, her brown eyes flashing.

"Well, at least Damen knows how to treat a woman and make her feel good," Haifa replied smoothly, knowing exactly where to set the barb deep within his heart, and his ego. "He's got style, class, a career, an education in business and marketing – he's everything you hate because you couldn't cut it yourself."

Seeing a rare opportunity presenting itself – his silence – Haifa continued, an arch smile spreading across her lips as she realized the strength of her words. Weapons.

"He's playing with a few of his friends from business school at Sprites tonight – it's a benefit concert for the Third World Free Trade initiative, you know, trying to bring some actual jobs to those people in Africa. We've rented a suite at the Hilton out in Three for the weekend – just to sort of spend some time getting to know each other."

Actual jobs. Those people. Free Trade. Three myths, or religious beliefs. Depending on who you ask. Condescending in any flavour.

Not only was Damen richer, smarter, and more successful than Khalil was – he was a clownish approximation of a musician. He'd learned a few chords at college while studying business and started singing pop-rock love songs at the student pub. Damen knew less about the heart and soul of music than the average fan at one of Khalil's shows. Yet, he was making more than Khalil was – lots of ringdweller weddings and retirement parties with hundreds of loaded guests wearing their best tails. For Damen, it was a "hobby" that girls really liked – including Haifa – who he was fucking on a regular basis. It was part of Khalil's soul, essential and intractable, a wild animal companion, a witch's familiar. A painful gift. The true artist was just that, a painbearer. Damen was a classy chameleon, a pompous poseur. The two could not be further apart as men.

"I don't need to know him to know what a colossal asshole he is. Folks like him are all alike – all claps on the back and big, bright smiles hiding a shrunken, reptilian brain. Sure – I'd love to hear his band play! He's a joke, a musician only in the sense that he knows a few little riffs and doesn't understand anything about what music really *is* or what music can *mean* to people. You're just a gold-digger in the first place – so remember this – you get what, and who, you deserve."

His words dripped with hatred, his tongue envenomed. A bitter black stream flowed from the wound of his heart out from his throat.

Haifa smiled the self-assured, Cheshire grin of a woman who knows she has left her mark on a lover's heart and is moving on to greener pastures.

She got off on his social and economic impotence – he didn't have a legitimate heritage and he no longer had her damnable beauty to explore. She was cuckolding Khalil and her shining eyes reflected an intellectually orgasmic satisfaction.

He didn't even own a car, and she drove – or was driven here in Damen's luxury cruiser. He just noticed it though the large side windows of the cafe, Damen himself in the driver's seat, fixing his hair and talking to someone over wireless. The large black crawler looked like it cost a decade's salary of a worker here in the city, shaking like a tank cut from coal and chrome. Time to go, Haifa – the bull engine rumbled an imperative. An order to keep up or be left behind with the rest of the garbage.

After she had toyed with the moment, languishing in it, Haifa adopted the tone one might use with a crying or distressed child, speaking slowly and with saccharine softness.

"It's okay, Khalil. I know you don't mean it – I know this is hard for you. You are hurt, I can see it. You need to settle down and get a grip. I care about you, really, I do," – lies, she was practically licking her plum lipstick clean from her lip – "and I think you should ask around for a job around here. I know Ches up the street is looking for someone to work the fryers and sweep the place up. Saw a sign in the window when I was driving down here. You could use the money."

"Yeah, okay. Thanks for bringing my stuff back." This strained politeness was testament to the fact that he could still hold it together, at least for the crucial next-few-moments.

"Not a problem."

Now, time for her final gambit – a weepy and sympathetic I-wish-things-had-been-different attempt at appearing empathetic – appearing human.

"Please, Khalil. You're a good guy, you've just been screwed over so many times that you don't know a friend when you see one – just enemies. You don't need to live like this – you can get over it and move on. I know you can, you're stronger than that."

"Yeah. Okay." He took the hard stance, shrugging his aching shoulders and staring blankly at some invisible object a hundred yards distant. There would be no good-bye kiss, or even mention of the word Love. He would make sure of it – his patience for lies and passive-aggressive formalities was worn through.

She gave him one last, twinkling half-smile before abruptly getting up from the creaking booth and walking away, her full-length wool pea coat and long brown hair swishing elegantly as she retreated farther away – turning the corner beyond the peeling cream wallpaper – instantly gone.

Out of sight, out of mind, right? That's what they say, though typically the perpetually indefinable *they* are full of shit.

He heard the small bell suspended above the doorway tinkle and a slight ruckus, a muffled exchange of pleasantries as Festif turned the corner, the sunlight flashing off the pieces of laminated text that he had sewn into his cloak. He heard the big black beast waiting outside roar in victory, screaming away from the Spartan.

Shuffling down the vinyl floor in the slim space between the window-booths and the wall, the old man Festif was muttering to himself quickly as he clutched at different portions of his cloak, demanding answers from the mute tongues of long-dead novelists and philosophers.

"Purple is for passion, purple is for prose," he muttered to himself as he sank down heavily in the seat, still warm from Haifa's presence. A welcome substitute. The aroma of cannabis smoke still clung to him, and his eyes were red – the pupils dilated. Those same bloodshot eyes quickly spied the stack of books tied up in the shopping bag that lie on the corner of the coffee table.

"Books! Treasures!" Festif grew excited, his voice rising in a ripple, slight enthusiasm breaking even over Khalil. Khalil couldn't help but smile at this childish curiosity. Khalil slid the bag over to him and he immediately tore it apart, taking a look at the contents. Dostoevsky spilled out onto the table and Nietzsche's moustache also threatened to do so. The rest stayed put for now.

"Ah, I have this one!" Festif exclaimed, snatching up the Russian novel and clasping it to his chest,.

"What man needs is only his own independent wishing, whatever that independence may cost and wherever it may lead. And the Devil knows what this wishing–" His brow furrowed "Now how does that end? What does the tortured Russian say of the Devil and his knowledge of the human spirit? I must be sure of it. I knew once."

Festif hiked his cloak up over his knees and onto the table, the flat plastic laminate slapping and snicking. He grasped tab after tab of ancient literary passages, highlighted to suit their subject matter, and grasped a few purple tabs, one after the other, mumbling.

The other morning patrons took no notice – Festif was a local fixture, a man who in days long gone would have been called a "character." To them, these idle and happy folk who came down to The Spartan for breakfast before work at their office complex, Festif was a genial, if crazed, elderly gent. Harmless. If they only knew how much harm a man like him might cause – that is, if he ever found replacements for those burned out fuses upstairs.

"Don't worry about the quote, Festif. You can borrow that one and scan-copy the passage you need for a new patch, if your old one is worn out."

At this, the urban hermit relaxed noticeably, tucking the novella into his cloak and smiling broadly. "Thank you, Khalil. A good book is hard to find, as you well know." An inside joke, and Khalil's own smile broadened to match.

"Too true. How are you feeling?" the musician had to ask. It was pretty potent weed and non-corp, non-pharma drugs were hard enough to come by as it was.

"Wonderful. Thank you again. Not many people would be so kind to a fucked up old madman! They say I'm *batshit*, you know!"

"Now, that's just not true. *Don't bullshit me.* You get coffee and bread from this place every day, and a few sweets that have fallen out of date on the weekends. As far as your state of mind – you seem better off than me, though I'm not sure how much that says."

Festif chuckled, which turned to coughing as his lungs rattled. He had to be at least eighty by Khalil's rough estimation. He never mentioned his exact age.

"That's just because the owners around here like my

colourful cloak – and I think that new missus over at the pub, you know – the Black Dog – takes a fancy to me."

Quite likely, she was almost as ancient and had a wild sense of humour. Good for him! "Sounds good to me, Festif. Maybe you can shack up with her, you think?"

"We'll see, son. I don't like being pegged. By the way, I bumped into your girlfriend on the way it – she looked like she was in a hurry–"

"*Ex. Ex*-girlfriend. And she *was* in a hurry – off to start a shiny new life with her new toy." He was bitter. It was impossible to hide, and Festif was very perceptive – so why bother?

"Ahhhh," an exhalation of knowing-all-too-well. "Well, let her have it! Like Dostoevsky said, our individual caprice is our greatest and most distinguishing feature. You have it in spades, Khalil. You are a rare person – a person who believes in something greater than what is simply material. Haifa, well, she's just less creative in her path. You diminish yourself by hitching your fate to hers. You're better than that – you can do great things!"

He was right. Fuck the money, the car, the trophy wife, and the house with the white picket fence. That wasn't the life that Khalil had ever dreamed of – it never was, and he never wanted it. More, he found that he actually despised everyone who did yearn for it, as if this glossy, empty-eyed version of the good life was something to sell your soul for. It was a driving disdain and one that coloured his personality. Khalil wanted, demanded, and commanded honesty, strength, love, hate, and above all – to make a difference. Change the world. Nobody did that by selling their agency to a 6 x 6 cubicle and a prefab house in the vast suburbs.

Then again, nobody did that by dying drunk in a back alley of the slums, either.

He sighed. This was all too much for a hung-over metalhead in the fading light of his prime. The coffee was helping alleviate the headache, and Khalil had endured the closure of his only relationship in the past five years – the only relationship which existed outside of that barren and bombed out stream of consciousness he called normalcy.

Exhaustion came over him, again, relentlessly. His shoulders collapsed heavily.

"You're right, Fest. It just doesn't seem like I'm winning, that's all. It's like one thing after another – I can't seem to become... what I want to be. There are so many obstacles. There are so many things in my way..."

Silence. Festif scrutinized the dark-skinned young man, not saying a word, his reddened gaze seeming to strip away the flesh and look beyond. He said nothing. The silence became somewhat uncomfortable. Khalil felt like he had to say something for the second time in five minutes.

"There's a show tonight, we're playing again. I know

you're not really a metal guy, but–"

"I'd love to. The Wreck, right? They do have some *excellent* wastage as well – one time I actually pulled a full forty-ouncer out of the dumpster behind that place! Besides, a little heavy metal might just put some iron back in this old spine. Fighting spirit, you know!"

Festif licked his lips in expectation – if Khalil was inviting him than surely he would be afforded a few drinks and tokes over the course of the night. His voice was high pitched and cracking with excitement – a man half his true years. Besides, he'd come to a few of Infidel's early shows just to see what all the fuss was about – then excused himself on future occasions claiming an "everlasting earache" when the band stopped offering free shots with cover charge.

Such fears were dispelled with the promise of beer and smoke. Tonight was going to be one hell of a show.

5. PLAY AT PIXELS

The synthetic strings and digitized voices of the video game arcade filled the air at Pixels, the retrogaming barcade and smoke shop set up on the basement floor of 141 Keane Place, the same building playing home to the Wreckage as well, on the second floor. With a squat ceiling of about 9 feet and comprised of wide, creaking beams – Pixels could feel a bit claustrophobic if one wasn't used to it. Small windows were covered over by posters of games from a long gone golden age of gaming – icons like Mario and Master Chief striking vastly different heroic poses. There were also newer games, a few Icon and Supermodel EX arrays with cheap contact suits attached for emulation, but they saw little use. This bar attracted a different sort of clientele with a different sort of interests.

Bright neon – green, red, yellow, purple, and blue – criss-crossed the ceiling in seeming disarray, attached at irregular intervals to the beams above, and casting a soft glow down upon the top of the arcade cabinets and the bartop. The walls were concrete painted black, showing through in several spots to reveal a barren, lifeless grey. The bartop was a black faux-marble installation, likely formica over chipboard – it too was scratched and showing several divots worn smooth by drunken, idle fingers.

He waved to the bartender, Elliott, who was busily inspecting the bottom of a whiskey tumbler and scratching his ribs.

"Hey, Elliott."

"Yeah, Khalil?"

"Did you shut Invaders off? The scores are reset to the default."

"Naw man, that machine has been fucked up for the last week. On its last legs, I think. Last Invaders PCB in the city, so you'd better play it before it kicks off for keeps."

"*Fuck!*"

"Yeah, I hear you man. These things are ancient to begin with, and they're cheap entertainment to occupy the drunks – and Mr. Condoin don't give me a budget for acquisitions in this place if you get my drift. If it works and it's cheap, we buy it. If it fucks up and I can't fix it with this–" Elliott shifted his glasses and reached under the counter, producing a plastic bin full of wires and electronic components, shaking it for good measure, "–

it's scrap metal."

Khalil nodded and shifted his attention to the *Space Invaders* cabinet others like *Pac-Man* and *Dig Dug*, another favourite. The marquee was punctured and cracked, showing several holes around the edges. The name "Doucet" had been scribbled onto the the top right of the marquee, highly stylized. The sideart itself was virtually nonexistent, having been painted over a few times to accommodate new boards – a simple vinyl peel-n-stick alien clinging on for dear life. The monitor was fuzzy, riddled with minor tearing and ghosting, yet the joystick was deceptively tight and nimble – most of the patrons were likely too interested in the three-dimensional fighting games or rail shooters to notice this antique. The hi-score had been reset, but that was no big deal – Khalil would be recapturing that particular trophy presently.

The game began as Khalil passed his forearm under the credit scanner attached rather crudely to the side of the machine and left it there until a dozen credits had accrued. He noticed only the slightest of dips in the blue bar glowing under the skin of his forearm, his personal account dwindling but not adversely affected by playing a few rounds at a dirt cheap price. The bright green figures filled the screen, and Khalil began to move and fire.

Space Invaders was an intriguing game, a companion to all of the other arcade machines of the late twentieth century in that the sole object of the game was survival. Survive longer than the rest, take a few of the bastards down with you, and you become a hero, at least until someone pulls the plug.

Even if the player takes cover under those crude arches, trying to hide from the onslaught bearing down on them from all angles, the bunker will eventually crumble. An unceremonious death was sure to follow. One bang. One explosion. A chirping sound file signifying victory played through ancient, crackling speakers.

Khalil felt the hard plastic of the joystick mould itself into his palm and he worked the controls swiftly, sliding back and forth, popping out from cover and pounding lasers into the advancing rows of glowing white aliens. Two thousand points – the whirring red saucer entered from stage right, a long shot but worth the points. The bloops and blips seemed louder than the new wave rock and dark wave trance that Pixels piped in through amplified speakers.

Khalil felt Elliott approaching, beer in one hand and tumbler in the other. His voice came over Khalil's shoulder, friendly.

"Hey, are you going to roll the score over? I don't think I've ever seen that."

"Sure, Elliott. Most times I end up around a hundred-twelve or thirteen thousand." A joke. Honestly, this was the best score Khalil had ever achieved. The time had drawn on, unnoticed. Elliott shook his head and pushed his thick-rimmed glasses back onto the bridge of his nose.

"That's pretty goddamn impressive. Not many people around here bother with Space Invaders. Myself, I kind of have a warm spot toward it."

No wonder the game had lasted so long – this layman engineer had been replacing parts in this machine long after other, newer models had gone dead and silent.

"Thanks. Me too." All of Khalil's attention was focused on the screen now, although idle conversation actually seemed to aid his gameplay.

The score approached rollover, and both men widened their eyes slightly, as if to capture the colour rising from the phosphorous screen as a photographic moment in memory. A slate of zeroes. Elliott shook his head and then continued paying rapt attention to the monitor. Khalil smiled to himself. His rough, calloused fingertips gripped the ball of the joystick and brushed the lips of the arcade buttons. He'd been playing between eight and nine thousand for months now, high-scores dominating the coin-op cabinet. He'd been trying to roll the score over for months – and now–

"Holy shit!" the bartender was beside himself, clasping Khalil's shoulder in a tight grip, the leather furling between his fingers. "Holy shit, Khalil! We have to put this on the board!"

"Not yet." Khalil continued playing, trying to slip in and out of cover behind bunkers that grew increasingly flimsy and depleted.

The aliens pressed forward, faster than he had ever encountered before. His shots were on time and on target, but were not enough. More skill, more experience was needed. His defender exploded in a shower of pixels and lo-fi sound effects. Game over. Khalil's shoulders felt an enormous release of tension, continuing throughout his lower back as he shook it off. Elliott's smile grew wide and he released his grip on Khalil's shoulder only to clap it in excitement once again.

"You deserve one on the house outta that – I've never seen anyone roll the score over in that game, not once!" He had already turned and was making a beeline for the bar.

"Sounds good to me." Free drinks were always welcome. Who says no? Khalil quickly noted his hi-score and then walked away from the glare of the cabinet toward the bar. Elliott had already unscrewed the cap of the forty of rum and was busy pouring a half-and-half with cola, over a bed of ice.

"Thanks." Khalil took a drink, the mixture of warm rum and ice cold cola filling his throat. He suppressed a cough – a strong pour indeed.

"No problem. That was amazing!" The bartender was already perched atop a flimsy looking wooden stool, reaching high above the bar to stencil Khalil's name on the champion's list in laser-pen. Not many classic arcade game titles stood on the board, probably because they were less popular and more demanding.

"I've been trying to roll the game over for months now. Damn!" Khalil smiled to himself and tipped the glass back into his mouth. The rum was spiced and warmed his palette.

"No problem Khalil. It was a sight worth seeing." The barman smiled, his close-cropped hair clinging to his forehead as beads of sweat took hold. It was exceptionally humid down in the basement level, which didn't help the machines. The bassist took stock of the arcade machines, laid out in jagged rows. *Street Fighter II, Mortal Kombat, Knights of the Round, X-Men, Defender, Terminator 2* (complete with working submachine guns!), *The Simpsons, Donkey Kong, Congo Bongo, Zaxxon, Afterburner* – noisy and glimmering beneath the soft lattice of lights above. Of the newer, non-immersive games the most popular were represented: *Gunbarrel, Feast Upon the Dead*, and *Sick Girl* being Khalil's personal favourites. These games were simple into multigame projection stalls and ironically cost less to repair than the antiques.

They were also less popular with patrons. Khalil had to admit that he had a thing for Sick Girl. Elliott always teased him about his holographic crush, the gothic girl of his dreams.

Khalil took another sip from his drink and looked over the counter at Elliott. Behind the bartender was a mirror coated in backsplash. It consisted of dozens of individual glass panels barely held in place with dried adhesive. A few had already fallen clear, leaving bald patches. A small vidscreen perched above the refrigerator flickered, timed out for a few seconds, then began a low framerate newscast from the capital city.

A brunette with perfect features appeared on screen, the reporter's hair pulled back in a rather severe ponytail and her eyes framed by thick, black designer glasses. Behind her, flames – roiling, belching black smoke into a black sky. The news ticker displayed "Southeastern Zone, MEU" on the bottom edge of the screen.

"What began as a peaceful protest against the increased jail time for non-corporate workers erupted into a full scale riot for reasons as yet unknown. Police have told us that the protesters began throwing stones at storefronts as well as toward the police officers themselves – in response, the police opened fire upon the crowd."

The feed flashed to earlier footage showing a handful of protesters sitting down in front of an advancing police line, a quick cut to a man throwing a small stone, and then a full-scale riot involving hundreds of police officers and bystanders.

"This instigation of violence, unfortunately, is hardly new. Food riots have been on the rise since abolishment of the minimum wage two years ago, from approximately twenty per year in the whole of the MEU to over fifty in the last month alone, leading some pundit analysts to believe that more stringent safety measures are needed to keep the domestic terrorists and criminal rioters in check."

Elliott looked up from behind the bar, craning his neck around to look at the viewscreen while his hands dug through the junk bin. "No shit, we're all hungry. Domestic terrorists!" He snorted.

The footage shifted, the reporter dissolving, replaced by a still image of a broken and battered figure clothed head to toe in black – a VISAGE officer quite obviously slain. The voice of the reporter took on a harder edge.

"Initial reports indicate that ten police officers have been murdered at the hands of the rioters, including Captain Eustace R. Rankin."

A pause while the textscreen fed the anchor more lines.

"Captain Rankin, better known as the Southern Cross, was one of the most decorated officers in MEU history – holding the record for the most confirmed kills of perpetrators, most summary criminal convictions, and the highest total number of arrested subversives in the entire southern bloc. He was a dedicated family man

– " the picture faded to show Rankin kneeling to hug his children on the beach, "a dedicated follow of God–" another frame popped into view, showing a fiery and passionate Captain Rankin standing at the pulpit, dressed in his uniform with a fist turned upward at the heavens, "and a dedicated officer. His death precipitates a further ten-point tumble in security sector shares and blue-chip corrections stock, causing investors and job-creators to speculate a devaluation of general currency and a spike in inflation."

The image of Rankin at the pulpit faded once more to reveal the live feed, the camera by now focused on the flames spouting from door and windows of the local VISAGE precinct – the fierce bald eagle perched above every precinct doorway burned a sooty black by hungry flames licking it from underneath the door-frame. The propaganda produced the opposite effect it intended for him; Khalil laughed, possessed of a dark humour.

"May he rot in his fuckin' grave." Elliott said as he turned the screen off, his lip curling.

"Amen to that, brother." Khalil smiled in response and took a long drink of rum and coke. It was still cool, if not cold.

"When they abolished the minimum wage I went from living in my own apartment with my girlfriend to living right over there." The barman pointed over to a doorway partitioned off with a piece of sheer linen. "No need to ask about the girlfriend, she wasn't about to live in a back-room." The sneer returned to his face as he looked down, transfixed, at nothing in particular. "Married a cop; now she lives in the rings. Less than a month after leaving me. Haven't heard from her since."

Each town or city in the Union had a ring – similar to the suburbs before urban blight and poverty had rendered the suburbs the new low income neighbourhoods and the city proper nigh unlivable. A concentric circle of filth and decay – Khalil, Elliott, Festif, and the rest with a high E (empathy) rating – the kiss of death during any corp job interview – all taking refuge at ground zero.

Inhabitants of the ring rarely entered the city proper, the rings themselves each possessing several industrial parks and at least one strip mall comprised of the exact same stores and products to be found in each community. Even the police preferred not to stab too deeply into the heart of the inner city, for reasons outlined by the earlier newscast, though they seemed to be growing bolder as of late. Out of desperation, Khalil figured, either political or economic.

It was nearly time to go upstairs and set-up for the gig, Khalil realized, polishing off the rum and sliding it across the bartop. "Thanks, man," he said and smiled at Elliott. "Take good care of that arcade cabinet for me, alright?"

"I'll have your score beaten by the time I see you again,

anyways," the bartender replied with a wink, scooping up Khalil's glass and setting to washing it out. The alcohol was starting to warm his senses, and Khalil took his time climbing the stairs, skipping the coffee shop and heading up towards The Wreckage.

6. AMINA

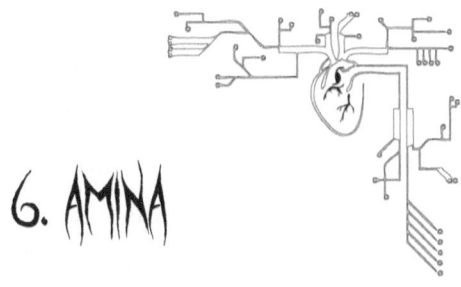

The ground floor of the small saltbox housing Pixels and the Wreckage was occupied by a 24-hour cafe, serving slightly crusty sandwiches and strong coffee for a few dollars each. While not particularly busy this evening, several patrons were seated in small groups. Khalil usually stopped in for strong coffee and small talk, but had skipped the pleasantries this evening while heading upstairs to the gig.

The bright red walls of the Wreckage were covered in posters of shows gone by, black and white copies hanging limply from wilted tape. As he crested the last stair, his eyes swept the bar, mostly empty with a few early-birds leaning against the bar or seated at the dimly lit tables on the far side of the dance floor. The television suspended above the bar cast a strong white glow.

The "gladiator" scenario of *Dark Carnival* was on again, two digitally constructed avatars slashing at each other with curved, wicked blades. Heba was hunched over the beer fridge, poking around for a customer's order, and didn't see Khalil come up the stairway.

Khalil always enjoyed stopping for a moment at the top of the stairs, sweeping his soft brown eyes across the scenery of the club, enjoying his dark paradise. The amps were stacked somewhat unevenly on the small, raised stage's fraying carpet.

A lean and studious-looking girl wearing an oversized blazer with elbow patches placed a bottle of beer on one of the amps, reclaimed her pool cue, and sidestepped around the corner of the billiard table in search of her angle. Ratty couches lined the walls on the near side of the room, sponge and spring showing through bare fabric.

A small group of middle-aged men were clustered on one of the couches near the fire escape, playing a game of small-stakes poker – the stakes being alcohol, pills, smokes, and weed. The bar smelled slightly of stale beer and inexpensive cigarillos.

He slipped around a couple having a heated exchange about musical and aesthetic taste (this gent had apparently been unwise to bring his lady love to such a *dive*) and walked over to a set of bar stools near the pool table, watching the game in progress. On the way across the dance floor, he caught Heba's eye and nodded. She'd be over with a few brews shortly – service with a smile.

The Brunswick table that the girl and her opponent were playing a close game of 8-ball on had seen better days. Felted in a strange mustard orange that looked decidedly retro, the cloth was littered with stains and gouges, long-standing testaments to drunken jump-shots.

It was free to play, however, and that made up for everything.

The bookish young lady adjusted her wireframe glasses and looked down the length of the cue at a tough cut into the side pocket, her mouth a tight line. Khalil couldn't help but notice her features, her small lips with a sheen of lip gloss, wide eyes nearly hidden behind a sweep of dirty blonde hair. She wore an intelligent and thoughtful expression. Her opponent, by contrast, was a greasy hulk of a man wearing a torn black t-shirt and a pair of oil-stained workpants along with a mean and toothy grin. He towered over her – she stood perhaps at just over five feet to his six and a half.

"Hey, honey. Don't take all night, will ya? I got other people to play too. Paying customers." The man chuckled to himself, wiping idle fingernails along his vast belly. The young woman seemed to ignore him, gently nudging the ball forward with her cue. The ball rolled lightly across the table and struck her intended target, sinking the 3 ball into the side pocket.

"Nice shot," Khalil offered from his seat on a barstool overlooking the dance floor. The girl looked up, breaking her concentration on the game, and smiled somewhat shyly at him.

"Yeah, not bad missus. Only three more to go! You're lucky I agreed to let you play for shits rather than money." The giant smirked, indicating his superior position with just one high ball left on the felt. A short fellow wearing a herringbone patterned newsboy cap snickered softly behind him.Two of a kind, Khalil thought to himself. Ignoring the barbs, the girl walked around the table, looking for an opening. The 8 ball was almost touching the cushion near the far-corner pocket, precariously close to the 6. Her cleanest shot, but with the potential of instant defeat.

"If you stay clear of hitting the six too close you can make it," Khalil offered. Heba had arrived with two bottles of Lab City Lager. She left them on the railing next to him before jogging back to the bar to deal with the influx of people showing up for the opening set.

She made the shot, though she chose her own, ignoring his advice. The white cue ball rolled ever so gently past the deadly 8 and touched the rail before kissing the 6 down into the leather pocket with a satisfying click. One left to go, then the 8. The lout started to lean forward on the table in a ridiculous show of intimidation, but was promptly ignored as the girl shuffled over to the far side of the table. Without skipping a beat, she pushed the next shot directly into the side pocket with a great leave on the 8.

"Nice going. Take your time on this one," Khalil said softly, brown eyes focused intently on what he was sure would be the last shot of the game. The small man with the cap was standing now, moving to the corner of the table to get a better view. The woman leaned forward, forming her bridge with a small and delicate hand, and gently tapped the 8-ball home. She then straightened, laid the cue on the felt, and extended a tiny hand across the corner.

Apparently, the larger man and his friend were no sportsmen. Snorting in disgust and shooting a dark look at the girl, the pair scuffled away, tossing the battered cue on the table with a clatter.

"Well, I guess I'll have to do the honours, then," Khalil said with a smile, hoisting himself from his perch on the barstool and walking over to extend his right hand, the left being occupied in bringing a beer along for the trip. The girl smiled slightly and accepted his offer, delivering a firm handshake that might have lingered.

"I'm Khalil, nice to meet you."

"Amina, nice to meet you… Khalil?" she said, looking at him somewhat quizzically as if testing the pronunciation in her mouth. It was close enough – men of Arabic descent naturally being fairly common throughout most regions of the MEU.

"Right on. Nice to see you whip that guy's ass. I've

seen him around a few times taking some easy cash from kids who don't know any better and haven't been around the Wreck for long. You should have taken his money and maybe taught him a lesson."

Amina laughed at this and seemed to appreciate the sentiment. "A good idea, but I don't really believe in playing for money. Don't have any to begin with!" More laughter, now, but more quiet and with a grim edge that seemed all too familiar to Khalil. "Sorry about the shot. Your advice was good but I liked my shot a bit better."

"Well, the beer is free. The first one at least. And the shot worked for you – I didn't see the angle on that one." Khalil handed her the fresh beer he'd brought over, having left the one he'd started back by his stool. Smooth as silk. Heba had been keeping an eye on the exchange and nipped past the railing, snatching up the bottle of lager and pressing it into his hand during her rounds with a subtle wink.

"Who says no to free beer?" Amina laughed lightly, turning around to place the fresh beer near to her own bottle. Khalil's eyes quickly roamed her body in appreciation, then returned to the table as she turned around.

"Want to play a game? Next round is on me."

"Sure, but don't worry about the drinks. I have an open tab."

Amina looked at him closely, her eyes narrowing as she leaned in slightly. "Right! I knew I'd seen you before.

You play with Infidel, right?" Khalil nodded, taking a wide stance and playing the air bass while banging his head. Amina laughed and clapped her hands in amusement.

"Not bad!" She took his air bass from him and began to play it herself, sticking her tongue out and tossing her head from side to side. The sleeves of her jacket nearly covered her hands, making the scene even more comical. Khalil couldn't help but laugh, a warm feeling that had eluded him as of late.

Amina looked down somewhat self-consciously to her sleeves, rolling them back up around her wrists. "Yeah, just bought this jacket today from the thrift. It's in pretty decent shape – and look!" She held the jacket open, revealing the lining along with a trim body and small, pert breasts. Paisley patterned chocolate brown on one side, over a field of cream silk – on the other, a stark black damask running amok over a blood red background. Quite obviously, this blazer was either designer or handmade, and several decades old. It didn't matter if it was a man's jacket, it suited her. A knee-length black skirt rounded out the ensemble, fringed in gray lace – she must live nearby or have a sub pass, walking was out of the question.

Her legs were slim and milk white, thrust downward into high-heeled boots that didn't quite seem to mesh with the rest of her outfit. Not that anyone would mind.

Khalil gave a low whistle of appreciation, casting his gaze downward at his own scuffed black leather jacket with tarnished steel zippers.

"You got mine beat, anyway."

"True. But it suits you. Very retro. You going to grab your beer and bring it on over?"

"Sure thing. One second." He quickly took two steps back to snag the beer from the runner, and then circled the table to place his beer on the amplifier beside hers. "Mine's the one that's near gone," he mentioned wryly, "just so you don't catch any germs drinking from the wrong bottle."

"In this place, everything you touch could be toxic. Part of the risk of setting foot through the doorway." More black humour. Khalil was definitely interested.

They set the rack for a game of nine-ball. Around them, the club became even busier – this was to be the last scheduled metal show for the season and as such, the crowd swelled. Elbows clad in corduroy, denim, and battered leather edged over the railing on the perimeter of the pool tables. Idle feet kicked against the rails.

The general clamour rose to a murmuring babble, a distinct bass note added to the canned music that was now thudding out from the amplifiers. A hand clapped Khalil on the shoulder, and he turned around, facing a wall of backs and shoulders and one smiling face.

"Hey, hey! What's goin' on, man?" Shawn had arrived

early, his eyes shining with the coat of a few drinks of liquor – the preshow was clearly underway.

"Not much, Shawn. Beer?" Khalil extended his second, untouched beer over the railing – it was enthusiastically snatched up, raised to parched lips and licked clean.

"Thanks! Nothing like Lab City." He shook his head in appreciation, then raised his voice above the din. "Who's your new friend?"

By this time, Amina had circled the pool table to stand near Khalil and had overheard Shawn's query. She extended her hand over the rail and the stocky drummer clasped it immediately, nearly dropping his beer in the process.

"God damn! What would cause a sweet thing like yourself to hang out with a bum like that!" Shawn nodded toward Khalil, grinning ear to ear. His favourite game – attempt to embarrass the bassist in front of any and all romantic prospects. This time, Khalil was quite certain, it wouldn't work in the least. Without skipping a beat, Amina flashed Shawn a brilliant smile, inclining her head coyly. "Nice to meet you, Shawn. I'm Amina. And if you must know, I find your friend here to be quite the charmer. It's not every day that you see a fellow double-fisting beer who speaks so softly."

At this, Shawn threw his head back and laughed. "Softly? Really?! My, my Khalil – it's a good thing you aren't our vocalist; I think you're going soft all over!"

Khalil transferred his remaining beer to his left hand and raised his right arm, curling his bicep, feeling the muscles strain taut against the leather. A half-smile crept over his face and he nodded meaningfully at Shawn. It was unlikely that he'd want to challenge the bassist to one of their many arm wrestling challenges – Shawn hadn't won, ever. That didn't stop him from trying, and Khalil had to respect his doggedness.

"Damn, never mind. Someone's been eating their spinach. You got a pillow in there?" Shawn jabbed lightly, knowing he'd have to retreat on that score. Khalil laughed and asked him to come around and join them in a game of cut-throat. Ducking under an arm and around a support port, the drummer joined them by the pool table, laying his beer down on the felt tabletop.

An hour passed quite pleasantly while the trio tried to talk over the opening set, Rain of Fire, as the band delivered some deep and resonant doom metal – the growls tearing over the crowd that had, by now, packed the Wreckage. A sea of bodies pressed together; a musky, stale, smoky scent.

Khalil hardly noticed. He couldn't keep his eyes away from her. Her thin, athletic legs leading to a tight, firm ass – half concealed by the fringe of her oversized blazer. Leaning over the table to try and reach a tough shot on the six – the swell of her breasts as her shirt pulled tight against the edge of the table. Her plump, cherry-stained lips curling upward in a sly smile as the six eased forward and clicked into the leather pocket. She most certainly caught him eying her over the course of the hour, despite his training in the art of masculine subterfuge, though she gave no notice nor inclination of offense – a tacit encouragement in his book. Amina enflamed him.

Shawn broke Khalil's reverie, walking up to him and snatching away the empty that he was clutching in his hand.

"Sorry brother, but it's time to set up. You two will have to catch up later."

"Yeah, yeah – you're right," Khalil turned to meet Amina, who was rounding the table as well, chalking the top of her cue between thumb and forefinger, "Amina, I–"

She pressed a bit close to him and looked up into his eyes, placing that same chalky finger against his mouth and smiling in the same crooked manner. There was a distinct playfulness in her eyes, and another look that he knew all too well. He could feel himself beginning to stir.

"Not now. I came to see you *play*. Don't let me down. I'll see you afterward." The smile remained in place, her bright blue eyes delivered their shining promise. He couldn't help but smile back, the alcohol by now having brought on a deeper delight than sobriety could ever offer in this circumstance. Things were starting to look up.

He felt himself being pulled away from her, Shawn's meaty hand hooked over his shoulder and spinning him around – the last thing he saw was her teasing eyes and lips. Shaking his head and placing his lager down on the railing, Khalil began to prepare himself for the performance. The crowd was pressing forward, a dull roar beginning as Rain of Fire unplugged their guitars and pedals while the members of Infidel set up their own kits.

The stage was broad and only slightly raised, perhaps two feet above dance floor. It was hardwood, deeply pitted, scarred, and stained. Three amps rested flat on the edge of the stage, while three more stood tall and proud beside either end of the drum kit, two on one side and one on the other. Wires ran nearly everywhere, corded together loosely with twine and brightly coloured rubber clasps. It was lit from above by a small array of stage lights, dull and dusty and only half-functional – time having robbed the use of many of the hued lenses which had been smashed or cracked through. In most instances, it was simply used as a strobe light of sorts – which probably explained the deterioration.

A large cloth banner was hanging behind the stage, pitch black and six-by-twelve, adorned with the INFIDEL logo – stitched acrylic stencils starting to come apart at the seams on some letters. The L was a particularly dodgy job, sagging slightly off to the right. Held on with some c-clamps over a wooden dowel, the banner had served faithfully as the stage backdrop for a few years now – enduring minor fires, thrown bottles, vomit, spilled spirits and any number of vulgar assaults.

By now Hassan had come up to join them on stage, his trademark locks bouncing enthusiastically as he climbed the stairs on the side of the platform. His Warlock guitar bounced against his hips, the wicked curvature of the body looking slick and oily black under the stage lights. He, too, was drinking a bottle of Lab City Lager which was nearly emptied.

"Hey fellas, seen Ratimir yet?" Hassan was curt and to the point – the band mates were friends, but Hassan played in a number of other outfits and treated each gig in a professional, scheduled manner. He brushed his hair over his shoulder and looked out at the crowd, which was pressing forward against the stage in anticipation. "Good crowd tonight, probably one of the biggest yet."

Hassan was right. Shawn and Khalil looked out over the crowd, packed into the Wreckage like penny matches in a matchbox, ready to ignite. The faces were primarily young, with a few older and wizened expressions mixed in, though these were the most dangerous men and women of all. Their eyes shone with a tempered, seething heat that had known years of hardship. Many of the individuals in this bar would likely never reach that golden age – that was the destiny laid at the feet of the corpsmen, soulless and fat in the outlying rings. This was not a place for servants of the establishment. If you worked for a Corp, you would have only the most marginal of reasons to visit the inner city in the first place. There was little incentive to visit the violent and ugly city centers except for the occasional call girl or weekend of slumming it. The unfortunate low-rung employees who had to commute to a city office building rather than telecommute or teleconference from the vast and concentric suburban rings took enough risks without coming to a nightclub like this – likely endangering their safety if not their lives.

Ratimir finally showed up after the three had set up their pedals, cable, and instruments; Shawn pointed him out to Hassan and Khalil. The guitarist was winding his way through the crowd.

Distinguishable by a white t-shirt and brightly coloured purple dreadlocks, Ratimir or "Rat" was a wild man to work with and undeniably one of the best shred rhythm guitarists around. He was also a fan favourite, and more than one beer was upended into his mouth by a rabid fan on his rather eccentric journey towards the stage. The front of his shirt was nearly transparent and he smelled like a brewery when he finally reached the stage, licking his lips, his eyes shining and intense. Rat loved coke and was probably feeling on top of the world. He could likely feel the strength and potential of his very *Being* flowing through his muscles and floating through his veins. Khalil knew the feeling intimately – better than an orgasm and a thousand times more deadly.

"Are you FUCKING ready!?" Rat growled at the top of his voice, whipping around to face the crowd and strangling the neck of his cherry Gibson SG. His free hand was busy plugging his guitar in and adjusting his control knobs. The crowd went into a frenzy, a chorus of voices and a wall of devil horns, clenched fists, and floating beers. Hassan strode up beside him and placed his foot on top of one of the beveled amplifiers on the outskirts of the stage, driving his voice down through the tarnished mesh of the microphone.

"This one's called Boot on Neck!"

The drums kicked in almost immediately; Shawn driving the pedals forward with such force and precision that there could be no doubt in anyone's mind – a war was beginning. A moshpit immediately exploded outward from the front rows near to the stage, a wave of kinetic power and human energy that threatened to spill throughout the entire bar. Rat was fixated on his own fretwork, his pick a flurry as he strove to keep up, chugging triplets. Khalil's fingers pulled at the strings as if he was tearing the life from the throat of an enemy, forcing the Thunderbird to groan and rumble into the floorboards.

No fuckin' money, soul in a vice

With a boot on your neck, you'll pay the price
Wasted existence, tears the words from your throat
Homeless and jobless, you'll starve and you'll choke!

Rat banged his head in a vicious circle, his thick-knotted dreads whipping through the air like some bizarre surrealist painting, a blur of colourful motion the perfect foreground for the surging energy of the crowd. The music, the screams, the chanting – collective effervescence and spiritual power brought into existence not from liturgy or law, but the total expression of a collective fear. And in the embracing of that fear – the perpetual fear and anxiety brought on by a state of poverty and powerlessness – a new and individual strength. A steely resolve. A promise torn from each throat not by state coercion or by religious decree but from absolute will. While the music continued, there was still hope gnashing and fighting to crawl out from beneath the boot, stamping on a human face – forever.

We're told that we're useless, we're told that we're
scum
Look at those liars, look what they've done
Dare to blame us, what a fuckin' bitch
It's not us poor bastards who lie, kill – that's rich
Pushed into a corner, no rights and no bread
Dare to be different and you'll be found dead

Battered, beaten, crippled and ruined
The State's fucking dictate will end fucking soon.

Khalil felt the orgasm of his music thunder through him, over him. It was the feeling of a prophet bringing truth to his people. It was the satisfaction of violent release. It was the rejection of his personal demons. It was unhistorical time, a closed horizon in which brutal and essential honesty flourished. It was the antithesis of the world he was born into. His lyrics torn from Hassan's throat, slashing across the crowd. The drum and bass bombarding them, destroying them.

As Nietzsche had whispered to Khalil from between yellowed pages years ago:

Only where there are graves are there resurrections.

The final words of the song, a hundred voices strong.

Chants now of "Boot on Neck! Boot on Neck!" began to arise from the fans as the song rose in volume and slowed in tempo, the machine gun blasts issuing forth from Shawn's drum kit slowing to a military march while Khalil's own guitar brought heavy rain down on the crowd. Rat's guitar wailed and screamed, low at first like an engine accelerating and gaining speed. The circle pit in the center grew wild – elbows, knees, and violent thrusts dominating.

The song ended as abruptly as it had begun. The band played straight into the next song without pause.

There she was, near the back, barely tall enough to be noticed above the undulating horizon of the crowd's edge. She knew the words – not simply lyrically, but she knew them. He could see it in her eyes. Khalil could only catch a fleeting glimpse of her before he was kicked in the thigh by Rat, looking for some stage antics. Obliging, Khalil turned on his heel to face Rat, banging his head in time and tune. Rat placed the head of his SG just below Khalil's arc of motion and raised a leg, making it appear as if the olive-skinned bassist was going down on the guitar. A smattering of laughter, hoots, and cheers were almost immediately drowned out by the clashing, dying guitars that signified the end of the song.

The set continued and climaxed in a sea of energy, sweat, and violent catharsis. The crowd was wild-eyed, letting hateful and despicable words and thoughts fall from their tongues and disperse, careening across the hardwood floor. It felt like nothing else in this world does, a euphoric high that could only be rivaled by the shuddering satisfaction induced by sex or drugs. A wave of relief washed over Khalil as the crowd slowly moved, en masse, towards the bartop and the washrooms to the side of the dance floor – also protected by a wooden rail. Heba would be a busy girl tonight, moving behind the bar like a blur – snatching slurred drink orders from the air and hoping for heavy handed tips in return.

Khalil snapped off his amplifier and unplugged his bass, wiping the sweat from his brow with the back of his sleeve. He picked up a relatively fresh beer that Heba had brought him before the encore and pressed it against his forehead. The cool beads of perspiration on the outside of the opaque brown bottle cooled him, the label sticking slightly to his skin.

Rat was bent over at the drum kit, snorting a line to recharge after the forty-five minute set. Snorting was the tried and true method of doing blow, but Khalil could never get into it – he preferred to smoke his with marijuana and tobacco or simply a quarter of a gram mixed into a tall rum and cola. Besides, it was a party favour for him, something that might be done a few times a year. For Rat, it was simply a way of life – his purple dreads rattling and clicking lightly as the wooden beads made contact, head bobbing to the tune of his ritual. Hassan had already left the stage and was headed to the band room down the long hallway behind the stage, as had Shawn – they'd likely be heading home immediately rather than sticking around for the amateur bands that would follow until the wee hours of the morning. They had families, or at least de facto wives.

A pair of meltwater blue eyes, wide with passion and excitement, peered at him from the front row of the stage. Her hair was mussed from the humidity and the surge of the crowd, messy and extremely sexy. Khalil approached the edge of the stage and sat down.

"You look tired! Did you enjoy the show?" A redundant question, but a good opener to see how things could go from here. She didn't really look all that exhausted to him.

Amina nodded enthusiastically, a wide and spritely grin forcing dimples into her cheeks. "You guys are always awesome, but I usually don't go anywhere near the crowd." That would explain why he'd not noticed her before, as the Wreckage was dimly lit at the best of times. Khalil couldn't help but chuckle at her youthful spirit, an enthusiasm crucified in the recesses of his own heart.

"Did you want to come out back with me and have a drink?" he suggested.

"Sure thing. Let me go back to the bar and I'll see you in the band room."

"Lab City – I'll have two. You can have whatever you'd like, just tell Heba to put it on my tab."

Amina nodded and moved briskly through the crowd, shoulder turned outward in order to sidle past the patrons lingering on the dance floor. Her blazer set her apart from the general visual clutter and he saw her approach the bar and lean over top. Khalil finished his beer, wiped his lips and his beard clean, and stalked down the hallway towards the band room.

7. SEX, DRUGS, AND DEATH METAL

Khalil always spent some time looking at the beams of light which thrust upward from rotting gaps in the hallway floor. It was a visual memory that always called him to take note, to enjoy himself for a few seconds. The hallway was narrow and quite short, extending toward another fire exit with a flickering OUT sign above the doorway. His mind was alive with arousal and euphoria. He turned the doorknob to the right of the fire exit – leading into the band room – and entered.

The walls of the band room were blood red, morose. Darker and moodier than the main bar. There was a small glass table in the corner with a sectional booth surrounding it, lit from below and projecting a cool blue glow. The floor patterned like a 1950s diner, a scuffed and chipping chessboard. There were two fake plants – a cactus and some type of weeping fern, positioned at either end of the sectional in order to offer some level of privacy to the occupants.

Rat was currently sitting, back on to Khalil, with a metal pipe inserted into his nostril, sniffing and snorting. To the left of the booth there ran a small bar, littered with half-empty glasses and liquor bottles. Open season on those, so the bassist strolled over to take stock of what might remain.

"Only tequila and bathtub gin left, bro." Rat's voice was hoarse and unsure, his speech coming quickly as the coke began to take hold. Khalil couldn't help but grimace – he had been hoping for a bottle of whiskey he could steal for later. There was a half bottle of Joshua Tree tequila and a near-full bottle of a clear, unlabeled liquid – the homemade gin. Deciding on the lesser of two evils, he picked up the tequila and walked over to the booth in the corner. Rat was actively sweeping the coke back into new lines.

"So who's the girl I saw you talking to after the show? Some new pussy?" Rat laid strong emphasis on the last word, leering at Khalil with shining, laughing eyes.

"Could happen. I'm working on it, anyways. She's coming back here for a drink." Khalil smiled through his beard, careful not to offer too much in case she happened to walk in. Letting Rat know not to run his mouth too loudly or loosely.

"Damn! She might even be hotter than Haifa! How the hell do you find these women, man? They must like foreign men or something. Exotic! Fuckin' wild, man!" Rat ran his hands through his long purple dreads.

"If it were about being exotic, I'm sure you would be knee deep in it, sporting those cute little dreadlocks the past few years. Besides, shes from the Old Eastern Bloc – it's in her accent – not really that different than it is up here in the Northeast Province."

Rat smiled slyly, bringing a tattooed hand up to rub at a somewhat stringy goatee. "Who the fuck says I'm not knee deep in it, girl? Eastern Bloc, eh? Yea, that's a hard place." He stood up and flexed his muscles, lean and whipcord strong. "Women die for *my* cock, Khalil. You wouldn't know a thing about it."

Amina picked an excellent time to turn the door handle, and Khalil turned to catch her expression as she entered to witness this scene. A crucial moment in time – a neon-haired white-Russian Rastafarian on a co-caine high flexing his muscles would be enough to send the more fainthearted fleeing down the hallway. Amina laughed, once again showing those gorgeous dimples on either side of her lips. A real team player and a quick thinker. Two of the most important and most attractive qualities in a woman in Khalil's estimation.

"Nice guns. Rat, right?" She extended a hand towards Rat.

He broke pose and clasped her hand enthusiastically, giving her a good look up and down. "Yeah, that's right sweetheart. Ratimir Volkov. What's a girl like you doing in a place like this?"

Khalil could see Rat looking at him from the corner of his eye, watching his game and how she might respond. He hadn't witnessed the rack of pool earlier or the look in her eye after they'd finished playing. Rat was in for a surprise.

She leaned around Tom's torso to take a look at Khalil, sitting down with his arm thrown over the back of the sectional in front of a few lines of coke.

"This." Amina brushed past Rat, who turned quickly to see what this girl was up to. Khalil leaned over in time to see her snatch the metal tube from the tabletop and lean over the table. With a quick sniff, half of the closest line disappeared. Her eyes fluttered and his mouth hung open in shock. This girl was live.

"You okay?" Khalil offered gently, his dark features sharp with concern. Amina simply stood there with her eyes closed, in profile to him. She rocked back and forth on her heels, and a slow smile crept across her face. With a gasp and a long sigh, she turned her face towards him.

"Wonderful. It's been a *long time*!" She couldn't contain her joy, and she ran over to him, tugging at his arm, her fingers grasping at the soft and beaten leather. She pulled him over toward the sectional. Khalil gave a helpless shrug to Rat, who was smiling like a young boy caught in the midst of a naughty deed. He knew what to do.

"Well, a pleasure meeting you Amina – good to see a hot piece like yourself knows how to roll–" he affected a gentleman's disposition, giving a sloppy and exaggerated bow, "–and I'll see you both next week at practice."

Khalil gestured towards the coke on the table; Rat shook his head and waved it off. "Plenty more where that came from. Later." Rat was big time and had his own means and methods. A gram or so was nothing to him. Khalil would have to thank Rat later; he had already left the room and locked the door behind him.

They were alone, and almost immediately Amina wriggled up into his lap, her warm, soft thighs and buttocks pressing against him, wrapping her arms around his neck and looking quite seriously into his dark, nearly black eyes. Her own eyes were wide and gaping, threatening to steal his consciousness in entirely. Her warmth and her beauty were mesmerizing. He could feel his sexual excitement rising, but attempted to keep it in check for a few moments longer. The images roiling through his mind were carnal and rough – Amina with her pale, milky thighs spread wide, riding him. Her breasts bouncing with each thrust, her lips parted wide and ready. Amina could clearly feel his arousal, and immediately shifted her weight so that she could undo his belt. Words were unnecessary, she knew how he felt –

what he wanted from her. She seemed to have the same sexual ambitions.

"I've wanted this for hours, just to be alone with you," she cooed softly. Khalil immediately felt a rush of blood; this girl really knew how to talk to a man. She slowly took off her blazer, allowing him to have a much better look at her figure. She was wearing a tight black t-shirt that clung tightly to her breasts, a slight screen-print pattern overlaying it like lace. She was slight of frame, her breasts firm and larger than he'd expected. Amina's eyes had not left his face, and she rocked back and forth, stroking him through his jeans lightly with a playful smile. He was harder than he'd ever been in his life.

Khalil leaned over the table and picked up a rolling paper and a pinch of coke. Hastily, he scuffed up some scattered weed on the tabletop and rolled a neat little joint.

"Keep going," he murmured softly, putting flame to paper and pulling a long hit. Her small hands played over his body, her right never leaving his lap while her free hand began to unzip and unbutton his pants. As the mixture of cocaine and cannabis flooded his mind with even greater promises of ecstasy, Amina made a show of licking her lips before leaning over into his lap. She was amazing. Haifa had been such a prude when it came to sex, and Amina was like nothing he'd ever encountered in the flesh.

He could feel her hands working quickly, pulling him free of his boxers and immediately stroking him – her soft hands tightened in a firm grip. The joint fell from his hand into a pool of beer on the table; all he could think about was how much he needed her. He felt a warm, wonderful sensation as she clutched the base of his shaft and took him into her mouth.

Khalil moaned softly, the gentle play of her tongue around the head causing spasms of pleasure to thrill up his spine. The drugs brought his sensual pleasure to new heights, as it did for her; he could hear her make soft noises, sliding her slick lips up and down the length of his manhood. Her tongue fluttered continuously against the tip of his cock while her free hand moved upward and gently caressed his stomach beneath his shirt. His surroundings fell away, all that existed in his world were her hands, her lips, and the imminent promise of further secrets.

Slowly bringing her head up from his lap, Amina kissed him hard on the lips – her eyes wide open, staring into his. Her taste was hot and feral. They both shuddered in anticipation and excitement. She quickly crossed her arms and grasped the trunk of her t-shirt, pulling it up over her breasts, exposing small, pink nipples – hard and erect. She hiked up her skirt around her thighs and turned away from him, reaching through her legs in order to better guide him into her.

She gently slid onto him, her warmth enveloping him, wet. Amina gasped breathily as she took the whole length of him, slowly sliding downward until he could feel her ass pressed tightly against his thighs. His hands moved of their own accord, snaking around her tiny ribcage and cupping her breasts, rolling her nipples between thumb and forefinger gently. He could feel her muscles tightening, gripping him harder and harder as she began to buck against him in earnest – pushing as deeply and as quickly as she possibly could. She was panting heavily, moaning and calling his name urgently. Khalil didn't think he could last much longer with such a beautiful woman using him like this; he could feel his climax building–

A crash.

Loud yelling.

Immediately, Amina sprang off of him and righted herself, pulling her t-shirt down and running to the door, leaving him throbbing and confused.

"Cops! The fuckin' cops!"

Shouting erupted from within the club, penetrating even the thick walls of the band room. An uproar and sounds of struggle shook Khalil's mind free of a blissful fog.

Khalil fumbled to get his pants back on while Amina flung the door open, filling the room with the sound of violence and combat. Shouts of pain and anger sounded like an furious river flowing down the hallway and cresting into the band room, rising in intensity.

"Stay back, look for a way out, and get the hell out of here." He looked her quickly in the eye, her fright very real. She could only nod, her mind likely still trying to figure out what was going on. "Be ready."

From craning his neck out and looking down the hall, it didn't seem as though the police had broken through the crowd yet. Khalil could only see flashes of arms and legs out in the bar proper. "Quickly, this way!"

He took hold of Amina's hand and briskly led her toward the emergency exit. Reaching the door, he heard the heavy sound of combat boots striking the steel grating – the cops were coming in the back entrance as well!

Almost immediately the door swung backward and a large man strode through the doorway. His face was the impassive cypher of the VISAGE collar – stone-hewn jaw with thin lips and dark, emotionless eyes.

Khalil made his decision in an instant. His elbow swung round in a vicious circle, connecting hard across the bridge of the cop's nose. He could feel bones or cartilage shift. Blood starting streaming from behind the false projection. The cop collapsed into a corner by the doorway and Khalil fell on him relentlessly, not allowing for mercy.

"Get the fuck outta here!" he yelled at Amina, frozen and illuminated by the moonlight in the middle of the long hallway. Khalil's calloused fists continued to rain down on the cop, each strike deeply satisfying. The man's feeble attempts at blocking were brushed aside by Khalil's dark and eager hands.

Khalil could feel the brush of Amina's skirt across his back and shoulders as she disappeared through the doorway, her light steps clinking on the metal stairway, fading away. The officer had stopped struggling. Khalil got to his feet and stuck his head out of the doorframe in time to see a flash of fabric retreating swiftly down an arterial alleyway. Meanwhile, more uniforms had rounded the corner and were headed for the fire escape. Not good.

He swung on his booted heel and ran down the hallway, careful not to lodge a foot in one of the holes in the floor. Nearing the entryway to the club floor, a total melee had broken out in the bar.

A stout, grey-haired woman wearing a brown leather duster struck a nearby officer across the face with a liquor bottle, shattering his VISAGE and cutting deep into his cheek as it knocked him to the floor. He was a pasty, doughy looking man – his eyes were rolled back into his head. Nearby, a tall officer was strangling a teenage male with long, black hair. His leather gloves were wrapped tightly around the young man's pale and slender neck; he had nearly choked all life from him. Khalil immediately reached up over the ledge of the stage and lifted his bass from the stand. Gripping the bass two-handed, he swung the thick wooden body like an axe, smashing the edge of the Thunderbird across the side of the officer's face. The cop's grip loosened, although not completely, and he dragged the boy to the bar-room floor as he fell in a heap.

Khalil felt a pair of arms encircle him from behind, attempting to bind him, forcing him to drop his bass with a thump, the neck stretched out over the teen's scrambling legs as he tried to break free from the grip of the unconscious cop. Khalil tried to pull free, but the officer was too strong to overpower with any ease; he began to lock Khalil's wrists up behind his back. Kicking his leg backwards against the side of his assailant's knee, Khalil felt the bone crack beneath his thick rubber heel, the heavy boots driving through the police-issue kneepad.

His attacker cried out and released Khalil, falling to the ground and cradling his knee in his hands. His face, still hidden behind the VISAGE, was placid and calm, the screaming coming from between emotionless lips.

By now the tide was starting to turn. By the far stairwell that ran down to the street, a dozen patrons had already been zip-tied and bound, helpless and shouting curses down on the police who continued to press forth into the bar, by now with reinforced numbers, firing stun-guns and swinging large electrified batons. Their faces were cruel – though unable to display wild emotion, it almost seemed as if a permanent leer was writ across their faces, curled upper lips struggling to break through the masks.

"Get down, now! You are all under immediate arrest! Any resistance will lead to increased sentencing!" A chorus of stern voices, all speaking in unison, even from the downed officers. The stereoscopic effect must have worked on a few people, because at least a third of the crowd immediately fell to the ground and placed their hands outward like starfish. They had been overwhelmed, overawed. The rest of the citizens, Khalil included, weren't going down so easily.

A girl who looked far too young to be here fell down beside Khalil, clutching at a series of metal spikes that had been driven into her chest – the hiss of coursing electricity flowing through the attached wires as she fell, her teeth clamped together and her lips pulled back in a morbid, uncontrollable grin. Khalil stepped over the girl to engage the officer who was coming over to tag and bag her.

"Come on, fucker. Let's see what they teach you pieces of shit nowadays," he hissed, rage and adrenaline boiling his blood.

A wild swing; obviously Khalil's taunt had provoked him. Khalil quickly pushed the cop's fist to the side so that it would brush past his face. Khalil took a quick step in, twisting his hips, all of his weight behind an elbow strike across the pig's face. The officer's nose broke flat from the blow, windmilling back a half-dozen paces before losing his balance and falling against the wall.

He didn't move. Khalil hoped he'd killed him. It felt good, exultant, almost religious. An an altar of violence, a cleansing. A burning angel, turning on his tormentor. A painbearer holding torturer's tools for the first time.

A sharp biting pain erupted in his right shoulder blade before exploding with even greater force in his skull. Stun-gun. He'd been tazed before and knew what it felt like.

Losing his balance, Khalil clumsily fell to one knee. The current continued to flow, even increasing slightly. His teeth slammed together; it felt like they would explode into powder at any moment. His jaw locked. He could barely breathe. His muscles pulled taut and rigid. He was unable to move. It took all of the bassist's energy to keep from falling forward on his face.

The current increased; now he couldn't help but gasp in pain. His muscles failed, broken, and he fell forward. Heavy boots on his back. A sharp kick delivered to his ribs.

Khalil could feel the steel-toe breaking his bones. He could feel the sting of a needle biting into his thigh.

8. THE NEWS FEED

Central News Agency (CNA)
– February 8th

Northeast Zone, MEU – A successful police raid by the Central Corrections and Enforcement Corporation (CCEC) on an illegally operating nightclub known as The Wreckage resulted in over four dozen arrests this evening. The club was found to be in violation of building codes, operating with an outdated liquor license, providing shelter for illegal drug users and drug addicts, and promoting black market merchandise sales. Fifty one criminals within were detained and arrested for noncompliance with arrest, assaulting central officers, and participation in the black economy. Amongst the criminals arrested is Khalil Madi, whom some might recall as one of only five fugitive corpsmen to have ever successfully escaped a Damocles installation in the past two decades, at the age of sixteen.

[A picture is displayed, showing a clean cut and intense looking boy with a swarthy complexion and a set jaw]

Madi and thirty one others are also facing summary charges of illegal drug possession, illegal alcohol possession, and illegal pharmaceutical possession. It is expected that all of those arrested will face immediate rehabilitation-via-imprisonment and a ten-year service labour contract upon conviction.

COMMENT ON THIS STORY (2,478) List (1-10):
[**Most Recent**] [Most Liked] [Most Disliked]

Lena Datsik: This is just one more reason why we should be cutting all that free money we keep throwing at the welfare bums in the inner cities. Want to live in the MEU? Follow our rules, shut up, and learn some culture while you're at it. Why do we let such trash even live in our society? Aren't we better than that?
LIKE: 215   DISLIKE: 34

Vernon Doucette: Summary charges? Presumed convictions? Tax violations leading to forced brainwashing under the eyes of Central Social Engineering Corp – and subsequent slave labour to drive the point home? The MEU is a fascistic and illegitimate state – that is the truth, whether you mannequins would hear of it or not. Good luck tracing this, I'm behind multiple proxies.
[Note: This posting is scheduled for deletion due to inappropriate content, pending an administrative investigation

as to the source of origin.]
LIKE: 5   DISLIKE: 598

Bashir El-Baz: I think the one thing that all the leftists are ignoring about this story is the obvious criminal element involved. Keep trying to paint these "poor little victims" stories, but it's quite obvious from the facts that these individuals are trash. Druggies, welfare cases, layabouts – more human waste that is better served on a prison farm or a road crew than sitting on their ass in the streets, hands out and begging for some of my hard earned money. We already pay enough taxes to coddle these jerks, let them find out what it's like to earn their way for once.
LIKE: 726   DISLIKE: 70

Tahira Fazil: It's about time that we started cracking down on these criminal elements that are ruining our cities and making out streets unsafe to walk – even in the daytime! I'm sick and tired of hearing people whine about the civil liberties of criminals – criminals gave up all their rights when they chose to break the rules. The rest of us follow the rules, work hard, and contribute to society. Glad to see they'll be put to work. Allah's will be done.
LIKE: 178   DISLIKE: 7

Jimmy Weasel: Hey! I've been to that bar a few times! To all the haters out there in the digital world – don't knock it until you try it. I hope it manages to stay open, but I don't think it's very likely. Glad I sat on my butt and watched Carnival instead of going downtown – a close call!
LIKE: 45   DISLIKE: 64

Greg Mercer: Why do I even bother reading the news anymore? All I ever hear about are arrests for crimes without a single exterior victim involved, and serious crimes like murder and rape that simply go unsolved or, in many cases, uninvestigated. Seems to me like the boys at CORRECTIONSCORP are more interested in filling jails with cheap labour to boost their numbers and keep their hands clean from the real dirty work in the city centers. Start doing some real "serving and protecting" rather than "snatch and grabbing" and I might begin to actually have faith in CORREC-TIONSCORP – until then, colour me unimpressed.

LIKE: 28 DISLIKE: 359

Virgil Sterne: Bring back the physical death penalty. You know, the permanent kind. Or send them to die overseas. One way or another, we shouldn't be spending a single dime of my tax dollars on animals like these. Can anyone tell me which would be more effective as a cheap deterrent – a rifle with a magazine of bullets or a gallows and a length of sturdy rope?
LIKE: 986 DISLIKE: 69

Ehsanuhlla Richards: The thought of violent and drugged up killers like this in my neighbourhood makes me so angry. I am trying to raise two little girls and I can just see people like this Kalil(sp?) Mahdit preying on them whenever someone isn't looking. Why do we continue to allow these people unto the streets? They should never have been allowed to walk free in the first place. That entire block should be leveled. I would do anything to keep my two children safe. I hope these druggies rot in their cells as an example to the rest of the sickos out there!
LIKE: 566 DISLIKE: 8

Benjamin Avery: As an ex-CORRECTIONSCORP officer *[linked Achievements Badges on profile]*, I can tell you that this is just one more example of why increased funding and congressional representation is necessary for our industry. Without the proper equipment and manpower, clubs like this would still be plaguing our national union – rather than being the exception to the rule as they are twenty years after the fact. I see most of the comments on this forum are backing us up, and I'd like to thank you all for that. Good citizens make for a great nation. Please pray for all of the courageous officers that were injured in subduing and arresting these violent criminals.
LIKE: 1,109 DISLIKE: 34

Yvonne Majaski: I have to question the impartiality of this type of reporting. Presumption of guilt is a very dangerous road to continue following – we've been going down this path too frequently in the past few years already. Time for sober, second thought. Let us not rush to conclusions and consequences.
LIKE: 132 DISLIKE: 679

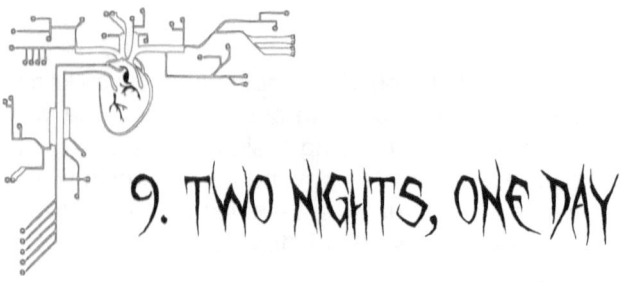

9. TWO NIGHTS, ONE DAY

The room was as cold as death; that was Khalil's first thought as he regained consciousness. He wondered for a few confused seconds if he was, in fact, alive. The pain that grew inside of his skull and shot through his battered limbs and bruised body put an end to this question. His chair was the only thing supporting him; he was slumped over a tabletop.

A high powered gas lamp suspended above Khalil was the only source of light in the room, casting his long, uneven shadow as well as that of someone else, sitting erect and opposite. She was short though well defined, articulate and feminine curvature accentuated by a pall-bearer's black business suit, long curly hair – he could see wisps of her hair standing out large on the clean grey concrete. It was an almost theatrical appearance, a juxtaposition of an arch and angular female intelligence set against a shadow portrait cast against the wall.

The pain began to increase sharply as the sedative slowly wore off. The dust in the air made his lungs shake and rattle, he coughed and felt a stabbing pain behind his eyes.

His left leg pulsed angrily, on fire – likely broken quite badly. His ribcage felt extremely tender and it hurt to take any deep breaths. Probably bruised but not broken. His teeth clenched together as yet more pain signals began to register as his vision, his consciousness, began to come back to him in sharper relief. Floating sparks and neon-pastel stars swam through already blurred vision. Khalil bit back another cry, shutting his eyes tight, long black lashes quivering. Khalil attempted to pull his upper body up from the table.

"Hey, now. Don't get too excited. You've had an awfully long night," a soft and raspy voice cooed gently from across the table. She was a smoker, that much was apparent. It lent a certain assertive edge to her tone. Khalil didn't much care for it given the circumstances.

"Fuck you."

She chuckled briefly; it sounded like sandpaper tearing through silk. "Nice to meet you too, Mr. Madi. I can see we'll get along like the very best of friends."

"Who are you?"

"My name is Maya Williams. You can call me Ms. Williams. I am to be your defense attorney as well as your convictions officer – meaning you are my responsibility.

An unwanted one, you can be sure."

"Yeah. A real pleasure to meet you, too. You have to get me the hell out of here." His mouth was dry; he could taste old blood and could barely spit the words out. The pain was worsening, particularly in his leg. Khalil needed medical attention; no amount of bravado or inner resolve could deny a fact of the flesh.

"We both know that isn't happening. You're a high-profile fugitive with subversive heritage. You're also facing summary conviction for multiple counts of assault against a corrections officer as well as multiple counts of illegal drug possession. The alteration of your subdermal is of course a felony. You're going down hard, and I'm not about to sully my career by getting invested beyond my barest obligations in helping you."

He was keeping one eye shut tightly to keep too much light from flooding into his vision. Only his battered body kept him from unleashing violence on her. His spirit raged, rattling a rusty cage that would not move.

"I know what I'm facing, but I need medical attention – now! My leg's broken goddammit!" His anger began to rise, impotent, chained to a harsh steel table. Khalil, at last, mustered enough strength to force his head upward in order to better see. The muscles of his neck stood out like a bull's, taut and rigid.

Williams' smile deepened into an entirely amused grin. She had the lean, wolfish face of a predator. Her smile was perfect, her teeth gleaming despite approaching forty. She was iron, entirely sure of her position within an unchangeable order. Fear was an emotion that rarely entered her mind, let alone what passed for her heart.

Khalil knew that this attorney was well aware of his medical distress, his past, and his psychological profile. She also probably had the E-rating of a cold stone, meaning schadenfreude was much more likely to pique her interest than any amount of pleading or altruistic diplomacy. Neither Corp nor Central lawyers achieved their lofty posts by tallying feelings and the intangible, zero-leverage concepts of ethics and humanity.

Besides, who could tell the fuckin' difference between Corp and State nowadays in any case?

Khalil spit on the tabletop, noticing his saliva was flecked with dark ruby blood.

"Look, Mr. Madi, it's nothing personal–"

True. For these cold blooded bastards, nothing could ever be personal.

"–but you really can't be serious. I am also here to facilitate your rehabilitation-via-imprisonment and subsequent repayment of your debt to society. You have quite clearly violated the responsibilities contingent to these assumed 'rights' you are speaking of. No rights are inalienable – each right comes with a responsibility to your country. When you shirk your responsibilities to Central, you also remove yourself from having any rights. Welfare

cases, service-dodgers, and particularly criminal fugi-
tives have literally no claim to any state-sponsored rights,
which are quite clearly the only rights that exist in human
society. I thought you were an educated man, Mr. Madi
– surely you've read Hobbes' *Leviathan* by now – with all
of that free time you have? I ask you: Is it better to be safe
within the belly of the beast or is it better to cling to life
as you do, gasping for every breath?"

Her intelligence drove at him, pressing at him like a
fencer's riposte. A challenge.

"I have natural rights as a man, no matter what the
mouth of this illegitimate state might say. You cannot
reach inside of me and strip my soul of its integrity. My
leg is broken. I am spitting up blood. I need a doctor, now.
If our society is to claim civilization over barbarism – a
patent lie – then you will allow me to be seen by a physician."

He tried to contain his rage. The smooth and facile
argument flowing from Ms. Williams' lips was infuriating
in its circularity. A closed argument was the firmest argument to her mind, analytical yet only on her own terms
and when it served her own purposes. Khalil pegged her
for a sycophant.

"Oh, certainly, Mr. Madi. That was never in question
– all prisoners are entitled to basic medical care to ensure
that they can properly serve. We are in great need of able
bodied prisoners such as yourself – the trite expense of

treating your physical injuries will easily be offset by the labour you will sell to us every day at the cost of room and board. If you plead guilty, as I have already strongly advised you to do, you will receive five years of total service. If you plead innocent, you will inevitably be found guilty regardless, and serve fifteen to twenty years of total service. Not only is your case quite obviously open-and-shut – I needn't remind you that you are a documented deserter and fugitive – but the public has no sympathy for your cause. You come from subversive stock and you are quite obviously of the same mould. Even amongst those political lepers in the inner city with high E scores, you won't pull much weight. Nobody cares about you, except Central – and they've been wanting you for a very long time, Khalil."

"I'm not guilty of anything. Fuck the law. I mind my own business and I never asked for anything from anyone. Get me a doctor and we'll talk. I'm through wasting my breath on you."

The pain was becoming more difficult to bear – each breath brought a new spike of pain from his damaged ribs. His headache increased to a near crescendo, and he couldn't help but wince as Maya leaned backwards, out of the circle of light entirely. Now, even her outline disappeared.

Hiding something.

Khalil turned his head away from the light and

slumped forward onto the cold steel tabletop. The freezing metal was sensual, soothing icicles pushing into a crushing headache, puncturing his skull and relieving pressure. He could hear the click of high heels advancing on him as he once again fell into a restless unconsciousness.

Khalil awoke in a brightly lit room, surrounded by bustling men and women in white coats. The windows opposite his bed told him that it was approaching nightfall, the sun nearly fully set behind the horizon.

His wounds had been dressed and it was quite clear that he was pharmacologically sedated – his mind was clouded and moved much more slowly than usual. He felt languid and peaceful, which immediately raised his suspicion.

Somehow, he couldn't bring himself to care.

The room was large, his own bed being one of at least two dozen. Long tubes of fluorescent lights ran the length of the room, casting their bright light against the sky blue walls. Windows flanked both sides of this oblong chamber, indicating that it must be a wing, most likely in a large hospital. A pretty young nurse with a cold, stern smile approached Khalil's bedside, staring down with wide, blue eyes.

"Mr. Madi. We have treated you for two broken ribs, a leg broken in two places, lacerations, and some minor head trauma. You have already accrued an additional six months in restitutive servile labour in surgical, pharmaceutical, and facilities fees. At this point–" she began as she methodically reached down to press a button that began to lift him into an upright, seated position, "–you are obviously alert enough to be offered further options. You may seek discharge immediately, purchase a wheelchair, and begin transport to your trial facility. You may also remain hospitalized here for another week, at the cost of an additional six months of service."

"I'll stay for another week. Thank you."

"That would be advisable if you wish to make a full recovery. Placing any amount of pressure on the leg over the next few days could give you a permanent limp, even with the bone-bonding agent.."

Empathy? Strange. Perhaps something more like standard congratulations on a medical consumer purchasing an optional upsell. Made more sense.

"I will advise the duty physician that you have opted for an extended arrangement. Please, also note that this is an armed and patrolled Central medical facility. Any attempt to escape your bonds or confinement will result in the use of deadly force." The mask slipped over, the blue of her eyes frozen to ice from autumn rainwater, the human entombed.

From his sitting position, Khalil could take better stock of the hospital room. As he had suspected, three dozen beds or so were placed in two rows along each wall, separated by a semi-transparent gauze screen, painted a variety of pastel colours. The patients in this ward appeared to be heavily sedated for the most part. He and one other man about fifteen feet to his right – two beds over – appeared to be the only patients awake. Khalil waited for the nurse to retreat through the sliding doors at the far end of the room before speaking up.

"Hey, hey there," Khalil whispered quietly to the small, bald man two beds down. The man was fixated, staring off into some distance with a flat, empty face. He blinked twice, slowly, and then craned his neck toward the darker man. He looked over Khalil's shoulder at one of the display screens suspended from the ceiling.

"Hello." A slow, plodding voice. Deliberately concise. Still gazing somewhere in his mind's eye; he was existentially *elsewhere*.

"Where are we?"

"Excuse me?"

Obviously it was a strange question. The man's expression was one of extreme puzzlement, as if he could not even comprehend a lack of this type of knowledge.

"I'm sorry, I'm in here for a head injury – concussion and such from a car crash – I just wanted to know where this hospital is located."

"61 Bonaventure Place, on the corner closest to the CORRECTIONSCORP processing center in the first ring." His eyes were now firmly locked on Khalil's face, searching it for any new information that the strange man might offer up inadvertently.

"Right. I don't often see much of the first ring." Khalil didn't feel it necessary to bother mentioning which side of the first suburban ring he inhabited, however. Inner city dwellers were untouchables, and this man was Khalil's only source of information, however begrudging.

"Me neither. The thought of being in here makes me sick. I am a busy man." The small man looked down at his hospital gown, stained down the front by some type of off-colour liquid. He had clearly vomited on himself recently. If he was distressed by this fact, it did not come through in his demeanour. He seemed to have been satisfied with Khalil's apparent distaste of the facilities and apparently decided to be somewhat agreeable.

"What are you here for?" Khalil asked rather boldly.

"No idea. Been throwing up a lot lately, feeling dizzy. Doctor's got me on eight a day, just to make sure I make it through the day. Pills, I mean. I *need my pills*. If I don't get them I get sick, and they're expensive."

"What kind of pills do you need?"

"Mindex. Calcula. Fibrella. Ultiknot. Zephex. A few others. I asked my doctor about them and he told me they would enhance my work ethic and productivity. I need a raise, and I need my pills. Things get bad without them." This man was fixated as well as deeply disturbed. Khalil could feel his stomach sinking, heavy and leaden.

His luck had truly run out, and he was within their power now.

"Can't help you with that, sorry."

Silence passed between them, and the short man returned to his position, staring into nothingness just beyond the windowpane. A chime struck, and the lights began to dim until they were completely extinguished.

Khalil turned to his own thoughts, embracing them as old friends.

Starlight poured through the large windows opposing the beds. The skies were bare, cloudless, and speckled like pin pricked velvet, bright dots – the light of the universe pouring through the cracks. He had always cultivated a deep love for the stars, a feeling that hit him right in the heart every time he would search the night sky. It didn't cost a thing to sit down on the cool cracked concrete and try to find a place without a streetlight blocking the view.

Khalil remembered his father wrapping his thick, muscular arm around Khalil's small shoulders and pointing out the simple constellations – Orion, the Hunter, and the Big and Little Dippers, and how to find one from the other. A little trick – if you closed an eye and measured the distance between the foremost two stars in the cup of the Big Dipper, and continued upward about four times – there was Polaris, the North Star. A meeting place for souls who cared to wander the universe – both time and space – together as kindred spirits, whether in their imaginations or after their heart failed to beat any longer. Khalil held a childish fantasy, though his inner demons taunted him for it; he imagined his father and mother together, as they'd promised him. Released from the bondage of flesh, together again in the glow of Polaris.

An eccentric belief, Khalil admitted, and filled with childish conceit. Nonetheless, he believed his personal religion.

Space was free. It was free from economic constraints – neither corporations nor Central state industrial pollution had successfully managed to block the view of the stars in the night sky, still shining through the clouds and smog at times. To Khalil, this view represented a place free from petty politics and the chains wrapped around his own neck, invisible and tightening.

He could feel himself approaching tears. He choked them down as he always did. Nobody would ever have known. His family. His freedom. Both physically gone, and now only existing in his memories and his dreams – poor substitutes.

They appear before him in waking dreams and nightmares, sometimes expectant – what would they ask of him? Merely that he keep them dear? Or that he honour them by remaining strong, and stand upright?

What is too much to ask?

When had Khalil suffered enough?

Khalil was not the only one suffering in the room,

however. Bereft of the drugs that made his pointless, droning life bearable, the small, pudgy man with the bald head and the blank eyes was sobbing to himself, curled up under the cold, cotton sheet.

"Hey," Khalil said, softly – discreetly.

Sobs continued to shake the man's body, obviously frail as his thin outline registered against the starlight. He sniffed a few times; Khalil could see his shoulder move – likely wiping his mouth and nose with the back of a forearm. The other patient cleared his throat.

"Yes?"

"What's your name?"

There was a small silence in the room, disturbed only by the soft murmuring of some of the more restless patients. Khalil wasn't sure if the frightened mouse of a man was going to squeak.

"My name is Thom. Thomas Hennings."

"Khalil Madi." If his name was familiar to Thom, he didn't really display any sign of it.

"*Khaleel?* Okay. Weird name, you must be from Central."

"No, born and raised here in the Northeast province. Well, pre-MEU really – I just got caught up in this shitstorm and I've been trying to keep afloat ever since." Khalil smirked, commiserating.

"I was crying." A flat statement, out of nowhere, gushing outward. Thom couldn't fathom why, so he spoke the words as an android, questioning the very reality of such an emotional possibility.

"Yeah, I heard. Are you alright?"

"I mean, I was *crying*. They've seen, and I'll be demoted to the first ring. That's why they have me here!" His eyes began to water again, and he bit his lip, drawing a thin bead of blood.

"You live in the second ring now?"

He nodded.

"You're right. They will have seen – and heard. You will be demoted to the first ring. The question, however, is why do you care? Do you have a family?"

He nodded again, curtly, the thin stream of blood rolling down to his chin, his teeth still clenched down on the white skin of his lower lip.

"Then they will suffer for your emotional sensitivity. Why do you continue to allow these people to control your life? You were born of a woman, of flesh and blood – not of Central or the MEU state."

He shot Khalil a wild-eyed glance, sweating heavily now. Khalil could see Thom's left hand gripping the sheets and pulling them upward, clenched. Complete panic – he was crying and he was now hearing subversive speech for, quite likely, the first time in decades.

He pegged Thom's age at not quite twice his own, a man of middle years, a soft-hearted dove of a man kept alive only because of his marginal economic utility. That utility had clearly come to an end, and now the play-pretend put on by his betters was over. Thom's life was over, whether he knew it or not.

Khalil pressed, having nothing to lose himself.

"Remember the times *before* this. You used to be a man. Don't let them screw you out of that. Take action. Do something! Fight back, goddammit! It's all you've got left."

Deep, wracking cries broke Thomas' chest. Khalil felt a twist within his own stomach as well. He must break this man beforehand and give him a glimmer of hope on the far shore – beyond the reach of what his allocated administrator would strip from him for his breach of emotional conduct. A minor offense but one worthy of residential and employment demotion. Thomas was a lower-class worker who clearly had a sensitive soul – they would either kill him to promote order or they would push him into the inner city. He wouldn't last a matter of months there. If Khalil could reach him now, Thom stood a greater chance of dying with dignity instead unlike the rest of his kind, sheep cooed to slaughter.

The threat of demotion from any ring to the first ring – One – was a lie. The cultural portrait of the first ring was, too, a lie. The first ring about any Union city – themselves built as rotting concentric circles – was a strict perimeter. A law enforcement industry that employed paramilitary control over a width of two kilometers. One was completely enclosed – ostensibly for the protection of those low-level employees working there, but in actuality to serve as a branch of the state prison-industrial apparatus. Combination of servile labour, behavioural therapy, pharmaceutical sedation (deducted an allowance company store scrip) and indefinite confinement. Checkpoints strictly monitored all commuting traffic. Offenders of any type (economic, moral, subversive) were cursorily charged and arrested.

There was no such thing as an appeal nor a pardon. Thomas was a criminal, worthless in terms of state secrets and in survival skills.

Khalil was doing him a favour and giving him the one weapon he had left. It was the same weapon Khalil was intimately familiar with. The cynic in him honestly didn't think Thom had the strength to use it. If Thomas couldn't help himself, who could, or even should?

Was a man like Thom worth saving?

Thom continued to cry, silently, his convulsions causing a rasping noise against the tight cotton sheets.

Khalil slept fitfully, waking often to look out of the window for pockets of starlight between the clouds.

10. DINNER AND A MOVIE

Maya Williams savoured the view, the entire panorama laid out before her. In front of her, a crisp white linen tablecloth draped artfully over a deep cherrywood table. Two tapered, ruby candles illuminating the main course at Bourani`s this evening – for her date, a steak smothered in caramelized onion au jus and for herself – an aromatic and spiced hazelnut chicken breast and garlic whipped potato. Standing tall and erect, beads of perspiration running down the smooth contours, two flutes of deep plum Marechal Foch. And beyond those, broad shoulders clad in exquisite pinstriped wool and a muscular chest hiding behind a pressed, pure white dress shirt. She savoured the thought of his hard body beneath her, the expectation even sweeter than the act. It was inevitable; Maya was a woman used to getting what she wanted.

Raymond leaned back in his chair and exhaled heavily, running an idle hand over his jaw and smiling archly at Maya. She returned his gaze flatly. She knew she was the most talented lawyer at the agency and one of the few who had lost fewer than five percent of their cases. While it was true that defense attorneys had a record-high rate of facilitation and plea bargaining instead of trials proper, Maya's losses in full trials could be counted on one hand. She savoured victory and the spoils of her personal wars of courtroom conquest. Innocence and guilt were incidental to her, as was romance.

Maya, for her part, had no intention of promoting Gates. He was a competent assistant and paralegal and an adequate lover, but no more. He was dangerous in the way that any subordinate was. Theirs was a relationship of power and leverage.

"Maya, I love this place! When did you discover it?" He smiled, bleached teeth sparkling. She remembered why she'd selected him in the interviews.

"I've been coming here for years, once a weekend." Bourani's was a political anchor in the rings and many influential people had been darkening the doorway of the establishment on an ongoing basis.

"Oh. I see. And have you brought any other men here?" A bad-boy smile, now. He obviously knew the answer. Another point for his wit, which turned her on.

"A few. None as ruggedly handsome. Certainly none as enjoyable." Maya was telling the truth – she didn't have any motive to lie in any case. He fulfilled her desires. He was the new and best thing going – and she liked to keep things moving smoothly.

She smiled coolly between black cherry lips. The waiter approached, bearing a carafe of the Foch.

"Madam, sir. Would you care for another carafe?" Elevated diction and a thin, penciled-on moustache perfectly suited to this gentleman, slender and smartly dressed, with suspenders criss-crossing his white cotton dress shirt. His advancing years added gravitas to his genial warmth and gave him a relaxing, persuasive aura which no doubt played very well for tips.

Robert was the name embroidered in fancy black thread above his breast pocket, stark against the crisp white of his shirt. He had been serving Maya and her dates here for the past year or so; she requested him as a matter of course after having been impressed the first time she'd been served by him.

Maya nodded curtly and the carafe was gently set upon the tablecloth, the wine sloshing gently within the neck while Robert sauntered off to his next table – two men wearing dark business suits and murmuring just out of earshot.

Her attention returned to Raymond, who was busy cutting a thick piece of bone free from his steak. Maya cut a piece of her own chicken and placed it in her mouth; she closed her eyes in feigned ecstasy, leaning back against the leather backing of the dining chair and pressing her breasts forward. She knew he'd be imagining the events that would be taking place later tonight – her curved, tanned body sliding against his body, her soft lips brushing against him, licking and searching. What he wanted mattered little to her, though. Maya would make him work for every caress.

Sex – an essential power, a human absolute. Maya was a master of many arts and intoxicated by the game itself.

An unexpected thought derailed her arousal. The sterile white of the tablecloth. The stainless steel of the fork and knife. The man opposite her, subordinate and yet starkly different. She was elsewhere.

"Something on your mind, Maya?"

"Been thinking a lot lately about this new cased I've been assigned. You know, Khalil Madi. High profile service dodger, subversive parents. Undoubtedly a subversive himself from the attitude he gave me yesterday."

Obviously not all of the truth was being spoken, but Ray would play along. He knew better than to press the issue when it was clear that the sex could wait – or not happen at all if he angered her.

"Oh yeah, the spitter. Well, what do you expect from trash past the first ring? The whole core is rotten, we just happen to be lucky enough to live on the upper crust. Besides, you've done dozens of requisite cases like this

— remember that Rourke or Richards or whatever that dirty old man was you had to represent last month? Besides, that's what the people in the inside get for their disdain of the enclave urban planning system." Again, that dazzling white smile, smoothing over the disgusting thought of coming into contact with such savages, human detritus.

Ray was a bit of a dandy and liked his women (and men) wealthy, successful, and attractive, either through natural or surgical endowments. He was not abnormal. The thought of Maya having to sit in close proximity to such a diseased specimen seemed to make him shudder, his painted grin faltering at the thought.

Maya smiled, reaching out a long-fingered hand to clasp over Ray's. Her hand brought warmth to his, cold from his wineglass.

"Don't worry, he didn't touch me. He's an animal, pure and simple. I don't like dealing with his case but it's my job, and if I foul it up, our firm might lose a major bid we have going on with CORRECTIONSCORP. We have a 98% facilitation rate with the state prosecution and if this Arab makes too many waves – we're shot. My job is to make sure he breaks quick and easy."

"Shouldn't be a problem. You've been facilitating for almost ten years now and haven't had a major hiccup so far – I'd say that's a pretty good track record."

"Very true. It's just that this comes at a very inopportune time for me, and I want to dispose of it as quickly as possible to lessen the risk of anything going off. This guy is not like the others. He's an animal. Deep down, a savage. I'd be lying if I said that I wasn't concerned about his behaviour, you know, keeping him in line. His behaviour enters the sphere of my direct interest. If some other poor bastard had drawn the name of Mr. Khalil Madi from the database instead, I would have been a great deal happier."

Maya finished the last of her Foch with a toss of the glass. She caught Robert's eye; he had been idly polishing some silverware towards the kitchen entrance, trying to look busy as he kept a watchful eye over his guests.

"Well, Maya, you're the best. If you say it's not a problem – I know it's not. Let's talk about something else for a while – for example, this place. I've never been here before!" Ray lit up again and opened his arms wide in a grand gesture, taking stock of their surroundings. "You don't see real wood and architecture this fine back in Three!"

Ray now lived in the third ring, quite a promotion from Two – which was where the vast majority of clerical and service industry workers habitated. This change in living accommodations had been cinched by a letter of reference from Maya Williams, esquire.

The second ring was mostly comprised of tenement

condominiums built in long rows, with small patios and narrow slits of concrete for commuting vehicles. Strip malls with budget or value brand consumer products shone brightly for miles in the second ring, stubby and short, shoulder-to-shoulder with sports bars and coffee shops.

Within Three, designer boutiques with full length mirrors and pretentious art replicas proliferated. Ethnic cuisine became a weekly social destination for various cliques of well-dressed management and lower level executive types – the new petit bourgeois.

Ray now had his own backyard, a twenty by thirty patch of grass and gravel that he'd promised to turn into the most wondrous garden next year, flush with buttermilk daisies and vibrant tulips. The summer climate this far north was wonderfully balmy during the few months that the frost retreated.

The ring in which Bourani's was located, and in which Maya lived, was Four – she was on the brink of being promoted to Five. Five was the largest and most spacious ring attainable by private citizens without personal invitations to join Central and dwell in Six, which was a near legendary position that all executives dreamed of. Her life as of now largely consisted of catered meals from the finest chefs in the subcontinent, long days of golf and imported beer at the Eaglepeak Country Club, and three-dimensional film and television screenings.

A promotion to Five brought the promise of unfet-tered global travel, unlimited sex partners (a thought which had previously intoxicated her but now seemed a faint amusement in light of her current satisfaction and more immediate professional concerns), and the prom-ise of actually owning her own real-estate in the lower rings for posterity.

She'd heard from transferred executives about Six in other cities, but never a word about Six here in the Northeastern Province. For now, it remained nothing more than an idle dream.

Maya joined her date in taking a more leisurely look at the interior of Bourani's, her assessment really un-changed from the last time she'd been here, with a wom-an who she kept on payroll for her lovemaking abilities – that had been nearly a year ago now, however.

Little had changed. A few stray petals clung to the ivory-white of the tablecloth. Crown moulding stretched the length of the ceiling, wearing intricate designs like some sort of Grecian ivy. Large glass windows touched with frost provided a beautiful look of a lake, small waves lapping against the posts of a nearby wharf.

"I can't believe the decor in this place!" Raymond said, craning his head to take in all of the architectural details. Robert had already come and gone, the dark wine nearly topping over the rim of the glass. An amateurish pour or a waiter with a heavy hand hoping for a generous tip, it didn't matter to Maya. She'd calculate 25% of the bill and leave that as a gratuity as she always did, even though she was secretly thankful for the extra alcohol – it would keep her a little more alert during the movie they were going to see after the meal.

"Shall we skip dessert?" Ray asked.

"You don't want any? Not even a look at the menu?"

"No, I think I'm full... and the film starts shortly."

"Soon. Let's finish our wine first. Can't let good grapes go to waste, Ray."

She smiled sweetly again at Raymond. Clearly the alcohol had already started to take hold; Raymond felt a slight thrill of happiness running up his spine and radiating throughout his limbs. He snatched up the wineglass and took a large gulp, enjoying the warm sloshing of the expensive Foch around his mouth and throat.

"What's the rush? Haven't we already seen this one before, anyway?" he asked, leering over the remains of his dinner at Maya. She glowered at him for his gauche misstep. Ray could be enthusiastic to the point of vulgarity, unseemly for his new station and surroundings. A few pairs of silent eyes began to circle their table.

"Oh, stop it! We're in public! Control yourself."

With an exaggerated sigh and a penetrating gaze, Raymond slumped against the back of his chair, drowning the last of the wine.

"How insincere of you, Maya. If you're so anxious, we can move on to bigger and better things." He stressed the innuendo.

Maya frowned as she scanned her subdermal identification icon over the in-table system with a wave of the wrist, covering the meal with a suitably generous tip. Dating the help too consistently was considered to be a bit too soft for a legal executor. His sarcasm was beginning to grow tiresome.

They rose from the rich wooden table and briskly walked toward the door, their shoes sinking deep into the lush carpet. Maya lead the way, Gates following closely behind. The dress clung to her body like a fitted glove, the silk of her blood-red dress outlining the gentle slope of her shoulders and the soft swell below those. Out on the sidewalk, Gates stopped briefly, his face taking on a look of consternation as he patted down the pockets of his wool topcoat.

"Damn! Out of cigarettes. Do you have any?"

Producing a beautiful stainless steel container, Maya flipped the lid to reveal a trio of menthol cigarettes. Ray pulled a slight face, curling the corners of his mouth.

"My deepest apologies." Now it was her turn to be sarcastic. She was much better at it.

Smoking had become infinitely more commonplace with the introduction of yearly nanite cleanings for most ring-dwellers – scrubbing the membranous tissues of the lungs, arteries, and internal organs along with the plaque from your teeth and the damage from your skin. It was a win-win-win situation – the tobacco industry boomed, the medical industry profited, and the suburbanites got a clean bill of health and a life of hedonism free from any pursuant responsibility.

"That's fine. They'll do." Gates snatched one from the container, lit it, and placed it in his mouth. He knew better than to turn his nose up at anything offered by the boss lady.

Maya lit her own after offering one to Ray. Tilting her head back and folding her arms, she inhaled deeply. The cool mint of the menthol tobacco filled her throat and lungs, providing some slight, unidentifiable tingling. The night sky spread out before them, unobstructed. Stars dull and bright spilled out onto a blue-black canvas. She was suddenly aware of feeling very small beneath such looming constellations, and snapped her vision back to street level, where Ray was busy chatting on his tablet with one of his friends from the office.

"–she took me to Bourani's! ... Yes, you know the place, up in *Four!* ... Don't lie, you know you're jealous!" Ray's voice took on a boyish, braggart's tone. "Best damned steak I've ever had. Amazing. Marechal Foch to wash it all down, Domaine de Anapolis." There was a barely restrained gloating in his tone, triumphant feelings enhanced by the alcohol buzz. Dating Ms. Maya Williams, esquire, made Ray a very important person, and the most popular fellow in his rather large circle of acquaintances. Maya was well aware of this and used it at times to leverage Ray, with or without his knowledge.

"Yes, I'll be back in the office on Monday. We can talk about the file then. Later!" Ray cheerily swiped the tab off and strode toward the curb where the car was parked.

Maya followed suit, dropping her exhausted cigarette to the concrete where it continued to cry smoke. Her long heels clicked against the concrete as she rounded the front of the vehicle and opened the passenger door for him; she'd overtaken him in no time with long, leggy strides.

"Getting in, Ray?"

He flicked his cigarette to the curbside pavement, the butt skittering, spilling bright ashes. Ray ducked his close-cropped head down and climbed into the passenger seat.

Maya walked around her dark sedan, sleek and oily black as if to match the fabric of her secretary's suit. She preferred a monochromatic design aesthetic – Bourani's opulent warmth and wood was a stark departure from her usual trappings. She felt she could control and manipulate the sterility of a minimalist aesthetic. The organic and asymmetrical design of florid Italy was distinctly European in its conception of liberty, her only complaint of her favourite haunt.

She swung the door open and slid into the driver's seat briskly, raising her subdermal to the ignition. The car sprung to life, a barely audible whisper signifying the engine had been engaged.

The interior of the vehicle matched the exterior – jet black leather and faux-chrome detailing. Digital displays and some three dimensional projections filled the space between her eyes and the road. Bright orange icons and tiles indicated the external temperature, humidity, and other miscellaneous trivia. Electric blue holograms analyzed the immediate surroundings of the vehicle as well as displaying diagnostic information regarding the car's internal systems – fuel, lubricants, and structural integrity. While a few years old, the sedan was a top of the line model, and turned more than a few heads in her gated ring.

"Where to now?" Ray inquired, running his hands over the thighs of his suit pants.

"The REscreen."

"What?! That place in the city core?!" Ray's eyes were wide and his voice faltered slightly. She hadn't hired him for his bravery.

"That's the one. We're going to a banned film." Clinical as always, Maya allowed a tight smile to touch her lips. The danger was a thrill.

"Maya, are you fucking *crazy?* It's not safe!" A daring

move by Ray. Such forceful and overt opposition to her authority!

"I have clearance. I go in once in a while to counsel some of the rougher clients. It's *not a problem*, so calm yourself, please." Now there was a hard edge in her voice, an unspoken threat. He took the hint, swallowing. He had spoken well out of turn.

"Okay. Okay. I just don't get why we have to take the risk–" Overstepping his boundaries again.

Maya shifted her gaze from the road to focus on him. He said nothing, then turned back toward the road.

Silence followed for half a minute before she spoke.

"The film is called *Metropolis* – a very old film, in fact. Silent, just like I prefer my company. A little culture would do a gentleman like you some good." As if she hadn't even heard his continued protest. Her voice was like a steel blade being drawn slowly over concrete.

The mood had darkened substantially, and Ray knew that Maya Williams would not forget his impertinence and subversion, however charming. She was, at times, a storm cloud of a woman.

"I'm sorry, Maya. It's just... you know how it is. I've never set foot in the inner city – all I hear about are the bloody rumours and news pieces, and what you tell me of your clients. I'm really quite sorry, it was rude of me to interrupt." His hand snaked towards her thigh, kneading the lean muscle beyond the sheer fabric of her dress. Her face softened slightly, the cloud above them dissipating.

"It's alright, Ray. I know it's frightening for you, even though it shouldn't be. We have clearance to get through the perimeter and the theatre is on the edge of town, not in the core itself. Trust me, I wouldn't endanger your life or my own so frivolously."

"I know. I should know better. I trust you." A lie. He trusted her inasmuch as he believed it was convenient to be having an affair with her at the moment, and that he treated his mistresses quite well. She wasn't foolish enough to believe that there was any underlying affection toward any aim beyond ambition and lust.

The vehicle sped through the streets of the fourth ring, sliding with ease around the flat, perfect asphalt.. Several eateries and shops passed by the windows as Maya peered out. Coco's Fashion Boutique (carrying only the newest in synthetic polyfibres and even some natural materials!) and a dozen other chain stores moved before her emerald green eyes. Raymond had insisted that Maya show him to each and every one earlier today; it was his first trip to the new retail outlets. He'd actually been somewhat disappointed in the selection – the same as every other store in Three, with minor variations. The food, however, was a vast improvement over the sports bars and chain Italian restaurants that proliferated across his own neighbourhood.

It began to rain, drops of water striking the windshield with increasing regularity as Maya wheeled that car into the nearest arterial leading toward the city center. The hum of the engine increased in pitch slightly as it began to wind up, accelerating with impressive speed and merging quickly onto the thoroughfare. The highway was largely abandoned at this hour – it was closing on midnight – and she couldn't help but lean forward slightly to glance again at the night sky.

"Stargazing tonight, Maya?" Ray asked curiously.

"Yeah. Don't really pay attention to it most of the time. Not sure if I like it." She brought her eyes back to the roadway, trying to focus on the yellow blur that marked the center line of the freeway. Her speedometer read 160 miles per hour – just under the limit.

"That's a curious thing to say. You don't like looking at the stars? You don't find them beautiful?" Now Ray was leaning forward, straining against his seat belt, trying to get a good look.

"I find many things beautiful. The stars, I don't know how I feel about them. They don't impact my life in any real way, nor can I impact their destiny. We are mutually exclusive. I don't really care about them at all, but they exist and so, persist in my mind."

"Well, I find them beautiful. Not quite as beautiful as a real diamond–" he smiled archly, then leaned back again in his seat, squirming backward into the leather with his shoulderblades "–but they'll do for a distraction for a few moments. And they're free." Ray laughed lightly at his own little joke.

Maya drove on in silence for a few more moments before the road began to narrow, approaching the first ring. She shot a quick look at Ray.

"Just let me do the talking. This won't be a problem."

He nodded briefly in response, but his fingertips scratched quickly and reflexively against the fabric of his outer thighs. He had a naturally high E-rating, Maya assumed. Perhaps she'd made a mistake in selecting an assistant with too much capacity for weakness and not enough self-interest.

Self-interest was predictable; the alternative was erratic, irrational, and in this way highly dangerous to well-laid plans and a logical mind. In other words, dangerous to *her*.

The vehicle slowed to a crawl as it approached the squat concrete and steel perimeter, painted black. Two corrections officers leaned over a computer within the observation tower about twenty feet above the perimeter, pointing to some unknown point in the distance. A bored looking officer with a wiry moustache and and a face lined by too many drinks looked up from his monitor and spied the car pulling into the checkpoint, one bushy eyebrow shooting up in curiosity. Casual duty officers were not required to activate their VISAGE system, but the guard snapped it on as he exited the booth, the projector morphing his aged face into a smooth, stern facade. He advanced on the vehicle, limping slightly – the technology couldn't cover everything – and rapped lightly on the window. Maya depressed the window button and it began to slide down slowly.

"Kind of late for a trip into the city, isn't it?" a cool voice demanded, his glove extended in anticipation of the necessary paperwork. If he was distracted or enamoured of her female form or her exposed flesh, all evidence was hidden behind his holographic mask.

"Seeing a client for last-minute counseling. Central is afraid that he's going to run, and I need to make sure he processes or it's my ass."

"Who's he?" the guard titled his head slightly, sizing Ray up and down with an unblinking eye.

"My paralegal." The truth; it was quite common for lawyers to be having affairs with their secretaries. Male male, male female, female male, female female, or other. The matter seemed to evaporate.

The guard then took a long hard look at Maya, who turned in her seat, placing an elbow and forearm on the window-ridge to meet the officer's gaze. The guard looked away and shook his head slightly after a brief pause to catch his breath. He hadn't even realized that she had already placed the pink hard copy of the paperwork into his fist.

"Let me have a look at this. I'll be right back. Don't go anywhere." The guard limped back to his booth, swinging the door open and sitting down in front of his monitor; obviously, he would cross-reference Maya's credentials against the corrections database.

The guard remained seated at the computer, his face failing to betray even a flash of emotion, the white glow of the monitor illuminating and permeating his false face. Ray was staring, despite her efforts to keep him from raising any unwanted suspicion.

"Stop staring."

He did, and his gaze fell downward. Much better.

After a few moments, the uniformed officer raised himself slowly from his chair and returned to the driver's side of the car, tapping again on the window.

"Your paperwork checks out Ms. Williams. You've got until oh-eight-hundred to be check back in. Stay safe." At this last, the projected face curled the corners of his lips upward before turning away – the man hobbling back to his booth with an unexpected speed.

The large steel arm blocking the roadway lifted upward with a jerk, and Maya accelerated smoothly back onto the now single-lane highway towards the city. The scenery had changed nearly overnight. Snow lay over ragged lances of dead grass, tall and unkempt. Dead and brittle trees and brush lay scattered in pockets on either side of the roadway, illuminated by the sedan's bright lights. Ahead of them, glowing an unearthly red-orange, the city. The new source of service labour in the form of enormous call centers, data entry, crude manufacture, and recycling industries – the dirty work. Even the snow looked sickly and ashen in the moonlight.

Patchwork huts made from scrap metal and building materials began to come into view, huddled together in small family clusters for protection. These were the true wretches who did not have even the meager amount necessary to rent a hostel room or a shared basement flophouse. Most of them exhibited a pale golden light that streamed out from under the poor foundation or through the many cracks in the improvised walls. Many of them looked more like igloos on the plain, as mounds of snow and ice were either swept naturally or patted into place overtop manmade materials to retain heat.

"People actually live in there, in those … things?"

Ray's lip curled in mild disgust with a look of fascination on his face; he wrinkled his small button nose as if he could smell something rank from within the car.

"Yes. I've never been assigned to process one but junior partners in lower level firms sometimes have to do so. Most of the time, they don't even bother filing the paperwork to request a public defender in the first place – either illiterate or ignorant."

Ray laughed at this, putting a hand to his mouth.

"Probably both, Maya."

She turned to give him a knowing smile as the car sped into the city proper, the squat and low buildings on the perimeter sitting dark. Debris and general filth sprawled across the sidewalks and spilled onto the edge of the street. Bent and stooped streetlights cast splotchy and faded light.

After making a left turn, Maya raised her hand and pointed. The REscreen sat on the corner of the street. A small, thin line of customers wound back from the box office, perhaps a little over a dozen would-be patrons shuffling and smoking in queue. The double-wide doors swung open; a pair of teenagers in motley maroon vests exited to place doorstops. The queue began to shuffle in uneven march, disappearing into the blackness of the theatre.

"Stay close to me. Don't talk to them unless they talk to you, and even then, keep it polite. Let me do most of the work and we'll be fine."

Maya knew he was afraid; his fear was nearly palpable. It was amusing to her.

"You are better than these people. Don't forget that. You are their natural superior, and they know it too. You have nothing to fear. I'm armed, and harming one of us in even the slightest capacity equates to an immediate death sentence." She delivered this speech while decelerating the sedan on the curb by the theatre. The overt shining fear dulled in Ray's eyes, even if his skin still trembled slightly and his breath remained irregular. Good enough. Maya was thinking that she might have chosen a bolder lover.

Maya opened the door and walked around the front of her vehicle to let Ray out. His wool overcoat made him appear a large black shadow; he was more imposing to these city scum than he understood. This was another comic irony.

Maya held his hand while he got out of the vehicle, reaching to the back seat in order to pull her long red winter jacket along with her. It had begun to snow, tiny flakes drifting down to cover the sidewalk. She tapped into the vehicle's computer, directing it to return to the parking facility just within the perimeter. The engine purred and whined slightly as it made a quick U-turn and slid off into the night.

By now the line had begun to advance, and only a handful of stragglers remained outside of the theatre, leaning against the brick wall beside the box office window, smoking. One of the taller bystanders fixed his gaze on the well-dressed couple as they approached the doors, his eyes burning behind thick eyeglasses. Maya held his stare with her own, but neither would break, and eventually the stranger inclined his head slightly and turned back to his fellows, accepting the cigarette being passed around the huddled circle.

Ray hadn't said a word, simply pressing deeply against her. She could feel him shivering, deep spasms that shook his body – he'd never spent much time in the elements, outdoors. The evening wasn't even truly that cold, perhaps minus eight to ten degrees Celsius – a crisp winter's night, but not an absolutely frozen one.

They reached the faded cut glass that housed the box office. Maya surveyed the display before her, a crude operating system that displayed a two dimensional menu with a primitive touchscreen, cracked at the corners and encrusted with dust and grit.

Only two films were showing – *Tombstone*, presumably a western, and of course – *Metropolis*, on alternating nights. She immediately raised his forearm to allow the vending machine access to her subdermal, deducting the necessary amount for two tickets. After a brief pause the machine signaled confirmation of payment.

Maya encircled the waist of her date and strode towards the doors, shooting one last look at the tall man who'd been sizing her up – the thug didn't seem to pay any mind, absorbed in low conversation with two other men wearing thick, worn jackets.

The lawyer swung the door open and gestured for Ray to step inside out of the cold, the wind beginning to whip small drifts of light snow around their ankles. She looked at him appreciatively and walked inside, her heel clicking softly through the thin red carpet within.

It was exceptionally smoky inside, the smell of cannabis and tobacco immediately assaulting her nostrils. Maya spied a few glowing cherries in the dark theatre, growing bright and angry as men drew smoke from them, dying to a blood red as they floated – seemingly, in midair. The smell of liquor and slight disinfectant added a more chemical after note to the general aroma. Ray smiled, a little devilishly. He was more familiar with seedier locales, despite the clientele being more bourgeois in his usual drinking holes.

"This place looks fun!" he hissed, clinging tightly to her arm and pressing her cheek into his shoulder. It appeared his fear was abating at a rapid pace as the warmth of the theatre hall soaked into his skin and bones. Maya felt more at ease as well; a stable Ray meant little trouble.

"Thanks, we try our best." A gruff voice came from around the corner. Then a tall, lanky man with greying hair appeared, wearing a dusty utility suit. He appeared to be a technician or maintenance worker, the cloth of his coveralls sharing the same maroon shade as the ushers Maya'd seen earlier.

As the man rounded the corner, his smile faded from his lips. His eyes grew hard and distant.

"Wait, who are you people?" he demanded.

"Customers." Maya said, smoothly, inclining her head slightly.

"Don't lie to me, you slick *bitch*; you don't live in the city – you're from the rings or I'll eat my goddamn shirt." He scratched his rough grey stubble vigorously with a dirty, calloused hand.

It appeared that this bent and greying man was beyond the age where her beauty and sexual appeal could influence him. Either that or he was a rare man of principle, disconcertingly common in these high-empathy wards. Like cockroaches, you could starve them, deny them access to the rudiments of meaningful existence, reduce them to chattel, and attempt to exterminate them – all to no avail as they thrived no matter the hellish conditions of their lives.

"You got me. We're from Three. Wanted to show my husband what a real movie theatre looked like."

The old man nodded, never lowering his eyes.

"You got guts, I'll tell you that, coming around a place like this. I'm not sure if I believe you, but I don't really give a shit as long as your money's good. You got tickets?"

He produced a small tablet and held it in front of him. The display turned green. He lowered his voice.

"You can go upstairs to the balcony if you want to pay an extra fifty. I'd advise you not to sit with the general admission, for your own damn good." The elderly man spat at a spot on the ground, scuffing at it with his boots. Maya could feel Ray tug at her arm, alarmed. That was nearly ten times the ticket price.

"Certainly, sir." Maya replied cheerily, extending her right forearm towards the tablet. Once again, the display flickered a strong green as his account was debited. The janitor nodded and produced a dirty magnetic keycard, handing it over to her. He rubbed at his short whiskers with the back of his hand and turned away from the couple, muttering something to himself and dragging his wheeled pail away.

"Charming." Ray said smoothly, his voice holding a sharp tone of reproval and irritation over what he perceived to be extortion.

"Cheaper than I thought we'd get away with. Sitting down there would be asking for trouble, and we don't want any. These people are not like us – life is cheap and short and dirty. But they'd still like to keep their lives, so they're well aware that it's best not to provoke the situation and force a confrontation. We're just here to enjoy ourselves... fifty is nothing – it's cheaper than our meal was. But if you'd rather sit down in the gallery..." she trailed off, not bothering to look at her date's expression.

They walked arm-in-arm up the short and narrow black staircase to the immediate left of the entrance, finally reaching a battered metal door, the black paint peeling to reveal rust beneath. A small monitor to the right of the door presented a scanning surface for the keycard; Maya waved it over the sensor and received a satisfying click in return, the lock sliding loose. She opened the door, holding it wide, leaning forward slightly with a roguish smile.

"After you."

Ray slipped past his outstretched arm, his body sliding against her chest. She felt the usual thrill soak through her. She let the door go and followed suit, going up another short run of stairs to a protruding balcony, overlooking the general audience. Three or four dozen individuals were spread out across the theatre chairs in the gallery below; some sprawled over two or three seats with their armrests hacked off.

Amongst those assembled, a few personalities in particular caught Maya's eye as she leaned over the tarnished brass railing of the balcony. An unkempt and unshaven old man with long, loose salt and pepper hair was smoking a marijuana cigarette in the front row, coughing profusely after every haul. His black leather jacket was spider-webbed with loose stitching. A young boy of about fourteen or fifteen sat near the back, his arm around what she presumed to be his girlfriend – a black girl with long, tight cornrows and a body to match. A few middle aged men wearing the same work uniform and each cradling a dark bottle of beer to their breasts, standing up in the aisle and casting ominous glances upward.

The lights began to dim, sullenly retreating back into their sunken sconces. A few ragged cheers went up from the crowd as the trailers began. The young couple in the rear immediately began to make out heavily with one another. Maya leered at them briefly before turning her back to the railing and softly walking back to the single row of chairs ringing the balcony and taking a seat. Ray moved close to her and placed his arm idly across her shoulders, his hand brushing lightly against her arm in playful circles.

The previews began. The first to screen was a gore-flecked actioner called *Vigilant / E*; a man from a city core had come home to find his wife violated and murdered alongside the rest of his young family. The ensuing killing spree brought a smile to his lips – in over a hundred years of cinema, not much had changed. The gallery seemed excited, Maya had a fleeting thought that this film would probably do very well in both the cities (where the appetite for realistic violence served as soul food) as well as in the rings (where the cheap gore and poor dialogue would cast the show as a cornball comedy). She squeezed Ray's thigh, excited by the grotesque imagery – a gallery of dismemberment and sexual fantasy. She could feel his anticipation rising, a tightness forming in his groin as her hand butterflied over his lap, teasing.

The second trailer was some sort of generic teen

romance that had been playing for the last four or five weeks in the rings – sometimes films moved a little more slowly into the cities, reaping fresh rewards from excited moviegoers in each ring as the release cascaded down. It was always new in each venue, never overstaying its welcome by more than a week before leaving the theatre for the next film on deck. View or perish – although you could always rent a digital copy from the Corp store from your entertainment center. She felt her gentle ministrations working their desired effect on Ray's lap, saw his attention shifting to her eager grasp.

They had a few minutes before the show started. Maya decided to make the best use of her time under the glow of the screen, despite the whoops and intermittent whistles from the gallery below.

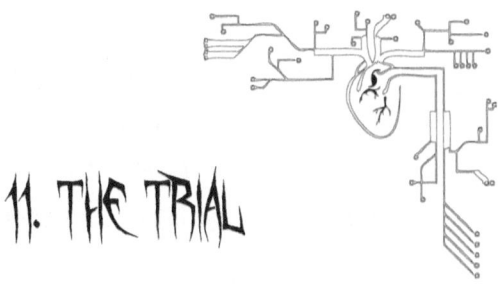

11. THE TRIAL

"Your name and citizenship number, for the record."

"Khalil Madi, 297728371."

The courtroom was nearly full, many members of the press tapping their tablets furiously, some daring to raise hand tablets to capture video streams of the proceedings. Bright red cherrywood and dark granite gave the room a distinct atmosphere of oppression: heavy, onerous and set in stone. The judge, a shivering ghost of a man with a shock of snow white hair, stared down at Khalil with a negative expression. He analyzed the accused with digital eyes. Khalil felt like he was being filmed while under a microscope, like some sort of disgusting insect.

"You naturalized or born MEU?"

"Born here. The northern territories. Old Russian."

The judge nodded, and took a moment to pore over his data. Maya Williams leaned over in her chair to speak under her breath with her client.

"Don't volunteer any information. I can get you a shorter term of rehabilitation-via-imprisonment if you stay silent. Cut down on the amount of sessions they put you through, for sure. Eight years medium labour. We're pleading guilty."

Khalil simply looked forward, expressionless.

"You are the son of two political subversives and anti-government agitators – Nakul and Eva Madi, correct?"

"Those are the names of my parents, but they were not agitators. They were right about this country and they loved it very much."

A shocked murmur ran throughout the courtroom, and by now all of the suited journalists had undone their blazer buttons and placed their recording devices in the air. Maya whirled in her seat, grasping Khalil hard by the shoulder.

"What in the hell are you doing?" she hissed. "You're making me look bad! You don't have a case! Are you insane?!"

Khalil swept the arm from his shoulder with a backhand, never breaking eye contact with the judge and his spotted, wrinkled face.

"Regardless, Mr. Madi, their criminal record quite clearly describes your parents as enemies of the state. Do you harbour the same seditionist sentiments?"

Silence. Khalil chose not to answer until the charges

were laid and his plea was expected. By now, the murmuring of the press and public galleries had grown to a swell, the halls of the sentencing chamber beginning to reverberate with the clamour of crude emotions, anger breaking through the veneer of cool logic.

The judge slammed his wooden gavel down upon his high podium and depressed the "order" sign, signaling bailiffs to silence the gallery if necessary in order to expedite the proceedings. Even this somewhat high-profile case demanded efficiency.

"You stand accused of multiple criminal counts. You stand accused of four counts of assault on an officer of the union. You stand accused of four counts of aggravated resistance of lawful arrest. You stand accused of two counts of trafficking in the underground economy, and one count of trafficking marijuana. You stand accused of one count of marijuana use, and one count of cocaine use as well as simple possession. You face seven counts of illegal employment. You face a felony charge for the illegal and knowing alteration of your subdermal implant. As you hold a negative net worth and have no material assets to place in collateral for the tendered services of a legal defense counsel, you have been appointed a public defender. As this legal defense comes at the expense of the state, you may not delineate these charges individually, thus you must render a plea to these charges en masse. Mr. Madi, how do you plead?'

Maya pressed her hands down on the arms of her chair to rise, but was halted by Khalil's own large hand pushing her down into her seat as he rose. Without blinking, or moving his eyes from the judge, Khalil delivered his own plea. His voice would not give an inch.

"Not guilty."

Maya sat with her mouth hanging mute, the colour draining from her face. She could kiss that promotion goodbye. Rage slowly filled her veins as the public gallery erupted with jeers, booing, and catcalls – the press gallery babbling like a human river of voices and exclamations of surprise.

The not guilty plea had not been invoked in superior court for nearly a decade; the last defendant to invoke the plea had been sentenced to immediate execution of the mind, followed by ten years of service and general labour. Khalil allowed himself a tight, sarcastic smile. Even the judge appeared to wake from his lethargy, his monotone now replaced with a tone of barely-contained excitement – a sentencing *for the ages*, he was sure of it!

"Very well, then Mr. Madi. We will proceed with the trial. The court would like the prosecution to make their introductory statement."

The state prosecutor stood, the bearings in his chair squeaking slightly as he shifted his massive weight. He was a giant of a man, though flabby and out of shape, draped in a long black suit. He cleared his throat roughly, placed a chubby hand in a bridge on top of the table, and swiveled his head to gaze at the galleries. While there was no jury system in place, the favour of the public and the press was a well-known tool to all prosecutors hoping to convince impressionable judges.

"Before we begin, let us colour the details of Mr. Madi's lifestyle and history – in particular during his formative years. The defendant was born in 2021, in what was known as the Russian territory of Karelia, now North-central Province – prior to the birth of our Union. His father, Nakul Madi, was a pipefitter and erstwhile engineer – his mother Eva Madi nee Smythe – chose to stay at home and work as a freelance journalist and reporter over the internet while raising the defendant."

All factual so far. Khalil had to wonder precisely where the prosecution was going with this – though he had a strong suspicion.

"Then things began to get a bit more interesting. As Russian nationalists opposed to the amalgamation of our nations into our union, the parents of the defendant staunchly opposed the conservative political movement seeking the founding of what would eventually become the MEU – the state we all live in and enjoy today. Their opposition gradually became outright subversion and terrorism – they protested unlawfully in the streets, resisted subsequent arrests, and wrote polemic pieces of propaganda to local and provincial newspapers decrying the formation of our state. For their continued treason – rest assured that they were given many opportunities, in person, to repent of their oppositional and rebellious positions – they were arrested during a labour organization march on the capitol, and rehabilitated-via-imprisonment as wards of the state. They have served as agents in sensitive roles ever since."

Khalil's knuckles tightened, gripping the edge of the table with one hand and the lip of his seat with the other. He began to feel the world move around him, melting away as if he was floating above his own body. His detachment was so powerful that he barely heard the rest of the prosecutor's opening statement. Even if his parents were technically alive, the spark that dwelt within that flesh was no longer animated by their souls. They had been dead to him for a very long time. He suspected that this was lie designed to unnerve him – it had worked – but reasoned that if they had access to a bargaining chip like this that they would have confronted him with it here.

"As terrorists, they instilled the same hate within their own seed, their own child – the defendant. Following their arrest and sentencing, the defendant was placed under the watchful care and guidance of our very best educational institution, the Damocles Corporation, in a campus on the western seaboard. At absolutely no cost to the accused – merely the standard necessity of fulfilling a ten year contract of service following graduation and discharge – Damocles Corporation raised the young boy into a young man, at great financial cost. Over a quarter million dollars per pupil, to be precise. The defendant was trained in state philosophy, advanced literacy, leadership and discipline, extensive combat and arms training, coercion and interrogation techniques, and general labour for physical endurance. In repayment, he orchestrated a jailbreak from the institution while on combat exercise in the surrounding woodlands, fleeing through the trees and escaping detection despite a lengthy manhunt across the entire region. This is the first time we have seen his face in any official capacity, nearly a decade later."

While the giant of a prosecutor was delivering this lecture, the multiple video screens mounted on the walls of the courtroom sprang to life, playing archival news footage from the day he had escaped from the installation.

He could see teams of camouflaged soldiers, guns firmly mounted to their shoulders, striking out briskly throughout the forest. The leaves were as green and vital as he had remembered. It had been a beautiful summer's day when he had made a break for it – the first time he had been free to explore nature in nearly a decade, and it had only been in desperate flight! The lies continually falling in the nuances of the statement of his accuser were deftly placed, connected to recorded events that he could not dispute, shielded by their proximity to an elementary truth, hindering the opportunity to strike back at the extenuating circumstances.

Khalil ground his teeth and tried to relax his grip, attempting to calm his mind in spite of his raging emotions.

"Even though the defendant had deserted from his duty to the state, and despite his skill in hiding his whereabouts at any given time, we continued to follow his file and collect evidence whenever we possibly could to help us locate him, pressing him to make as many mistakes as possible. The data we managed to collect over this passive investigation was colourful, but not extremely useful to us until the last legs of this race. For a few years, we couldn't even gain a trace on his general whereabouts – until we received an anonymous tip that the defendant had taken up temporary residence in the Northeastern Province – the fringe of our Union. There, laws were laxer than is the standard, in the habit of any border province, due to less manpower and a population more sympathetic to regional concerns than the broader concerns of the state at large. This made it very easy for the defendant, despite being a visible minority, to find safe harbour amongst like-minded subversives and traitors."

Khalil could hold his tongue no longer, his heritage burning hot in his veins, his beard bristling with anger

– he shook like a leaf in the midst of a taunting, teasing tempest.

"Lies!" The word exploded from his mouth. He pounded a thick fist down on the wood of the table with such force that Maya jerked back in her chair involuntarily, spilling some of her documents across the desk. Khalil stood rigid and pointed a long, calloused finger at the prosecutor – his dark brown eyes darkening to take on the aspect of glittering jet. His hand was shaking slightly and he feared he would misspeak. He spat his words free, each syllable envenomed.

"You are the traitors. Every single one of you who sells his manhood and his own integrity to a corrupt and cowardly approximation of law and justice. You who lie to advance your own agenda at the expense of the powerless, and who use their station to gain domination over your countrymen. You call me a traitor!? *You* are the traitorous dogs who live to tremble under the grip of your master's palm. Corporate sluts and self-centered whores – never include me in your ranks! Fuck you. Fuck all of you!"

Khalil had no doubt that as soon as he had risen from his chair, the state livestream would be slowed in order to edit or censor his words on official broadcast. The teeming press gallery would undoubtedly capture his entire speech to be broadcast on various subsidiary shows on the net. It was the least he could hope for. If he was going to die – and undoubtedly he was, he had known it from the moment he had been taken into custody by the police – he had resolved to go out as loudly and with as much strength as possible. He lowered his finger, yet remained standing, staring with a stone expression, piercing the prosecutor with a predator's gaze.

The fat jowls of the attorney seemed almost to shake in fear as if he thought this madman might physically attack him at any moment. The judge nodded towards the bailiffs flanking the bench and they immediately moved into position at either end of the defense table, their faces implacable under the damnable guise of the VISAGE. Their intentions, even in light of their masked facial features, were crystal clear.

The judge scowled down at Khalil fiercely. By now, the bassist was convinced that the judge held no illusions of holding a fair trial, inwardly prejudiced. The press gallery was going wild, screaming questions at Khalil's back. The public gallery was on the verge of a riot – some people hurling racial and personal slurs – *sand nigger! camel jockey! fuckin' pussy!* – and others crying for his immediate judgment and sentencing, the more likely scenario.

"Mr. Madi, you are clearly in contempt of court. Being a witness to this myself, I declare you guilty on this count. I will be adding this to the list of official charges, which we will begin enumerating immediately, explicating each. Would the prosecution continue, beginning with the charges at the first of the list?"

The old man never broke eye contact with Khalil once, though the prisoner detected the phantom of a cruel smile turning the corner of his dry, cracked lips.

"The prosecution prefers to proceed in order from charges of least severity to those of more egregious character, your honour."

"Proceed. The defense will be allowed a cursory defense of each charge, lasting no longer than five minutes." Khalil remained standing. Maya had buried her head in her hands in shock, her long and luxurious hair spilling out over painted plum fingernails onto the tabletop, enshrouding her. The pudgy white hands of the state prosecutor snatched a slim, sleek tablet from the tabletop and he tapped it idly. His face betrayed nothing.

"Regarding the charges related to simple possession of cocaine and cannabis, both illegal substances, the prosecution offers the official evidence collection report garnered by CORRECTIONSCORP officers at the scene of the arrests, the Wreckage nightclub and bar. I am distributing the report now, asking that this evidence be taken into direct consideration by the court."

The prosecutor pressed a thick, sausage-like thumb down on the screen of his tablet, which chirped in mechanical compliance. The report had been filed.

The judge looked as if in a daze, the information be-

ing projected directly onto his vision via optic implant –
the fastest way to read. After a period of nearly a minute,
he shook his head and tapped his temple softly to release
the image from his field of view. "This all seems quite cut
and dry to me. Does the defense have anything to say?"

Maya shot up like a buoy restrained deeply underwa-
ter, nearly exploding to her feet. The effect was visible as
male and female eyes alike swept her suited figure.

"Your honour, I would like to renounce my client in
lieu of his egregious violation of my professional advice,
and take no responsibility nor interest in the stake of his
case."

The judge looked down at the well-heeled lawyer
with a mixture of pity and bemusement; in this judicial
system judges were prized for their low empathy scores,
which logically led to more impartial rulings. The judge
knew that this *distancing* was not in the least possible.
Once assigned to a case, a public defender was obligated
to see it through to completion – even if their client ended up being one in a thousand that shirked the bonds of
responsibility and proper conduct. The stray wisp atop
his bald pate bobbed as he lowered his head in commis-
eration.

"Ms. Williams, your record in courts of law is well
known to all. You serve the state and your clients with
equal acumen and eloquence. It is well understood that
you share no part in the outrageous actions of your cli-

ent – but he remains your responsibility regardless. You would do well to entreat him to beg the mercy of the court, for it appears we are off to a very poor start already." His wrinkled hands gestured toward the tablet on his desk, the tablet responsible for the official court record. The judge's way of telling Maya that it was nothing personal did nothing to lessen the shock of the moment as it continued to unfold.

Maya was fighting to recover her composure and leaned forward, resting a hand on the rich mahogany surface off the desk, breathing deeply to stave off the panicked hands of anxiety reaching for her on the inside.

"Yes, your honour. I am simply asking for it to be made an official point on the record that my client has expressly violated the professional advice I have given him and stands in opposition to my wishes and counsel as his public defender. Judge accordingly."

Khalil turned his gaze, sidelong, at Maya. He conveyed the message with his eyes.

You are a coward, and I don't give a fuck about your career or your image. He turned away from his lawyer, facing the judge once more.

"The coke wasn't mine; it's not uncommon for drugs to be left out in the band room. The weed was mine, and the law standing against the possession of such violates laws born well before the institution of your false ones. Habeas corpus, or the great writ, for one – and the fundamental assertions of the natural law, for another. It is incumbent on you, in the interest of true justice, to prove by what vehicle the simple possession of the flowers of this plant, one which has never killed a human soul, violates the harm principle."

Khalil spoke, his voice only faltering slightly at the beginning under the heavy crushing weight pressing down on his already strained nerves. The whole world was watching – most would get the highly cropped version, but some might be privy to see the entire proceedings. Big words – he normally saved them for Festif so as not to come off as a smart-ass to everyone else. Right now, he needed those words.

The judge drew back, high and aloof in his chair, his eyes assuming the aspect of a pit viper. He had not expected any form of deep eloquence or nuance in the arguments of the accused – from time to time lowborn criminals would attempt to deny their charges with simplistic arguments and lies in common courts, though never in higher channels. The accused's passionate outburst at the outset of the trial bore the marks of a burning soul, but not necessarily a cerebral one. This was something dangerous. The prosecutor, Khalil noted in his peripheral vision, stood wary and slit-eyed.

Williams had assumed a cavalier air of nonchalance, leaving no doubt that she had severed any further connection with the actions of the accused madman. The old man pursed his lips briefly, steepling his fingers, before replying.

"Mr. Madi, a few glaring errors undermine your points. The first is that no man lives in a state of natural law, particularly in such a civilization as we have now. We, the public and the state, require concessions of the individual in order to ensure a thriving, healthy, civil society. With regards to your reliance on the harm principle as a course of legal defense, no such precedent stands in our law – we do not require proof of harm in order to categorize something as an offense. It is abundantly clear that the abuse of illegal drugs, no matter which particular intoxicants, is a detriment to the workings of a productive and wholesome society. This alone justifies the enactment of laws against the possession, let alone the traffic, of such substances. You have admitted to the crime itself, and thus I pronounce you guilty of this charge, both counts."

Once again, a general clamour arose in the galleries – this would be the first sentence in a long string of such; the press and the public had scented blood and now yearned for more. The ruby colour of the wall and the cherry mahogany were stained with the blood of thousands of victims before he; as a man familiar with fate, Khalil did not show any outward sign of surprise.

The prosecutor, in the meantime, continued on as if nothing had slowed him, his nasal voice pronouncing the second allegation between thick lips.

"Related tangentially to the first charge, the prosecution now calls for sentencing of the second charges related to the trafficking of marijuana. Photographic evidence collected from public safety cameras show the accused distributing marijuana cigarettes to citizens. I will now relay this evidence to the court." Again, the prosecutor pressed his thumb against the tablet. Khalil broke his stare long enough to peer at his own tablet lying face up on the table in front of him.

It was a static image of him, a few days previous on the morning which he had gone to meet Haifa at the Spartan. This particular image had been snapped off before he had entered, however, while he had been with Festif in the adjoining alleyway – his hand was extended to the mad philosopher, offering him the joint. Open and shut case here as well – Khalil ground his teeth slowly. He opted to speak of his own accord, knowing that he would receive a guilty verdict on this charge, regardless. His deep voice rose above the general excitement rushing throughout the courtroom.

"He's an old homeless man who kicks around the neighbourhood, though he's always very kind and never starts any problems. He begged me for some relief for his arthritis and I gave it to him over a morning chat. I took no money from him, or from anyone else, in exchange for marijuana. I am not a drug dealer, though I do believe that marijuana can be useful in alleviating some of the pains of this world. Is that type of behaviour and belief now insidious and evil in the eyes in this court of blatant injustice?"

The judge shifted his shoulders as if he grew somewhat uncomfortable in his deep, leather chair. He thought for a moment and then opened his mouth to reply.

"Mr. Madi, once again you gesture towards anecdotal evidence that has no bearing on the relevance of the charge at hand. The circumstances of your crime do not exempt you from the fact that you have committed the crime in and of itself – nor do they mitigate your sentencing in the least. Compassion is an impediment reserved for religious services and war memorials, not a notion of any weight on the blind scales of justice. This evidence, along with your testimony admitting to the crime, draws a verdict of guilty on the charges of trafficking."

These two sentences in tandem would be enough to merit five years of servile labour in a state work camp. Blood had been drawn from the accused, and even the bailiffs, imperturbable and inscrutable behind their projected faces, seemed to relax a bit. Taking a moment to scan the faces of the crowds behind him, Khalil noted a dark, sexual lust for punishment rising in the souls of the audience. Many even went so far as to lick their lips unconsciously, the blood hot and feral in their veins. The defendant turned his chestnut eyes back to the pulpit of the judge, who was busy delineating the next array of allegations.

"–trafficking in the underground economy, and seven full charges of illegal employment. Does the prosecution have any evidence to substantiate these charges?" The judge finished on a note of manufactured curiosity – of course the prosecution would have corroborating documents. This was a show trial and if legitimate evidence could not be found, it would be produced nonetheless.

"Indeed we do, your honour," the prosecutor continued smoothly, as if on cue. "We have photographic evidence that the accused is plying his trade as a musician for direct deposit from the Wreckage," he said, his fat fingers stabbing the tablet again, "as well as affidavits from three witnesses who have seen Mr. Madi performing in other venues as well for undeclared pay. Our most conservative estimate is that Mr. Madi has received nearly a hundred thousand dollars in pay for his services as a musician over the course of the past ten years within the underground economy."

The crowd gasped in shock – such gross tax evasion was unconscionable. Furious epithets were torn from a few rowdy mouths in the public gallery. Khalil turned half-way around to smile at them broadly. Continuing to face down the now-seething mob, he spoke directly to them.

"I work for myself, to survive. Do the math. I made ten thousand a year playing music. How else is a man going to survive? A can of cola costs you three and a half dollars. I contribute nothing to this perverted state, and keep everything I earn to myself – and I'm damn proud of that. I'm more of a man than you cowards will ever be." He smiled, cruelly and honestly, at the men and women surging against the rail.

A man in a dark polo shirt and khakis placed a tall leg over the rail, his eyes wild and aggressive. The taller bailiff left his post and moved to halt the enraged man, his presence alone causing their roars to quieten.

"Guilty on all charges. Now, we move to the unpleasant business of the capital offenses." The judge cleared his throat, as if deeply disturbed.

The prosecutor was high on his internal chemistry, excited and tense – the accused's death writ was nearly a surety at this point, everything but signed and sealed. Sweat had appeared on his pink, porcine brow – he was facilitating a prosecution that was sure to result in the death penalty. His inculcated duty bolstered his spirits, and he spoke free from tremble or falter in his voice, despite his obvious outward distress.

"The accused is further and most seriously charged with the murder of two CORRECTIONSCORP officers, Sergeant Jack Abatangelo and Officer Steven Whelan, as well as two further counts of attempted homicide on other officers who shall remain unnamed for their continued safety. This is in addition to the counts of resisting lawful arrest. We have multiple testimonials written by officers on the scene, a few bystander reports, and multiple sources of footage corroborating these allegations taken from the sensory recordings captured by the VISAGE devices worn by each and every officer on the scene."

The tablet chirped one last time and delivered the evidence into the official court report. Meanwhile, two photographs of the officers outside of their masks were projected onto a large screen on the far wall of the courtroom in memorial.

The court fell silent. Khalil's gaze washed over the burgundy walls and the black granite portico and benches places along the perimeter. He thought to himself, this could quite possibly be the last opportunity that he would ever have to speak with his own voice.

"Those officers *deserved* to die."

Khalil nodded his head backwards slightly to indicate the public and press galleries.

"You will never break me. I am *above* you. You *fear* me."

Khalil lifted his shirt in a sudden motion and tossed it in a heap on the floor at his feet. He stood bare chested before the court, thick black chest hair curling over a muscular chest. Light, livid scars crawled over his back, shoulders and arms. "Here. The whole world can see the truth. Nothing you can do to me will ever hurt me again."

To accentuate his point, Khalil leaned forward and spit on the floor of the courtroom at the foot of the judges pulpit.

For several seconds, there was absolutely silence. Millions of minds attempting to reconcile what they saw with what they knew.

It was an eminently dangerous moment, a quiet which produced disquiet.

The bailiff nearest him struck him a backhanded blow across the face, whipping his long, black hair about and turning his head aside.

Calls for death and punishment rung out once more, now a cacophony of screaming, lustful demons screeching over the railing. Maya stood up abruptly, pale as winter's frost, and strode out of the courtroom, abandoning her counsel to his fate and distancing herself further from the madman. Khalil himself was coiled like a viper, his anger seething within him, wanting to grasp the bailiff's neck in an iron grip and tear his throat out. He grit his teeth and dug his fingernails into his palms, biting deep into his flesh.

The judge peered intently at this man before him, a tall, strong, defiant wretch from the inner city who had defied authorities for over a decade, had contributed nothing to his society except for death and exhortations to death, and had showed utter contempt not only for the society in which he lived, but also the gravity of his courtroom.

"Guilty on all counts. Due to the severity of the charges, coupled with both your contempt for the rule of law as well as for the honour and integrity of this court-room, the law demands severe sentencing."

The public gallery grinned wolfishly as one, rising from their seats, nearly giddy with anxious expectation. The press gallery sat stone-like, awaiting their byline and the real beginning of what was sure to be a momentous story within the news cycle for at least a few days.

"In light of the evidence presented before the court, as well as your own admission of intent along with a complete absence of remorse for your crimes, Mr. Khalil Madi, you are sentenced to *multiple, consecutive,* and *cumulative* execution until deemed Free. Following your rehabilitation-via-execution, should your physical self survive, you will endure a *twenty-five year sentence* of servile labour on our eastern border, with no opportu-nity for reintegration until after such time, not including any additional servile time you have accrued."

Khalil shut his eyes against the sentence, attempting to project his consciousness away from here, to some-how escape his corporeal bonds and live apart from the last failing vestiges of his life. He dug his nails in harder, welcoming the brief pain that reminded him of his continued existence. The world spun about him.

No amount of willpower and integrity can shield one from the fear of certain death.

The bailiffs approached him, and with a professional and robotic coolness, latched their thick and muscular arms under his own. A trail of catcalls, threats, and scornful laughter buffeted him from every angle as he was led towards the far exit of the courtroom. Flashes from multiple video and still cameras lit the room intermittently, casting his olive skin in harsh relief against the dusky rose of the walls.

The whole world was watching, including the small corner of it which had been Khalil's former haunt.

Elliott hung his head low, slumped heavily forward onto the bar at Pixels, face buried in his arms. Festif sat perched on a nearby stool, watching the glowing screen, his wrinkled and whiskery face wet with tears, his frail body shaking beneath his motley cloak.

Less than twenty kilometers away, Haifa drank a glass or two of expensive red wine, starting off an exquisite evening of fine dining with Damen; she was hanging out in Two a lot more lately and rarely watched the news.

Hassan never watched the news and Rat was sitting on the carpet in a hotel room, bare chested, with a needle in his arm and his mind awash in a sea of inventions.

Shawn and Heba were alone in their apartment, eating microwaved dinners and quickly losing their appetites. They held one another closely. Shawn was on the verge of tears. He hadn't cried in years. Heba was his rock, the most stable person in their shrinking world. She held him against her chest and gripped his shoulders.

Millions across the nation watched it in their homes. Some cursed violently at the uppity camel-jockey – he would get what was coming to him soon enough. Some found themselves conflicted.

Some, particularly nearer to the beating heart of cities, clenched their fists.

Some switched the feed off.

12. FREEDOM OF EXPRESSION

Gregory Nottingham's STATE OF THE UNION – Great Americans for a Strong Tomorrow

"Live Feed from the Beating Heart of News to Your Screen"

The executions will take place in less than six hours, this very evening, and our nation will be cleansed of one more arrogant dissident who threatens our democracy and spits on our flag. I can honestly say that I'm as shocked as you all are in seeing the absolutely disgraceful conduct perpetrated by Mr. Khalil Madi, a man convicted of more crimes than I thought we had on the books – including the murder of two of our youngest and bravest.

Cursing in our Supreme Court? Spitting at the foot of His Honour? The whole thing seemed rather

theatrical and staged to me, as if this devil was act-
ing out some sort of mad gambit in order to gain new
converts. Well, huffing and puffing is to be expected
from core city trash, but then he actually had the gall
to reveal those sickening scars! As if our profession-
ally trained and disciplined law enforcement officers
would enact such punishment on a small child, as he
claims! Hyperbole is certainly the name of the game
in this case, and cheap theatrics and big words don't
mean jack squat when you're trying to gain converts
on the way to the gallows.

Tonight's pay-per-view is already attracting an
unheard of amount of buys, already surging towards
the all-time purchase record set by the execution
of graffiti vandal and pulp-fiction propagandist Sois
Chalance nearly four years ago. He got two hundred
million buys and we're showing a projected total of
nearly three hundred million. [1]

On a more personal note, was I the only great
American who nearly shook with rage when that
bearded, bristling terrorist spouted such disrespect
for our armed servicemen? These officers put their
necks out on the line, day in and day out, dealing
with violent, drug-dealing scum like Madi everyday –
and yet he's the victim? After brutally murdering two
officers serving in the line of duty, performing legitimate arrests on violent criminals? After abandoning

his initial period of service to our country – as a cow-ard – and then hiding in the filthy underbelly of the core, dealing narcotics, getting drunk, and scream-ing vitriolic and obscene sedition in an attempt to agitate the mob to violence? Yet, somehow, in some strange and bizarre universe, we are suppose to not only sympathize with this drink- and drug-addled bum, but further to tolerate or even agree with him?

Great Americans work hard, long hours. Many of us do not have much to speak of, but we treat what we do own with dignity and reverence. We fol-low the rules, upholding them as an example of how – if we all work together and all share the same goals – we can create a better country that all of us can ap-preciate, an unquenchable flame of freedom that our enemies beyond our borders seek to extinguish just as violently and callously as Mr. Madi and his ilk have attempted to do from within. We sit at our desks and we work, and we work hard – turning the gears of in-dustry and ensuring a bright future filled with oppor-tunity for our children. Men like Khalil Madi, though I hesitate to even grace the condemned animal with such a word, are not a symptom of a failing society – as he would have you believe – but rather the cause of it. Their own inadequacy is projected, writ large, so that other failures can find a reason to hate suc-cess, hate progress, and in doing so, hate their own nation and their own countrymen.

So what do we do about it? Do we take this insult, this disgracing of our time-honoured laws and traditions, lying down? No. Do we, as proud and productive Americans, accept a terrorist spitting on the judge's bench and uttering threats and profanities? No! What we do is wait these ponderous six hours, spending them spreading the news of the atrocities committed by this Godless murderer to our friends and families. Share this story on the social network and spread the news* to all of your acquaintances and associates. Watch justice take its course tonight as the craven and unapologetic coward is brought to sobbing, pleading contrition and beyond.

I know that's what I'll be doing.

-*Gregory Nottingham*

*by clicking "Share", you will be e-mailed a discount code offering you 10% off the purchase of this evenings pay-per-view as well as entered into a contest to win one of three Grand Prize packages including airfare and accommodation to visit Median Studios for the live taping of the Repatriation Ceremony in approximately six weeks. © American Philosopher Media Properties

[1]: Now is the time to invest in Median News and Events Corp, the private-public partnership entity producing and distributing all of your legal and political news! If you hold a Patriot Portfolio, your membership is guaranteed! If not, perhaps now is the time to buy in! Tonight's sales alone will produce sizable dividends for all stockholders in addition to being a strong message of affirmation in the strength and pride in our union.

EXERCISE YOUR RIGHT TO FREE SPEECH!
READER COMMENTS BELOW *(Displaying Results 1-5 Order: Oldest to Newest):*

TruPatriotLuv12: I think it's sick that this terrist is allowed to even eat his last meal! Why didn't the guards at the courthouse kill him for real when he started cursing? My dad got so angry when we were watching this on our screen at home that he threw the controller and almost put a hole in the wall! I can't even pronounce his name, or even write it, he's clearly not one of us and doesn't have any rights at all. I hope we get to talk about this trial in school tomorrow so I can tell them what I think.
LIKE 10,241   DISLIKE 402

Valeria: We don't need idiots like this polluting our gene pool, and we rightly clamped down on rulebreakers. Too bad we didn't manage to catch this particular waste until now. Off with his head, again and again.
LIKE 23,422   DISLIKE 1,056

TheSoundandTheFurry: Don't know how people were even willing to sit through that whole manifesto? I tried a few minutes of listening to the idiot talk and it was just crazy rant material.

guy had a problem with cops, guy took it out on cops via force and threats, cops responded with force and he ended up with a death sentence. That's really what it ends up as at the end of the day. Not a question of who's to blame (he is), or whether the problem he had with cops was brought on by others or he caused it or not.

LIKE 18,684   DISLIKE 789

WingMan1984: I think it says a lot more about the limp-wristed justice system that we have in place that we even give this joker a trial. We shouldn't be wasting time and money on this EXPLETIVE FILTERED, after all bullets are cheap and so are shovels.

LIKE 9,130 / DISLIKE 1,521

TazMaRazz: I love the fact that you are speaking openly and frankly with us, Mr. Nottingham. I listen to your web-cast every day and I make sure to tell my co-workers about the way things are REALLY going on in the world. You can't trust those alternative news networks that are so biased that they openly admit to it on air! What happened to objectivity? Fairness and balance in reporting? Do these idiots even think before they open their know-nothing mouths?

It's good to see American journalism reconstituted each and every week with some courage and some backbone here at the SotU. Keep up the great work.

PS. Can't wait to see that sucker fry.

LIKE 13,422 / DISLIKE 65

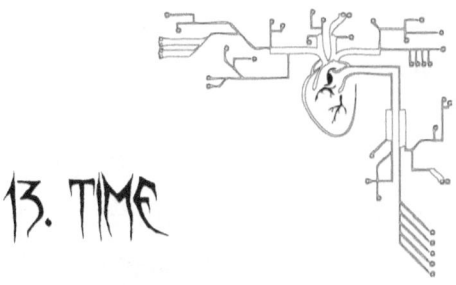

13. TIME

As soon as Khalil exited the courtroom, escaping the cameras and the insults, he felt his spirits flag and his shoulders slump. It had been a lot easier to be proud and courageous when he'd known the whole world was watching. That had been two weeks ago, and his courage was failing him.

Khalil's mind spun slowly, unbalanced, chemicals firing into oblivion.

He didn't *feel* there. This didn't feel *real*.

He found himself staring down at the remnants of his last meal. Khalil had requested a T-bone steak, medium rare, and a heaping mound of garlic mashed potatoes with real butter. He asked for a pint of Lab City Lager and got that, too. Now the bone lay in the center of the plate, sitting in a pool of pink juices, every last bit of meat torn from it. Same for the potatoes; only a few skins were left strewn on the plate. Truth be told, he couldn't finish all of the beer – it started to set his stomach in motion and the last thing the musician wanted to do was puke on his way to the gallows.

If he was going to die anyway, time after time, it would be better for himself and for those poor bastards like him, angry and silent on the streets, to retain as much dignity as possible. Khalil hoped he meant something to them.

He wondered – briefly now as the bailiff standing behind him placed a hand on the shoulder – if Haifa or Amina watched his trial – what would their faces look like?

Haifa's face appeared in Khalil's mental vision, beautiful yet vicious, a twist of her lips indicating disapproval. His third eye had drawn every feature of her face in stark detail, high contrast. Her terrible and lost beauty tugged at him, a short gasp barely audible.

She would not have cried – Khalil didn't think so at least – but rather shaken her head as if to say "That's a shame!" Of course, that would have quickly been followed by "After all, you brought it upon yourself – and I told you so."

But Amina – he did not know if she'd even gotten away. Khalil barely knew her. Still, a large part of him deeply wished that she was safe, even though he knew it was unlikely.

His parents. He kept thinking about them. Their "executions" had probably been a great deal more mundane. Certainly less theatrical. Perhaps that was for the better.

After they were done with him, it was likely that he would be a brainless husk willing to serve the bidding of Central. Not if he could help it, but he wondered if he'd be able to resist for any meaningful amount of time. Nobody else had, and there had been plenty of offenders brought to those cables and wires.

Khalil felt himself being lifted from his seat at the cold steel table by the bailiff.

Time to go.

Khalil took a deep breath, appreciating the sterility of the remanufactured oxygen. Only a few breaths left before his soul was to be stripped from him once again. Last time they did it with whips.

This time they'd do it with psychoactive drugs and the murder of his sentient self. His consciousness was to be placed on the rack and pulled and torn loose from its moorings, moulded like clay. Then, hardened. Smooth and strong in appearance, entirely artificial.

"This way."

The security officer had Khalil's shoulder in an iron grip, pressing him firmly toward the doorway leading to a thin, long corridor. The floor was of that same flecked ceramic that Khalil recognized from crumbling schoolhouses and hospitals in the cores. The walls of the corridor were painted a flat black. At the end of the hallway was a small opening, almost like a hatch, which led into the immersion chamber.

Khalil took his time. He was acutely aware of the feel of his own body. The fabric brushing against his chest. The tightness of the band about his waist. The expansion of his lungs drawing in dead air.

Would he remember the torture and simply be forced, for the rest of his life, to act against a buried will?

Would he be wiped clean and replaced with a simulacra that affected his soul without truly possessing it?

Would he simply cease to exist and enter a period of eternal blackness and unconsciousness?

One could only hope. Before that question would be answered, however, there was a great deal of pain to endure. Khalil shivered slightly as he and the guard reached the end of the hallway, facing the squat metal hatch.

"Put your hand on the scanner beside the door, and then step back." The guard's gruff tone was further deepened by a built-in vocoder within his VISAGE. Death's voice was deep and gravelly, digital and emotionless. Khalil lifted his hand up to the scanner, felt the cool glass under his palm, followed by a wave of slight heat from the scanner washing over his handprint, bathing it in alien light.

He was registering for his own procession. Khalil couldn't stifle a bleak chuckle. Couldn't he be fashionably late? And these clothes! A snow-white jumpsuit that clung tightly to his body – not exactly a tuxedo and coattail. The humour fled as quickly as it had come, yet Khalil was deeply thankful for even small mercies.

The hatch sprung open with a hiss and swung wide, forcing the condemned to take a tentative step back into the stun-baton of the guard – thankfully not activated. The guard jabbed Khalil with the point of the baton between the shoulderblades, forcing him to proceed into the chamber.

The room was fairly small, perhaps twenty feet by thirty. The walls were also black, as was everything else in the room – the banks of computer servers, the harnesses and wires hanging from the ceiling like diseased vines. The empty coffin of the contact suit hung limply from a constellation of cables.

The overhead lights were extremely dim – it was apparently important for the sake of the immersion to restrict as much light as possible from interfering with the visual apparatus. A bespectacled man, tall and thin with gaunt features and pale, nearly translucent skin was also dressed in a long black lab coat, seated in front of a computer workstation, tapping furiously at the touchscreen.

"Ah, yes, yes. Bring the condemned in."

He turned his face to look at Khalil, seeing almost through him. As the surgeon – Khalil could see the distinctive scalpel insignia on the doctor's breast, above the pocket – looked him up and down, Khalil suppressed a shudder. This surgeon was studying the dark man as an objective piece of meat rather than as a living human being. Khalil felt like livestock.

"I have a name, you sick bastard."

The crackle of the stun-baton activating behind him. A brief pressure applied between his shoulderblades. Pain coursed through Khalil's entire body, his muscles burning and tensing as he fell to one knee. The steel of his handcuffs made a musical tinkling. He could still hear the humming vibration of the baton floating in the air behind his neck.

"Now, now. I am fully aware that you have a name. You will have a new name within a few hours. I suggest you relieve yourself of the attachment to your name as soon as possible – your transition will be a lot more seamless if you relax and allow your sentence to transform you into a vital member of our society." The voice of the thin-lipped grey doctor was high, nasal, and aloof. "Strip him."

Rough hands tore his jumpsuit free. Buttons lining the seams made it a fairly simple process.

The doctor approached, holding a long syringe. Khalil tensed to spring, but felt the butt of the stun baton pressed against the nape of his neck. No funny business.

"This drug will allow you to integrate nearly seamlessly with the immersion suit, substituting your reality as you know it now with the reality provided to you – a psychedelic psychoactive alongside dissociation in order to facilitate your processing."

He grasped Khalil's arm, searching for the vein in the bend of the elbow. Finding it, he gently inserted the syringe and depressed the plunger until nothing was left. He removed the needle.

Once again he was prodded to his feet by the officer behind him, wearing the executioner's mask.

Now, all time slowed to a crawl. All details became important, total focus was near. The moments left in the life he had lived could be counted on a single hand. His consciousness of this fact blended seamlessly with the sledgehammer of the drug coursing through his veins.

Let's get it over with.

His last clear thought.

There were only three stairs up to the railed platform where the immersion suit hung. The black metal of the platform was scratched in a few places and even dented along each of the stairs – apparently many victims came kicking and screaming.

The contact suit itself was comprised of a wild assortment of electronics and harnesses designed to simulate the feeling of complete freedom of movement. Steel rings would be punched into his skin at over three dozen points on his body, attached to a long feedback cord.

Khalil would dance like a marionette inside of this black room.

He would run in place from his captors. His body would hang in full suspension, all of the rings embedded in his skin pulling taut.

Khalil could not drive this image from his head – his skin being pulled up in so many points as miniature tents of olive flesh, ripping and bleeding freely. Maybe if he fought hard enough he could, ironically enough, expire from blood loss in the physical world.

The mask became the center of his attention as he took the first step up to the platform.

Only two more steps left to go.

The mask cast its gaze downward, tilted at a forty-five degree angle. Two virtual definition projectors were placed just above the ocular vents – there were slits to allow for venting of the indigo-hued gas that would be constantly applied to his respiratory system.

The mask, like every other aspect of the room, was also black. It clung tightly to the face, in the shape of a grim death's head.

The dissociative began to take hold, and it felt like two spheres of his mind ripping apart. A placid calm stole over his body and he stopped shaking. He began to feel like he wasn't even there any longer; perhaps there was no loss after all.

He mounted the last step, facing the opening of his mask.

"Strip him."

Khalil felt cold, rough hands expertly tearing away his jumpsuit, which was merely closed by snaps on one side. The suit came away from his body in one smooth motion, leaving him naked. The bailiff stepped down from the platform, and the surgeon spoke from behind his console.

"Prisoner. Do not move from your present position. Your body metrics are being scanned in order to proceed with the suspension ring fitting. You may speak to the Reverend, if you'd like, to cleanse your soul, at the additional cost of two months of servile labour following your cognitive restructuring. Do you elect to add this option?"

Khalil leaned over and spat on the floor, feeling himself make the motion and simultaneously viewing the scene from without. It felt like two near copies of his consciousness beginning a journey in separate directions, getting farther apart by the second.

The computer made no reply, a negative response seemingly the default. Khalil felt the strength fading from his limbs. His body felt oppressively heavy. A trio of robotic limbs extended with a whirr from the ceiling – two of them held him in a firm and steady grip while the third began driving the steel rings through his flesh. Each stud drove through the skin and some small amount of muscle with a pneumatic hiss, like a spike being driven into soft wood.

With each stud and ring a new piece of the contact suit was fitted, drilled tight to the flesh and anchored in place. Sweat and the slick flow of blood kept the suit from digging too deeply into his skin, but he had yet to be suspended and to feel the force of gravity pulling at the plates.

Whether the pain was truly mild or not he could not tell. His material senses had begun to fade. He was now firmly in the grasp of the surgeon's drugs, and reality was a word that had lost any singular meaning for him. Again and again Khalil felt the clamps grasping his limbs and pinching his flesh together for a new piercing, the most notable sensation being the cold steel against the skin. He could feel tiny streams of blood running down his neck, shoulders, arms, back, legs, and heels.

The doctor advanced on him, his lab coat swaying dramatically as he approached Khalil. Khalil was fascinated by the folds of fabric – how they moved as he drew closer, a textile ocean.

The doctor climbed the steps to stand next to him. His head felt like it was going to float from his body, away from his shoulders, gore rolling down his back. Khalil could see this with his mind's eye, more real than the skeleton-man standing in front of him with the sign of the scalpel on his shirt.

Khalil could see the surgeon leaning over his back to inspect the installation of the suspension rings. He wiped the prisoner's back down with a stinging antiseptic pad.

"All of your rings have been fitted properly. You will undergo your sentencing in less than two minutes."

It was all he could do to nod, black curls of his hair falling in front of his eyes. He stood, barefoot and bleeding. The contact suit fit him like a velvet glove as dark as the night sky, the shining metal hooks like stars dotting his flesh.

"Do you have any last words?"

Khalil tried to make his lips work, but the feeling was foreign. His body was numb. Khalil gurgled slightly in the back of his throat while the doctor leaned closer, his pale face reeking like sterility.

"Yeah. *Fuck* you." It was barely a whisper, bubbling past drug-relaxed muscles.

"No, prisoner. Fuck *you*." A thin smile rose to the doctor's lips, and a bright pink flush coloured his delicate cheeks. He looked like some sort of painted jester to his prisoner, leering, grinning, leading Khalil to his doom. Khalil tried to hate his torturer but could not summon his animal instincts from beneath the great sea of drugged lethargy.

His muscles would not move again until his new life

began.

"Execute the prisoner," the doctor hissed to the large array of databanks around the perimeter of the room. The command was verbal and voice-matched to bypass security protocols and to sign the death warrant. The computer set to obey.

Khalil felt the rings grow taut, like a pulling hair, and he was lifted into the air, inclined slightly forward, inducing a rather strange sense of vertigo. The incline was not so great as to be painful, not so steep as to restrict his movement in any meaningful way. For some strange reason, Khalil felt whole again – the dissociation seemed to pass slightly as the mask began to lower itself below him, and tilt up towards his face.

The mask grew even closer, now only inches from his face. Then it pressed about his skull. Khalil felt human hands reach for leather straps, tying them expertly about his head.

He could barely breathe. There was no air!

The gas began to be pumped through the oily black tubes attached to the mask, a thin wisp of blue-grey smoke rising from the jawpiece and up to meet his nostrils. The smoke smelled sweet yet slightly stringent, chemicals mixed with some sort of earthy compound that was reminiscent of peat. At the very first breath, Khalil began to feel his eyes widen and his muscles return to action, quivering with energy. His eyelids refused to close as the mask completely ensconced his face.

All Khalil could see now was darkness, the absence of all light. The sightless oblivion of the coffin.

The smoke continued to rise up into his throat and nasal cavity, burning his skull. He could not choke nor gag. His body would not respond until the transfer of his consciousness was complete. His eyes would not close, fixed in place upon the miniature projectors above the ocular slits and the small amount of gas escaping from them.

The inert projectors sprang into life, driving bright images directly into his immovable gaze – the flash of cameras. Stereoscopic speakers built into the death's head helmet crackled, activating and spilling the sound of a cheering audience into his ear canals.

Khalil ceased to struggle and simply was.

14. SLEEP TO DREAM

I wake to the gentle shaking of a hand on my shoulder.
"Wake up, honey!" *My mother's voice. I open my eyes, blinking to try and clear the sleep from my eyes. She looks down at me. Her face is young and vibrant. The room is bright with sunlight, streaming in from a nearby bay window. We are at our summer cottage on the south shores.*

"Were you having a bad dream, baby?" *She brushes a loose lock of chestnut brown hair away from her eyes. She sits on the edge of my bed, a cup of coffee in her free hand. She likes it black, and I could smell the strong grind.*

"Yeah," *I say.*

The sound of the ocean waves crashing on the beach can be heard from the cottage, which is so close to the ocean – less than a minute's walk from the front door to the bubbling surf. A slight breeze, salty and cool even in the hot August summer, brushes the thin curtains aside.

"You okay, big guy?"

My dad is standing in the doorway, tall and powerful. A wide moustache graces his face, his skin – already naturally dark – deeply tanned by many summer days spent out in the sun.

"Yeah, no problem, dad."

"Heard you hollering some. Bad dreams?"

"Yeah. Same as before."

He nods brusquely, considers the matter closed. My mother continues to look at my face, showing me her small, private smile.

"Time to get up big guy. We're going swimming!" *From behind his back he produces a pair of my swim trunks and tosses them onto my sheets. He gives me a wink, raises his own mug of coffee to his lips, and turns away from the doorframe.*

"Well, you get dressed and we'll meet you out there, okay?" *Mom leans close to me and gave me a kiss on the cheek. I smile. I feel a lot better. I squirm a bit and she smiles even more.*

"Love you!" *she says, standing up and taking another sip from her coffee mug.*

"Love you too, mama."

She turns and leaves the room. I can feel the spring and light vigour of childhood, a drastic contrast between how I ... had felt before.

What before?

This thought troubles me, and a gripping feeling of deja vu builds inside my stomach, like an iron ball.

I shake my head to try and shake the troublesome thought – no doubt a lingering touch of a disturbing nightmare – and swing my legs out onto the floor. My room here in the rented cabin is the same every year, a light pastel blue with a nautical theme wallpaper that was peeling in spots – an anchor and a lighthouse alternating.

I leave the room and clip through the hallway toward the living room slash kitchen of the cottage – a single room with a small LED television and basic cable. I see that the Saturday morning cartoons are just finishing up – I'd slept in longer than usual and I'd even missed breakfast. I watch briefly as two poorly animated knights do battle atop a castle rampart, the black knight beating the white knight into the flagstones with a comically oversized iron mace.

Two plates and two mugs sit unattended on the drop-leaf kitchen table.

I open the kitchen door out onto the open-air patio and see mom and dad taking a swim out in the deep blue water of the ocean. The waves are almost black, growing clearer as shallow surf flows over the white sand beach. The grains of sand on the southern shore of the maritime province are almost like dust, and flecks of them glint like gems in the sunlight. A far cry from my much colder, much grimmer home further North – though both are beautiful and speak to me inside.

I walk onto the beach, feeling the heat of the sand beneath my splayed toes. Perhaps my blood stirs – all I know is that it feels incredible. The iron ball in my gut melts away into a distant wisp of memory. My parents splash at each other, laughing and sneaking a kiss when they think I'm not looking.

I feel the song of the family in my heart.

I call out to them, cupping my small hands around my mouth, teasing – they wave at me to come join them out in the sea. The surf presses against my shins and legs, lapping at my waist as I rush into the freezing water. Most people liked to dip a toe in, or their feet, slowly absorbing the balmy temperature of the Arabian Sea. I always ran headlong into the crashing, bubbling surf and relished the feeling – a moment of time in which you just knew you were alive, that you could feel.

My parents are further away than I thought. I make a dozen strokes and yet it doesn't seem like I'm getting any closer.

I come up from the water on the next stroke. There is something strange about how my parents look, bobbing in the water ahead. I plunge again into the water. My head breaks above the water again – deep strokes now – and my parents are both turned away from me, treading water.

I notice that the sunlight has dimmed, and somehow the sky has now been filled with looming, grim clouds. I am almost there, and can now feel the return of the sick feeling in my stomach, can feel the gaze of these swelling clouds beating down upon me. I cry out to mom, I shriek for dad to help me.

My parents turn to me, and they are not my parents. My mother bears a face that is not her own. My father's face is an empty space. The two figures are snatched under the waves, as if pulled from below. I can barely hear a soft, relieved sigh. It may have been my imagination. I can feel my heart beating in my chest now, hard against my ribs.

I can't breathe. I feel the iron ball in my stomach begin to weigh me down. A soft hand grips my ankle; the grip increases in pressure, almost crushing. I feel heavy raindrops whipping against my hair, my face. I look up and my eyes are stung shut. My mouth fills with a sick and sour metal taste.

I can't breathe!

My lungs struggle with convulsions, gagging and retching noises erupt from my throat and nose.

My hands grab at my mouth, tearing. I open my eyes again and the sky is weeping blood from coal-black clouds. I feel the hand gripping my ankle crush my foot. The pain itself is distant, surrounded by terror.

My head is drawn under the water. The pressure mounts on my skull, crushing me as the descent accelerates and my consciousness fades.

For the first time, I know what it feels like to die.

15. TICKETS TO THE DARK CARNIVAL

"Well, ladies and gentleman, what a *terrific* start to the show!"

The deep tenor of the stage announcer swept out of the virtual studio into millions of homes, institutions, and drinking establishments across the Union. The bronze and handsome face of Mr. Lyndon Blackmarsh was split in a blinding smile. He stood in front of a semi-circular array of high definition, three dimensional capture cameras.

The audience that was visible was populated by viewers wealthy enough to own their own contact suits. Thus, the audience could attend this exclusive pay-per-view broadcast from the comfort of their own homes, transported to an exotic locale for sport with the swipe of a subdermal with enough credit.

Contact suits were a consumer version of the immersion suit, minus the gas mask and the suspension rings.

They allowed complete tactile and sensory experience of the subject's consciousness, though they could not, of course, gauge or replicate the subject's inner dialogue or emotions. They had to rely on their own individual emotions to supplement the pure sensory experience.

This made it a lot easier to lie within the simulation, hidden behind a digital mask. Guilt, rage, fear, and others would only show if intentioned.

Maya Williams was one such viewer, linked directly into the audience with her own contact suit. She removed her mask and reclined on top of her four-post bed, staring up at the blue silk canopy. Sweat ran down her face and chest, her breasts heaving in fear. She had not personally used the contact suit to witness an execution before – the thought had usually disgusted her.

In this case, she felt it necessary in order to better understand the client that had already begun to ruin her career.

Ray had already begun seeing one of her associates at a competing firm. He'd likely hatched the power play as soon as he'd smelled trouble after the trial, a week or two ago. Ray was cunning enough to hitch his wagon to a rising star rather than a shooting one, leaving her bedroom empty for a few days.

Maya could not handle another experience in the contact suit. She turned on the wall mounted display to watch the show in a more old-fashioned manner. A young blonde intern from Two was lying next to her in bed, squirming against the silk bedsheets, apparently continuing to relish his own immersion. She looked at the perfect skin of his toned back, muscles articulating against his fair skin as he shifted.

She turned her attention to the picture projecting from the wall, the square-shouldered Blackmarsh with perfect – though graying – hair and the kind of chiseled jaw that only a plastic surgeon could produce.

Dark Carnival was the name of the rehabilitative stream, and it was shown whenever there was a criminal of note who would stir the excitement of the crowd. The perfect synthesis of capitalism and corrective justice. Publicized punishment and reinforcement of proper mores with a price tag and a profit margin. Beneficial to the public and to a private purse.

Executions were fairly rare, multiple executions rarer still, but other forms of less harmful punishment were enacted on a weekly basis. In *Gladiators*, for example, prisoners were placed into the bodies of virtual contestants, facing off against vastly superior opponents – both in terms of skill and in terms of weaponry. While such bouts rarely went to the death, they were still extremely painful to the hapless prisoners, who were struck multiple times by seemingly real weapons, producing undeniably real pain.

The host, Lyndon Blackmarsh, had been the emcee

of the gladiatorial arena for nearly a decade now, never missing an air date. Gregory Nottingham was his co-host for this special event, however, and threatened to steal his spotlight; Blackmarsh had to go the extra mile in terms of dressing up his avatar. Blackmarsh's hair was slicked to the side in a long swoop, black with streaks of grey that never seemed to change with the course of the years. His tall and powerful frame nearly filled the screen; he looked like a man who could handle himself in the arena with ease.

The introduction to this particular, special edition airing of *Dark Carnival* had been short but sweet in order to accommodate the abnormally large amount of executions to screen in the special three hour streamcast.

The three-dimensional camera arrays had swept in from a darkened corner in the subterranean suspension room in which Mr. Madi's body was currently held in suspension-immersion. As soon as the injection took place, the effects crew began to transition their focus to the virtual studio hosted by Mr. Blackmarsh, and the viewership nearly moaned in anticipation when the gas began to flow into Khalil's mouth, nose, and lungs. The show had begun, and Williams, her intern, and millions of other people had just witnessed the first kill.

Now came perhaps the most intriguing part of the show, the revelation of the Wheel of Fate. Whether the wheel was truly spun at random or – more likely, Maya

guessed – there was a veiled itinerary of specific programs that would be run in order to produce the intended results, nobody knew.

It didn't really matter. Simply the unveiling of the
pinwheel itself was a monumental thrill, each bladed
rudder containing a picturesque landscape with a brief
title that alluded to the horrors within. There was hardly
time for the audience to read each blade. The camera
panned over the large steel pinwheel so quickly and with
such rapid camera cuts that it was nearly a visual blur,
thoughts and pictures revolving so quickly into the that
it was hard to grasp or recall any particular image.

Maya could feel the sheets move; she looked over to
see the intern's short, soft fingers clutching the bed tightly, his knuckles white and shaking with anticipation. His
breath was coming quickly, excited.

She could feel her own anxiety building within her
as she watched the oversized wheel began to spin. The
coloured arcs acted in a hypnotic fashion as Blackmarsh
began to narrate in his sonorous voice.

"Yes, the Wheel of Fate spins, shaking free the dust of
years that have settled on its blades since it last claimed
the life of another murderer."

There was a steely timbre in his tone that seemed to
suggest that Mr. Madi was getting all that was deserved,
what was coming to him. "Where will it settle, where will
we be thrust next?"

The blades began to slow, and the stage lighting dimmed in the background, leaving the multi-coloured steel pinwheel cast in a striking light. The scenes became more visible as they passed from darkness into the spotlight.

There was a desert vista, sand dunes rising high against a moonlit sapphire sky. This scene receded into the background, like an old watercolour in pastels.

A dimly lit study, a pair of beautiful wooden chairs, and two ghostly figures. This blade, too, edged its way out into the shadows.

The pinwheel slowed to a halt, leaving a single petal exposed to the spotlight.

The picture burst to fill the entire frame, exploding even beyond the borders of the video screen to wrap around in panoramic view to those who possessed a high-definition set or, better yet, the full contact suit.

The vignette painted in sharp, contorted colours was extremely graphic in nature, a darkly erotic portrait. Naked young flesh, saliva, ejaculate, an open and expectant mouth – swallowing and smiling devilishly. Lovers reveling in their lust, contorted and ambiguous.

Large sex toys, light leather whips, a hand wrapped around a pale and delicate throat, squeezing.

A few scattered, stifled moans from the audience, a human cry for release. Those whom remained silent were no less aroused.

"Why choose between the two? We now watch as Pain and Pleasure sail into view, fleeting and disloyal and deliciously addictive."

The scene approaches, growing larger over the audience, each individual being isolated slowly and then enveloped by the image, within a cocoon or a waking dream.

16: PAIN AND PLEASURE

I am in the back seat of my parent's car. My girlfriend, Jennifer, is in the process of taking her bra off. It's flesh coloured and padded – her chest is somewhat flat, her breasts not quite a handful.

Her nipples slip out of the top of the cups as she winces, reaching behind with both hands to work at the clasp. They're perfect, small and hard and almost pink. I can feel myself getting rock hard, the type of erection that you get over a half-dozen times a day when you're a teenager and that you need a blowjob for when you're hitting thirty.

She pulled at my belt, leaning over my bare chest and brushing me with her nipples.

My left hand cups her, squeezing her gently and rolling that small nipple between thumb and forefinger. She was breathing heavily, and a low moan slipped from between her lips – almost a whine of anticipation.

She'd gotten my leather belt off and was hurriedly picking at the button-and-zipper of my jeans.

I reach my right hand downward, around her neck and back, slipping my fingers beneath the waistline of her boyshorts and grabbing the soft, warm flesh of her ass. Now my jeans had been unzipped, and she pulls at my hips to pull my pants and boxers free.

She is hungry, she loves sucking cock, she would do it for hours.

Her hand pulls me free, long and rigid and jutting up from her fist. Her eyes are shining and wide, her small breasts shaking slightly.

"Khalil, you make me feel so good. I want you. I'm going to taste you, and show you how much."

She uses her free hand to brush her hair away from her face and begins stroking me with her fingers, lightly brushing up and down the length of me, leaning in to kiss me passionately. Her small, soft breasts press into my chest; I can feel her nipples against my skin.

She sucks my lower lip into her mouth and bites it lightly. She flicks her tongue in and out of my mouth, and when I return suit, she holds my tongue in her mouth, gently sucking it.

I feel the blood surge again and again to my cock, causing it to rise away from my abdomen and fall back again as her hand wraps around and pulled at it. She smiles at me, a sweet little smile that I still...

Still?

I don't think that's the word I'm searching for, we haven't been seeing each other that long...

But none of that matters now.

Her head is in my lap and her mouth is sweet and warm and her tongue is eager yet gentle. I feel the vibrations of her moans in her throat as she slowly turns her head from side to side, exploring me.

She takes the entire length and drives a wave of pleasure through my body, making my fingers and toes clench and curl, my right hand making a fist in her long, blonde hair.

And now, the pain. She likes to bite a little bit, teasing nibbles at the fringe of my foreskin. The act itself arouses me. She shifts her weight onto the bench seats in the back, turning sideways and spreading her thighs to allow my hand purchase – she needs me now.

She continues to kiss and nibble me and reaches an arm out, her hand grasped tight around my wrist, leading it between her milky thighs. She'd shaved herself; the bud of her clit is firm and engorged. I can feel the heat coming from her, and I know she is already wet, I can feel it on the inside of her thighs as I rub her, gently.

I feel the heat from her mouth around me again, and once again I throw my head back, resting against the seat, my eyes looking up through the rear window. The sky is overcast, the stars concealed from view. There are no city lights here and the darkness is near perfect. A sharp and brutal pain shoots up through my groin and abdomen, and I immediately curl forward, my teeth clenched.

"What the fuck!?"

I cry out, looking down and trying to get a glimpse of what is going on in the low light afforded by an obscured moon. Jenn raises her head up from my lap and I can see a smear of near black across her lips. I smell blood. My eyes instinctively flick to my groin, and I see that my cock is bleeding, a ragged bite strung along the top of the shaft.

The pain is almost unbearable. Her head bows again, smiling and licking her lips clean. My hands reach out to grasp her by the throat.

The world seems to bend and shift and break apart around me, I feel like I am being lifted away from my body – loss of blood perhaps.

I close my eyes, squinting them shut to block out the pain. I feel my hands tighten around her neck.

I begin to exert some deal of pressure around that soft little throat in anger.

The pain around my groin recedes to a dull ache. I hear a scream as if from far away, drawing nearer, until it became a series of short, gasping, desperate sobs.

I open my eyes.

"What the fuck!?"

Haifa cries out, desperately squirming against the wall and slapping my hands away from her neck, red and beginning to show hints of bruising.

Where am I? I'm so confused.

I was in my car... with...

"What the hell is wrong with you, Khalil?"

I don't understand. One minute Haifa and I are having sex, and the next, I just black out?

Why am I in my room, back at my apartment?

I'm having a waking dream, something about my life a few years back that just sidelined me like a freight train. I feel my erection, still throbbing.

"I—"

Haifa stares at me, wide-eyed and fearful. Her eyes are locked on my face, her hands still limply holding my wrists – a useless gesture, really. My physical dominance is well established; she couldn't stop me even if she wanted to.

She trembles like a frightened animal. She has always been afraid of the scars running across my body – almost like unfinished business or a debt unpaid that would be called into reckoning someday, and I'd just snapped.

My mask had slipped, and she'd almost paid for it with her life.

"I'm... I don't know. I just blacked out. I'm sorry... I'm so sorry."

I feel hot embarrassment flushing my cheeks, the rising feeling as if I were going to start crying.

I never wanted to hurt her! I wasn't that kind of man! I was better than this!

But there were my fingerprints, starting to show purple through her delicate skin.

She is hysterical, still pressed hard up against the wall.

"You almost killed me! You were choking me, and wouldn't let go! I didn't know what to do! What the FUCK, Khalil?! Are you fucking crazy? I'm getting the fuck out of here!"

She springs to her feet and attempts to move past me. My hand shoots out, catches her ankle in mid-stride, her body tumbling down face first on the corner of the mattress.

I drag her back, effortlessly, into my arms. I can feel her shaking against my chest, her large breasts spilling over mine.

"Shh, shh shh."

I put a finger to her lips. She moves her knees apart a bit so that I can press against her slit. She wants it more than ever before. Her arousal mingles with her primitive fear, creating a toxic combination. I can smell it from her. It just makes me harder. My erection rises again, a rush of blood and the flexing of my shaft pressing hard against her.

"You liked it," *I breathe in her ear, my breath hot.*

"Oh, please. Oh please," *she begs, crying, tears springing from the corners of her eyes.*

She relinquishes her feeble grip on my wrists and runs her hands down my back, grabbing and squeezing my ass as hard as she can with her long, athletic arms.

"Hold me down and fuck me as hard as you can. Use me."

I grasp her small wrists and held them together with one hand, using my right hand to spread her knees and hold her in place by her hips.

I am just about to enter her when I feel her pelvis collapse beneath my weight,.

The bones shatter and the skin rips free in my fingers.

Her body seems to deflate from the inside, the breath escaping from her lungs and whistling from her lips. Her skin feels weak and brittle under my hands. Bones begin to puncture her skin. Her breasts fall flat and distended against her ribcage.

Her bones begin to animate, tearing from the flesh entirely and coating my lower body in blood and gore. I instinctively try to jump from the bed, tearing my shoulders away from the skeleton.

I feel wet bones, still slick with blood and ichor, pinning me, hugging me tight. These brittle bones now seem like iron bands across my back.

I try to close my eyes but they won't move. My muscles won't respond for some reason. I am paralyzed.

The flesh on Haifa's face hangs from her jaw. Bits of hair are still stuck and matted to the top of her skull. I scream.

She screams back, from I know not where – just a sick, high pitched, terrified scream coming from between her filthy teeth. They are a sickly colour, like the inside of a boiled egg.

Her teeth begin to blacken and rot in front of me, falling back into her skull with a slight rattle.

I free an elbow and manage to bring it down, hard, on the exposed skull. I feel it crack and split slightly around the temple, and with a grunt I strike again, as hard as my muscles and position will allow. Her skull splits apart from the blow of my elbow, her jaw breaks free.

Still, with no rhyme nor reason, she continues to scream. It it getting louder – it's so loud that it feels like my eardrums are going to explode.

As I close my eyes and cover my ears against her shrieking, I notice that the faded floral wallpaper coating the room is starting to strip from the walls, curling artfully downward.

What the fuck is going on?! Am I dreaming? What is this?

Wake up!

The thought bursts through my brain, screaming to match the high pitched whine of the grinning figure between my legs. I open my eyes and witness the impossible.

The long strips of wallpaper are crawling over the bed, nearly covering the entire surface in some kind of undulating weave.

The screaming stops as a long strand of the wallpaper, the colour of tobacco stained parchment, winds itself over Haifa's skull.

I already feel loops fitting themselves around my bare thighs, my wrists, and my chest. I pull and pull against the seemingly fragile bonds, but the paper will not relent. The edges are sharp and draw blood as I struggle. I feel yet another tendril wrap itself firmly around my testicles, looping around the girth of my now flaccid penis.

Haifa begins to sit up again, the paper falling in curls from around her face and down her torso.

Except that it is not Haifa, is not a skeleton – it is Amina.

Her tiny, naked frame seems different, somehow, than how I remembered from...

When had I met her again? How did I know her?

She purses her lips sweetly, freshly coated in a bright-red lipstick. The cuts in my arms and thighs overrule my sexual drive for the moment. My mind is still trying to work its way through a massive labyrinth of confusion.

I am trying to connect the dots. There are far too many.

"Khalil. Always the gentleman. Last time I saw you like this was just before I went down on you, remember?" *Her eyes flash, meeting mine.*

Her eyes are brown, rusty almost, tarnished in some way. The particulars of the room seem to fade into the background, leaving me, Amina, and the paper straightjacket. The dirty red walls of the Wreckage seem to close in around us. The lights in the room dim even further until it's just as it had been. Ghostly liquor bottles in soft focus are standing on top of the band-room bar in my peripheral vision.

A paper snake winds its way around my neck and, try as I might, I can't turn my head. I am beyond panic.

"That's better. Now, where were we when we were so rudely interrupted last time?" *she asks softly, her eyes quite clear in delivering her message. Amina rises to a kneeling position in front of me. I relax my muscles for now – struggling only makes the cuts deeper. I am already faint from mental exertion and loss of blood, which is flowing somewhat freely from many weeping wounds.*

She lowers herself closer to me. Her small and perfect breasts graze the inside of my thighs as she brings her red-rimmed mouth closer and closer to my cock. I can feel myself growing hard yet again, the hot breath from her mouth stirring me despite myself. I feel helpless.

"You are a very bad man, do you know that, Khalil?" *she asks prettily, licking lightly at the exposed head and keeping her eyes fixed upon mine. I am fully erect now, giving way to more primitive, essential desires. Lust courses through my veins and again I try and tear free from my bonds – again the paper sinks deeper into my wounds.*

Now, blood is streaming at a fairly consistent rate down my limbs, across my back, even down and around the base of my penis. My blood sinks into the paper, which seems almost to wriggle and writhe in joy at being fed, sucking the blood from my body in sexual excitement.

"You are a very bad man, I said. If you can be called a man at all," *she adds with an unsettling smile. There is a deadness in her eyes that terrifies me. I do not comprehend the meaning of her last words until I feel the sudden constriction around my genitals, watching as Amina lifts her arms.*

The skin and tissue of her torso is grotesquely distorted, a strand of gristle from her hands in a long thread, wrapped around my erection. It bites into me with invisible teeth, drawing beads of blood at first yet increasing in pressure.

I bellow in pain. I call her a whore, a slut, my desperation explosive. I can feel the ligaments and muscles literally snapping as my cock and balls are wrenched from my abdomen.

I kick and arch my back, trying to break free. I howl. Blood gushes from the open cavity and stains Amina's breasts, stomach, and thighs.

She closes her eyes in some sort of ecstasy.

With my last conscious breath, I heave my body forward; I spit across her placid, upturned face. Blood continues to stream from a dozen slashes and a gory abscess, down into the knife-edged folds of the wallpaper straightjacket.

I die a second time, naked and mutilated on a bed of iron roses.

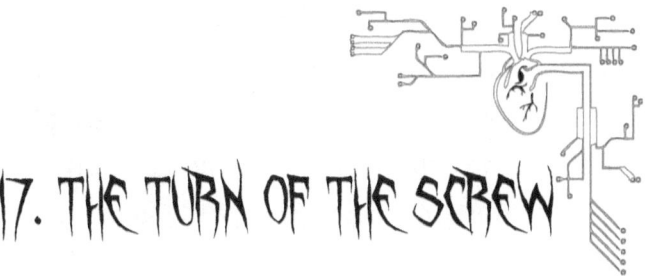

17. THE TURN OF THE SCREW

The crowd assembled at Pixels turned away from the monitor behind the bar. Some patrons continued to play the arcade games, although Elliott had been sure to hook the sound system up to the live broadcast to overpower the electronic bleeps, chirps, and chiptunes of the cabinets. Most had pale faces and many had been sweating or crying. Some had streaked to the bathroom to vomit. Many of them had known Khalil either quite well or at least casually, as a fellow patron of the bar, a classic gamer, performer, and friend.

*"I can't do this..I can't deal with this I **can't**."* Elliott spat under his breath, scrubbing furiously at a worn patch atop the old wooden bar that never seemed to get clean.

A few customers had remained at the bar, watching the intermission of the broadcast with blank stares. It had been a very long time, many years in fact, since the last pay-per-view execution, and in this case, the prisoner in question was one of their own. Still, some lined up at the bar listlessly. Others preferred to simply be here, playing games and trying to avoid as many of the gory details as possible, hearing only the general drift of the night's events.

"That was fuckin' terrifying," an older woman muttered to him, nursing a tall drink of vodka and soda. She looked like she'd seen the other side of forty and had been working here in the core city for her entire life. Deep age lines cracked her face, but she maintained that small, cynical smile so common around the area. Equal parts bitterness and black humour were represented in that secret smile. She took a long pull from her straw. "I've never seen anything like it. Last time it was a single execution and it was standard stuff, a virtual lethal injection and then off to sleep. Why are they taking it this far? Is it for the ratings? There can't be much left of him now..."

She trailed off, seemingly replaying the grotesque and graphic imagery in her mind, in a faraway place. The barman replied.

"They just want to make an example of him; show the rest of us what to expect if we stand up to the authorities and defy Central. I hear that the war overseas is going poorly and *that* kind of talk alone can get a man jailed. Spitting at the feet of a court justice and spitting on their entire culture at the same time? What did he expect, that *stupid bastard?*"

Elliott nearly shook with anger as he spoke, his emotions completely spinning out of control. Of course he believed what Khalil had said – what the man had said was truth. But why say it, what could he possibly gain from being so antagonistic against an enemy that held all of the cards?

The woman took another long drink. "He expected that we'd all watch it. And he was right. Everyone and their damn dog is watching this broadcast – doesn't matter if you're some rich cocksucker in his suit out in Four or sitting here watching it on an old vidscreen like us. The whole of the Union is watching this case and he knows it."

She pushed the mostly empty hi-ball forward and Elliott snatched it up.

"I don't want to watch it but I have to. I don't want to see my friend go through this, but I have to. I know he's making a statement. I believe in that statement. In my heart I do. I would say almost all of us who live here believe in his statement – we're powerless and we have nothing. He is showing us that we still have something." He gestured with an off-hand palm towards the liquor display, and the middle aged woman nodded, her graying hair falling over her face as she did so.

"Yeah, whatever the hell that is. I don't have anything

except my own bones and a body that's giving up on me two decades too soon. I'll be dead in a few years. Real dead. Corpse rotting in the ground gone. Not like that," she said, gesturing at the announcer currently on the screen. "I can feel it. And for what?" she snorted, snatching the drink from the barman's hand before he could finish pouring the mix into the glass.

"I feel for Khalil. I didn't much care for his music, but I loved the energy that he gave off – something wild, something crazy, something you couldn't tame. If anything, this is just one more sign that God doesn't give a fuck about poor bastards like us, and seems to love giving an easy lay to people who don't deserve it and never worked a day in their lives." Her eyes were heavily lidded, hatred her native tongue, a language well understood by Elliott and anyone else within potential earshot.

"The more things change, the more they stay the same. I heard that in an old movie once, and I never forgot it. It's the truest statement I think I've ever heard in my life. If you believe that, though – why bother making yourself a target? Why subject yourself to this?" The tall, lean barman nodded at the screen behind him.

"And the more you two yap, the more goddamn distracted I get!" growled a deep voice from the other side of the bar, wedged in between two arcade cabinets.

His back was turned to the bar, long and straggly salt and pepper hair falling down loosely over the upturned collar of a long tan topcoat. The coat was almost a jester's motley by now, stained in so many places that it retained very little of it's original shade, having taken on a more monochromatic palette in the interim.

His name was Josef Aubienov but most of the regulars just called him Grampy or Gramps – he and Festif were perhaps the two oldest men in the community.

Josef was seventy-eight and was only now just beginning to stoop with age. He was a tall man, over six feet tall, muscular and lean like whipcord. He was unshaven, with white, wiry stray hairs along his jawline. He was always found wearing a well-worn flannel sweater and a long pair of patched navy workpants. Both were typically stained deeply with oil – the war paint of the working class. Joe had worked on cars, homes, plumbing, and pretty much everything else.

Most of his work was under the table. He'd worked in some places outside of the city as well on a special work permit. His stories of the rings outside of the perimeter always drew a crowd, but years had passed and now his tales were as tired as his bones. Not many people listened to his stories anymore, and he had little work to do in an age of gadgets beyond his comprehension. He could fix a manifold or a piston but he couldn't figure out how to use a tablet, even one with an OS built for schoolchildren. He did, however, have a deep love for pinball, and Elliott paid him a small stipend to come in and repair the two working pinball machines still present at Pixels.

"Sorry, Gramps!" the woman bawled out over the bar, to which the old man gave a curt nod and returned to his game. The clanking and slapping noises of the mechanical pinball machines were largely drowned out by the booming digital speakers of the later arcade machines that proliferated in the arcade, but Elliott had placed the pins closely enough to the bar that he could still hear them. It was the rhythm of life to him and gave them both some comfort – the sounds of play for the bartender and readily available alcohol for Josef – a win-win situation.

The middle aged woman tossed back the rest of her second drink and then shambled for the doorway, waving goodbye to Elliott as she stalked her way down the narrow corridor of cabinets next to the stairwell upwards.

Shawn was also here, somewhere in the mess of machines, playing a few games during the intermission in order to try and take his mind off the plight of his friend. A few of the customers had already begun to pass out. Some were so ridiculously drunk that they slumped forward over their joysticks or fell asleep on their seats.

The atmosphere was depressed yet tense, like a rusted spring bound tightly, lubricated with rotgut liquor. Business was good, at least, small and pitiful consolation though it was.

The intermission drew to an end, and Elliott and the

rest of the bar turned their attention back to the video screen. He tapped at the volume control and brought the bass-deep voice of the announcer into the room.

"Welcome back, ladies and gentlemen, a very warm welcome back! It certainly has been a very moving night, has it not? We've seen sights of terrifying heartbreak, sensual lust, and horrific gore – and we're not done yet! Let's have a few words with some extremely lucky members of our studio audience just to see how they think things have been going."

Nottingham's simulacra walked across the stage to mingle with audience members. Given that this was a controlled digital set and none of the participants were physically in danger, public figures such as Nottingham had adopted an increasingly personal and casual rapport with their loyal and passionate viewers. They touched at the creases of his stunningly fitted designer suit jacket, eager fingers plucking at his lapels.

Countless smiling faces of the pale elderly and the idle rich were upturned to him beneath one of his outstretched hands. Beneath the other palm, the pinched, angry masks of the perceptually oppressed – working-class social conservatives who blamed their lot on "the welfare" and other cathartic dogwhistles, unlucky capitalists with narcissistic personality disorder and a sadistic streak; those with an appetite for blood and pain visited upon others.

All belonged to his flock and bent to his gospel of prosperity via punishment. His digital demographic was influential in so many ways; his blog reached tens of millions of paying subscribers. To see him here, to literally feel his presence as an avatar, was mana to them. The energy was palpable. This was a historic moment.

Nottingham reached the periphery of the crowd and extended a hand, waiting for his producers to select a transmission to usher forward. After a few moments of suspense, the cameras panning over a few likely candidates – a senior woman wearing a long and luxurious wig, a young man with his newlywed wife, holding hands and cheering, a stern looking businessman with a blond moustache – finally settling on a sour-lipped rake of a man looking side-to-side on the edge of the mob.

"You sir! Yes, you!" Nottingham called out, pointing a long index finger at the man, who seemed to snap out of his own thoughts and place his hands on his chest with incredulity. After a moment, the audience member took a few tentative steps forward to join the host, who immediately wrapped a large and brawny arm around his sloped shoulders.

The other announcer, Blackmarsh, stood with his arms lightly clasped behind his back, showing off his physique to female admirers, smiling at the proceedings but not really paying too much attention. A showman, Blackmarsh was unlike Nottingham in the regard that he didn't particularly care for political nuance or intellectual pursuits; he did care for the paycheque and the lifestyle it afforded. He was not an ideologue in the same sense as his co-host.

"And what's your name, friend?" Nottingham asked, tilting the microphone downward so that it might reach the mouth of the thinner man he held in the crook of his arm.

"Chris... Christopher Winters." The small man was shaking, slightly. He'd not planned on being thrust into the spotlight with hundreds of millions, if not billions, watching. There was a patina of sweat forming on his bald head.

He looked small and wilted in his oversized blazer and ill-fit dress shirt.

"Well, Chris, welcome to the show. Our producers tell me that you're a teacher – is that right?"

"Y-Yes."

"And you teach high school history and classics, am I correct?"

"That's right, at L. Shaw here on the West Coast."

"Well, Chris, now is your time to shine. You get to spin the Wheel of Fate and decide what exhilarating scene we're all going to enjoy next – and after that, we'll be offering you digital copies of our library for use in your classroom as well as a free trip to Las Vegas for TWO WEEKS!"

Nottingham nearly shouted this last, prizes were commonly given to audience members or "contestants", but rarely of this size and expense. Mr. Winters shook like a leaf, and now the sweat was like a thick film on his brow. Nottingham clutched him closer, drawing him near to his breast, pressing the microphone even closer to his lips.

"What do you think of that, Chris from the West Coast?"

"It's... It's great."

The tiny man did not seem capable of displaying anything other than extreme anxiety. He looked about to faint.

"Well, come on up and spin this wheel! Let's see what fate has in store for Mr. Khalil Madi next!"

The crowd roared in unison from across the globe. Meanwhile, tweets and forum postings flew like wildfire, burning with increasing violence.

18. THE DARK AND FORGOTTEN SPACES OF DIGITAL EXISTENCE

On sop.wolfpaws.net, port 6666, several characters were currently stalking through the dank corridors of the Miskatonic Asylum, avoiding crazed inmates and other dangerous, aggressive mobs. Multi-User Dungeons, or MUDs, were an archaic aspect of the early internet that had largely faded into obsolescence, but a few thousand players still ran private servers on small, regional intranets that still accepted the telnet protocol. Essentially enhanced text-based chat-rooms complete with monsters (or mobs), quests, and treasure – hardcore gamers still sought out servers to engage in some old-school roleplaying from time to time. Shadows of Paradise was one such server, with ten players currently questing.

```
<2395hp 894mp 102942/200209xp> The Mis-
katonic Asylum - Northwest Wing
```

You stand in the hallway of the northwest wing of the famous Miskatonic Asylum. The walls are painted black and there is but little light to show your path. The howls of escaped lunatics reach your ears, echoing throughout the cracked ceramic hallways. There is a long trail of blood leading to the north, growing more fresh as you reach the end of the corridor.

Obvious exits are: North, South, West.

A gibbering mental patient is here, struggling to free himself of the straight jacket.

Brule the Dragoon stands here [PARTY]
Caballo the Nimble stands here [PARTY]
Lysis the Lyrical stands here [PARTY]

Lysis: Are you guys watching this?
Brule: Yea, it's fucking crazy. Did you see the last one?!
Lysis: I've never seen something so bru-tal. And he SPIT IN HER FACE!
Caballo: That bitch deserved it. What's

up with the gore?

Caballo: Can we just get on with the
game? I need five more lunatics for
this quest and two syringes for the drop
quest.

Brule: Yea, yea, hold your horses.

The party moves North...

<2395hp 894mp 102942/200209xp> The Mis-
katonic Asylum - End of the Line

You stand at the end of the corridor
of the Northwest arm of the Miskatonic
Asylum. The trail of blood ends here, a
headless corpse lying prone in the left
hand corner of the hallway. A hunched and
shivering form looms over the corpse,
clutching a severed head and bowing low
to feed upon it. Guttural noises and the
sound of chewing flesh are all that you
can hear. The lamplight is especially
weak here, as nearly all have been broken or extinguished.

A huge inmate kneels here, eating the
flesh of his dead companions.

Brule the Dragoon enters from the south...
Caballo the Nimble enters from the south...
Lysis the Lyrical enters from the south...

Lysis: Everyone ready?

Brule nods his head affirmative.
Caballo laughs mercilessly at A Huge Inmate.

Lysis backstabs A Huge Inmate!
Her dagger slice DECIMATES A Huge Inmate!
A Huge Inmate tries to trip Lysis, but fails!
Brule joins the fray!
Caballo joins the fray!

[Lysis: Feeling Fine FOE: Scratched]

Lysis' circle attack SUCCEEDS, confounding A Huge Inmate. CRITICAL STRIKE!
Brule's spear strike IMPALES the shoulder of A Huge Inmate.

A Huge Inmate CRUSHES Lysis with a bear-
hug!
Caballo grapples with A Huge Inmate,
but loses the test of strength!

[Lysis:: Wounded, FOE: A Bloody Mess!]

Lysis' circle attack FAILS against A
Huge Inmate.
Brule's spear strike RUNS THROUGH the
chest of A Huge Inmate.
A Huge Inmate is DEAD!
Party gains 10,002 xp and 103 gold piec-
es.

Caballo removes A LoNg SuRgIcAl SyRiNgE
from the corpse of A Huge Inmate.

Brule: Easier than I expected.
Caballo: Yeah, well, last time there
was just two of us.
Lysis: I can't believe that we're watching this type of stuff on TV now. Where's
the dignity in this?
Brule: I know what you mean. It's insane.
Lysis: I think it's sickening. The guy

```
obviously  killed  those  cops  in  self-
defense.  We  ALL  saw  what  happened  in
court.  Did  any  of  you  see  the  surveil-
lance  videos?
Brule:  No.
Caballo:  When  do  we  get  to  kill  more
stuff?
Brule:  Can  you  link  me?
Lysis:  Just  one  second,  and  make  sure
you  set  up  a  few  proxies  before  you
check  it  out...
```

On the Usenets, now a disambiguated and decentral-ized set of semi-connected and secured intranets, sur-veillance video and handheld video from the night of the raid on the Wreckage had made its way into thousands of eager hands.

A massive thread had been turning over, roiling, for at least a few weeks following the initial posting of the first video. Subsequent videos had followed, spurring further debate. The text body of these threads was per-petually being stored and resubmitted across the net-work, meaning that several copies of the same thread spanned the Usenets and were commented on in a frag-mented fashion.

One such discussion was currently taking place as Gregory Nottingham led the hapless history teacher to the Wheel of Fate, calling for absolute silence as the little bespectacled man prepared to heave the wheel one final time.

In alt.news.centralmeu.northeast, the discussion raged on hardest:

Initial post by M. Haggar:

As we can all see in this video, the accused "murderer", was simply performing with his band this evening, and had no intentions for violence. After his set, he disappears down the corridor leading to [inserted later: we now know that this corridor leads to the band room out back, thanks to local poster J. Faustus] the band room. The camera shows that he stays in that room until approximately three quarters of an hour later, when armed officers storm the public house and begin beating the crowd indiscriminately.

At approximately 1:34 in this compilation video of the raw feed, we can see two officers wearing a VISAGE mask holding down a young woman and beating her senseless after she was fully restrained. At 2:09 we see an CORRECTIONSCORP officer utilizing a stun gun on an elderly patron near the pool table. You can see him collapse after the first shock, and then convulse onto the floor as the officer applies what appears to be lethal current. At the very least, this man is unconscious, as he does not move an inch for the remainder of the footage. Our first glimpse of the accused comes at 2:54, where he comes running from the hallway, presumably over the noise of the conflict in the main bar, and you can SEE the look of shock and anger on his face. He immediately grabs his bass guitar from the stand and strikes the officer here, at 3:03, across the skull. It may have been a killing blow, but it's impossible to tell given that all of the officers are wearing their VISAGE projectors.

A brief melee ensues for the next thirty seconds or so, where we see Madi cripple at least one officer as well as delivering an elbow across the face of another – another possible killing blow which would account for the two alleged CORRECTIONSCORP fatalities. The question is not "Did Khalil Madi kill two CORRECTIONSCORP officers at The Wreckage" - most of us believe that he did – but rather "Was this killing justified"? And a great many of us believe that it was – it certainly seems obvious from the surveillance tapes that have been leaked to us. These officers are obviously storming into a public house and randomly beating everyone within, sometimes to apparent death. Who is the real criminal here? Why do we continue to allow ourselves to be ruled like this? Are we men or are we slaves?"

>>>> Turbocat says:

"Can't agree more brotha. Let the idiots who watch the Central streams believe whatever they want, they haven't seen this footage and even if you showed it to them, they'd say some shit like: "Well, those fuckers deserved it, they're all criminals anyways." What is a criminal in this society? Someone who doesn't fit the mould precisely? All of us here on the Usenet are already criminals – we're accessing a non-monitored and non-moderated forum which became a crime in the Digital Communications Safety Act less than a decade ago. I'm behind enough proxies and firewalls that I don't mind saying that Central is a fascist organization in the truest sense of the word, and I'm sick enough to tell you all today that I think Khalil Madi is a hero. I don't care who is listening, or reading, or trying to trace me. I'm dying anyways, slowly or quickly it doesn't matter to me. I know he can't hear me and that he'll never read this, but I just wanted to get that off my chest. And I'm not the only one, believe that. Do they really think they can bury this leaked video? This is going to explode, and I'm ready for it. I have nothing left to lose."

>>>> All Those Evil Eyes says:

"This makes me sick to my stomach. You can clearly see these coward cops just slaughtering these people who were just there for a show. This is just another crackdown on people who don't have SHIT. Instead, we work call centers, process frozen food in run-down fuckin' factories, and rot to death. If we don't rot, we live sick. Fuck Central. I'm going to start talking to my friends and see what we can put together. FUCK CORRECTIONSCORP, and FUCK THIS FARCE. Live free for once, you bitches! The cops better hope I don't catch one of them unawares, by themselves. A lot can happen in the dark."

>>>> Expand: [145 more posts]

On the *State of the Union Official Forum*, things were certainly a fair bit different. Not only were the clientele posting from their citizen's accounts directly, but they were also all elevated citizens – living in the rings encircling respective population centers.

Gregory Nottingham encouraged all of his viewers to comment as much as possible in the name of "inclusive, comprehensive public discourse from the grassroots upward."

And so, his followers posted in droves.

Gregory Nottingham's STATE OF THE UNION –
EXERCISE YOUR RIGHT TO FREE SPEECH!
READER COMMENTS BELOW *(Displaying Results 1-5 Order: Oldest to Newest):*

Please note that ratings have been temporarily disabled.

Melissa Zoltan says: Just to correct everyone talking about this mysterious "surveillance tape", none of us have actually seen this alleged tape, nor has anyone else – to my knowledge. It seems that once again the loony left is up to their usual tricks of obfuscating the real issues – ie. The fact that Khalil Madi is a proven murderer – and trying to draw sympathy for the devil. Isn't the current state of our rotting, disease infested central cities testament to why we shouldn't allow these people to have a say in how our society is structured? Why would you let lunatics and layabouts determine the course of our culture? Frankly, I'm riveted by Nottingham's performance on this show and I think he's doing an excellent job in conducting the rehabilitation service.

Catherine Finch: Is anyone at all a little grossed out by the kind of mind that this pervert has? I mean, in all of the other executions the visualizations were fairly barren and sterile, but this time it's just so sensational. Blood, gore, graphic sex – I had to put my young ones to bed shortly after the second sentence was being enacted! I'm paying good money for this program, using it both as an education tool for my children as well as instilling proper values in them. This is shocking! Is there no way to restrain the prisoner's imagination or his thoughts in order to make this event more family friendly for those of us trying to raise the generation of tomorrow? Or, at the very least, a refund?

Lee Garehte: Melissa – the surveillance tape is certainly real, and I've seen a few bits and pieces of it myself on various blogs and other newsfeeds on the net that are surfacing even as we speak. While I won't speak as to the content of the video, it does place these events in a very unusual light, and I find myself more than a little confused as to what the official narrative on this case really should be. That being said, there is no doubt that Mr. Madi is a murderer (this is confirmed in the video, I've seen it myself) but the circumstances of his crime have not, as yet, been discussed to my satisfaction.

Tifa Shalani: This is the best PPV I've ever seen! Why do we not do this more often!? I can barely wait for the next scene! To Lee, that guy above:

Ahhhh yes...... Finally a cop hater offers his/her worthless opinion so other cop-hating posters can applaud. Congrats! You win the Internet.

EVERYONE covers up their transgressions if they think it is possible. Whether it's the police, the church, normal citizens, organizations.... It's all the same. The police are just an easier target than most because they tend to be disliked by a sizable percentage of the population.

This SOB was a killer of police, innocent citizens.... Personally? I don't give a damn if they kill him in-

tentionally or unintentionally. I don't care if he was convicted under false pretenses or not. Have a grief? Take it to Central.... Don't stew on it for a few years then decide to resist arrest and kill as many people as possible.
Game over Khalil Madi....You lost.

Tim Mayfield: This is easily the most effective rehabilitation session I've ever watched on Greg's show. All these people asking stupid questions like "is it right?" Doesn't matter, in a legal sense. He represented a clear, articulable, and immediate danger to life. Using deadly force is authorized, regardless of type. If you're justified in using deadly force, it doesn't matter what kind you use. They'd have been justified in shooting, stabbing, starving, burning, or bombing him.

In households across the nation, families reacted. Couples argued over the sentencing. Fathers told daughters to go to bed and to leave the adults to adult things. Mothers told sons that this would be the end product of their errant ways if they kept it up. Sons and daughters alike snuck the signal into their rooms and watched surreptitiously.

The world held its breath and a silence fell over the globe as Christopher Winters, an until-now anonymous

History and Classics teacher, tottered over next to the Wheel of Fate for the final spin of the evening.

"All right, Chris. Now remember, it has to be spun hard enough to make one full rotation or else we'll have to discount your attempt and allow another to take your place as the prize eligible contestant, so really put your back into it okay?"

Nottingham clapped the small man hard on the back with the flat of his hand, fingers resting atop his shoulder. The microphone danced in his hand and the audience laughed as one. Mr. Winters did not reply, setting his mouth in a firm line and reaching his arms up to grasp the spokes of the wheel.

The music, a bass-filled classical piece with an ominous character, began to fill his ears and those of the audience, building to a climax. Winters heaved downward with all of his might, and the wheel immediately spun into motion, silent as death, as the orchestra grew louder. Cymbals and drums like heavy rain joined the accompaniment, now a rollicking and bursting crescendo.

The wheel began to slow.

A euphoria was evident, a charged collective effervescence that rose from the spine and seemed to scream out of each and every body. The history teacher had already slumped his shoulders in apparent relief, Nottingham rubbing excitedly at his shoulders while he described the blades that began to come into focus as the wheel came to a gentle rest. The crowd seemed to deflate, a slight moan of disappointment rippling across the studio and then across the continent.

"The Art of Conversation! How appropriate that would come up, coming from you, Mr. Winters!"

By now, the teacher's complexion held a firm note of ague, and it was evident that he was on the verge of losing his grip. The beaming host gently led Mr. Winters to the edge of the stage, and pushed him forward back into the crowd.

"Thank you very much for your time and assistance, Chris. We'll have our agents get ahold of you after the broadcast to deliver your prize package!" At this, the applause signs were projected again, and the crowd delivered a somewhat tepid round of applause.

This particular execution, the final one of tonight's proceedings, seemed anti-climactic. Without further ado, Nottingham once again placed his arms akimbo and drew them downward in a universal sign of silence, or sleep, and the crowd followed his lead, deep.

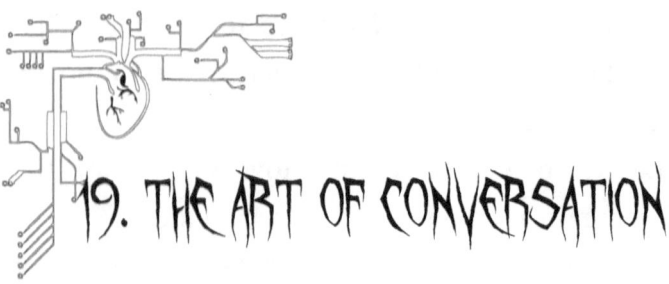

19. THE ART OF CONVERSATION

I feel like I am nodding off – perhaps the drink was too strong. I tilt my wrist from side to side and watch the deep amber of the scotch roll against the sides of the glass, the shrunken and depleted ice cubes clinking against one another. A bottle of Chivas blended scotch sits on a small round table to the side, flanked by two more glasses, empty and upturned. The residue from the lips of previous partygoers rests on the glass lips, the slight remnants of previous contents hugging the corners in the bottom of the tumbler.

The walls are lined with bookshelves, deep cherrywood that has an immaculate stain and smells rich and spicy. The wallpaper is a dark burgundy, like the colour of the deepest Italian red wines, changing in colour to a near rose when approaching the light cast by small pot lights placed in each wall, subdued.

I take a quick inventory of the books on the shelves,

picking out the titles I am at least familiar with. A great deal of economics textbooks, primarily the works of Friedman, Von Mises, and Hayek. I shudder to see Ayn Rand nestled next to Machiavelli. A great many volumes of history, largely outdated and with a firm emphasis on the sociobiological. A number of philosophical works by the early Greeks. Not much in the way of fiction whatsoever.

"Ah, I see you are paying attention after all. I had feared that my endless ranting in tandem with the strong drink may have caused you to drowse off." *A smooth voice, baritone and strong, with a charming quality.*

I bring my attention to a man I'd never seen before. He is seated in a chair directly opposite me. I find it exceedingly strange that I hadn't noticed him before. I take another drink from my glass, feeling the hot and languid fingers of the scotch stretching out into my throat and burning into my stomach.

"Yes, sorry, my apologies. I must admit, I felt a bit tired for a moment," *I manage to say.*

"Well, that's to be expected. You've had so much to drink that I doubt I could come even close to matching your display of fortitude!" *Here, my host pauses. In the light I can make out the fine contours of his face.*

His complexion is hawkish and lean, with prominent cheekbones and a tall, towering forehead. Long black hair flows back from his hairline, slicked back and trailing down to his shoulders. His eyes are dark and mysterious, possessing a vital shine that does not seem to match the rest of his rather conservative countenance – a smile that doesn't belong.

He's wearing a dark brown suit with an ivory collared shirt, complete with a silk necktie bound by a full-Windsor knot. Slight pinstripes punctuate the fabric of his suit and wind about his lean, almost skeletal limbs. Steely fingers grip the arm of his leather recliner so tightly that his fingertips bleed white. The other hand delicately cups his own rocks glass.

"Right, well, that's fine. I'm back with you now. What were we discussing?" *I probe, trying to gather as much information as possible without tipping my hand. I have a deep and unshakeable feeling that my hand was already face up on the table.*

Music began to touch my ear, and I notice that Rachmaninoff is being played at a muted level from a vintage turntable in the far corner of the study. Not my thing, but I was familiar with a few pieces of classical music; even though I didn't really care for the genre as a whole, Rachmaninoff was better than most else. I like his aggression and wild abandon.

"We were discussing ethics – you remember, we're talking about capitalism." *His eyes narrow slightly, scrutinizing my face. Looks like the pleasantries were coming to an end. I feel naked, as if lying would be both impossible and foolish.*

"Ah, capitalism. I see you've got some economists lining the walls here, though none that I can say that I identify with." *I gently shake my head for emphasis, and to try and clear it.*

"You identify with theorists? I just read them," *he says, laughing softly to himself. I don't really find the joke that funny, finding myself deciding whether or not to gratify him with a smile.*

He seems to read my thoughts. "Now, now, Mr. Madi – there's no need for you to observe such a tired joke."

"It wasn't that damn bad."

"It wasn't that good, either. Now tell me, what do you find so objectionable about the democracy afforded by the market? Don't you think that the market is transparent? What kind of life would we have without an open and free exchange of commodities? Everything in your life is a commodity, even your time. In the old America, they used to say – Time is money. Why can't you understand that? Or perhaps better, why do you refuse to admit it?"

I shake my head. There were too many questions at once. I extend a hand, palm first, face down. I lean back in my chair and take another burning drink of the scotch. A familiar warmth floods my stomach and radiats throughout my body. I feel a little more sure of myself as I put the glass down and lean forward.

"To your first question, I don't agree that the market

is democratic. That's the first lie in the game. If you mean to tell me that my fuckin' vote means the same as your fuckin' vote does, you're a damned liar. Good enough to fool a lot of idiots but not good enough for me. Some people are born into wealth, in fact most rich people nowadays were born that way, while the majority of the rest of us work to survive. Reality is, we're not going anywhere. Money buys commercials that make the ignorant believe things that simply aren't true. I could tell the truth from on top of a soap box all I want and maybe a handful of people will listen. You could spout bullshit all day long and back it up with all of the technological gloss and social networking projection that money can buy. And money can buy everything. Almost everything. To those who are blind, perception is reality."

He raises himself up in his chair as if to interject; I wave him off and continue. His annoyance is written all over the tight skin of his face.

"Ignorant people exist, and it's in the best interests of rich bastards like yourself to ensure that a great many folks remain ignorant as to their material relationships. Basically, make sure they never realize how poor they really are and always will be. Things are going to get worse. They have been for a long time, not even that fuckin' flag can cover the infection beneath."

I realize, then, that I had overstepped my boundaries. My social ineptitude wasn't lost on my host, with eyes that seem to burn now like fresh embers in a well-stocked fireplace. The whiteness returns to his fingertips, his hands curling and uncurling unconsciously – like claws – over the deep leather of his chaise.

"Continue." *An imperative, brooking no dissent.*

I feel an icy lance of panic shoot through me, an anxiety that seems to burst into my brain. I try to keep my hand from shaking as I pick up the quart bottle from the table between us and pour a double into my glass. I take my time reaching forward to grip a few ice cubes from a wooden decanter. I have another long drink, nearly draining the double shot, wiping the spicy wetness from my beard as I continue.

"The bottom line really is that you can only squeeze so much blood from a stone before it crumbles, or splinters, in your hand. And delicate hands, hands that have never sweated with labour nor built up callouses from hard work, may find that sensation very novel indeed. Frightening, even."

The long and skeletal fingers detach themselves from the armrests and come up to support his chin, his fingers peaked and steepled so as to obscure the details of his expression. He considers my threat as if it were nothing more than a theory, without the slightest chance of materializing.

He acts as one indulging an angry child or an idealistic youth. Paternal and patronizing.

It really pisses me off.

"But this is extremely profitable, Khalil. Just not in the traditional sense. Sometimes, there are qualitative profits to be made that exist on the level of essence, of just living. If I am what you say I am, an overman, a capitalist titan, more powerful than you will ever be, a thousand of you even... why should your mild threats disturb my thoughts?"

"Because you are not more powerful than I am. You are a shadow of a man. A pale fucking joke. A bowel movement of a sick ideology. And there are more than a thousand of me. They just don't know it yet."

I turn my gaze from the rim of the glass upward to the smouldering eyes of my adversary. As soon as they meet, they hold for a moment.

It's enough.

I am so weak. I should never have pretended to be strong.

Now I will regret it. I feel the surety of this inside of me.

I feel like I have been possessed, like something is ripping through me. I feel empty. My mind begins to deteriorate. I can feel my words slipping back down my throat and choking me into a stunned silence. My host breaks the steeple he has been forming with his hands and gestures wildly, throwing his hands up in the air and casting a long shadow on the far wall.

"Ideas?! What are ideas but pithy words and trite comments made offhand? Who has truly great ideas? To you, some illiterate core dweller blowing his skull out with cheap chemicals is some type of hero – what great ideas has a man like that ever had? Only a handful of men ever have great ideas, and great ideas rise to the top. I have great ideas. I have written volumes on subjects that you'll never even learn of – advanced scientific engineering that exists only as a crude awareness in your mind. I've built things with my bare hands that will outlast anything you will ever create. Yet you presume to hold the Truth above me? Your arrogance is only exceeded by your ignorance – and it is truly comical to see such a small man as yourself struggle to run with the rest of us. We were born for this. You are a poseur – a good one, admittedly, but all talk nonetheless. An angry croaking against the rising strings of progress. And now, not even a whisper passes your lips."

The knife edges of the skeleton-man's lips curl upward like cold steel thirsting for first blood. This is the first and last time I'd see his true face.

It was true; I can't speak. My tongue is heavy and thick in my mouth, mute. I can barely breathe, like the air is being pressed out of my chest by stony, powerful hands. My muscles relax despite my terror, unresponsive. Even my thoughts begin to run too slowly to be effective. A dim and dull panic is the best I could muster, a primal frustration being the only thing lending any life to my limbs.

I place a hand down against my knee, a difficult move in and of itself. I begin to brace it, preparing to rise in an attempt to exit the room. I apply pressure to my wrist and feel my biceps and forearm grow taught. I can't help a barely stifled grunt of exertion. The devil's mask doesn't change, but continues to stare out at me with bleak, laughing eyes.

"Oh come now Khalil – that's not very diplomatic of you! Drink and dash, is it? I'll have you know that this is expensive scotch, probably the best you've ever tasted in your life, I'd wager. How poetic that it would be the last lifeline I would throw to you before we wipe you clean – one last binge of excess and fear in the name of your own religion. Now it's time to join ours, and pay your respects to the ones whose blood, even now, stains your hands and your mouth."

The taste of black iron fills my mouth, washing over my gums and teeth. It is too much and I open my mouth. Blood rushes forth and stains the front of my elegant dress shirt a deep plum. I have a sickening thought – it matches the cherrywood stain of the room quite nicely. I've wasted my one cogent moment; I have lost my mind.

And then I am lost.

I claw frantically at my mouth and tongue, unable to form words with a dumb and swollen tongue. The blood continues to flow like a thin river, running down my chest. I tear at my necktie, forgetting the weakness of my limbs.

It's useless.

I fall heavily to the floor. A sickening wave of pain and immediate nausea as I hear my leg snap. I'm crippled. The dull, dim panic bursts. I growl, choking, writhing on the floor.

The skeleton-man leans in, his features now in sharp relief as the soft light from the walls wash over his rigid features. The same smile never left his lips the entire time.

He leans in close.

I can smell the musk of rotting fabric emanating from the lapels of his dinner jacket, and the faint sterility of chemicals. His colorless eyes drill into me. He opens his mouth to speak; his breath smells of rot and decay. I jerk my head away and vomit, blood and bile.

"How thin the line between man and animal?"

His voice sounded like the grating of stone on steel, pitting and scraping. Was this Death?

It is. The blood comes faster now, so quickly that it fills my mouth in an instant. I drink it down, choking on it, slamming and snapping my body around on the lush carpeted floor that strokes my face at every pass.

As if to say – there, there.

I can feel my spirit pulling free of my body. I hear the rising sound of low strings, resonating deep.

20. AN ERSATZ EXECUTIONER

"God dammit!" the old man cursed, slapping the side of the old pinball machine with his right hand, shaking the cabinet about. "I was ten grand away from my high score!"

"*Shut up* you old bastard, can't you see we're watching on the screen?!" Elliott hollered over the bar to Josef.

The wrinkled, deeply lined face of the old man set in a furious scowl.

"Who gives a shit about that? I like the Paki but I have a god-damn game of Atlantis on the go over here. He's dead fuckin' meat anyways! Nothin' we can do 'bout it." Spoken like a veteran of nearly seventy years on the inside of the city. Admission of empathy and admission of powerlessness. Josef had ceased fighting a long time ago.

"Just *shut up*, got it?"

Elliott spat, and old Josef just snorted and waved his

hand back in dismissal, returning his attention the game in front of him. The scraping and snapping noises of the electro-mechanical pinball machine drummed out an erratic backbeat to the proceedings. Now that the executions had been completed, there was only the Ordeal of Repentance left over to conclude the pay-per-view. Given that the final vignette had been less sensational than the two previous, the audience was irritated and anxious to climax.

The atmosphere of the bar as the extended commercial break came to an end was one of anxious dread – like the tight-lipped panic of a prisoner held in the stocks of the guillotine, awaiting the taste of the blade. By now an enormous crowd had assembled behind the bar, many of them holding their caps with fidgeting fingers or downing their tenth or eleventh double to keep those same fingers steady.

Festif had left an hour ago, unable to watch the torture any longer. Shawn was fall-down drunk, lying on the barroom floor, one leg steepled and leaning back against a Joust cabinet, staring ahead, seemingly hearing nothing. But he heard every word of Nottingham's voice, every threat of the nightmares, every cry from his best friend's throat. He was contemplating suicide.

There were several wild-eyed men with lethal expressions talking amongst each other, gesturing violently. The grumbling had grown to a level where Elliott had to turn up the volume to drown out the increasing clamour of the crowd. The sound of shouting could be heard through the windows. There was an unnameable electricity radiating outward and immersing everyone. The speakers rumbled and the screen once again flashed into vibrant existence.

The show was back.

"*Alllright then*, ladies and gentlemen, now we've seen the prisoner endure his punishment! We've endured it alongside him! We've walked in his shoes and we've shared his burden. Now that burden has been relieved, and our prisoner has walked through the valley of the shadow of the death. He finds himself, now, at the gates of the arena, a purified and bright-eyed lamb. He will sacrifice himself on the Altar of the Games immediately following this pay-per-view in order to lend his blood to the sand beneath – a sign of goodwill and honor not only upon the proceedings of tonight's Games, but also to Central and to all of us, as her citizens. We're going to segue straight into that segment, so stay tuned and thank you for performing your civic duty by watching the program."

Nottingham folded his hands and the camera swept in close to him, placing him slightly off-center and on a forty-five degree turn with a full pan of the audience behind him, following suit. He closed his eyes and bowed his head. The lights dimmed, the swelling music ebbed back into background muzak. The camera swept away over the crowd, faster and then so quickly that it become a long-tailed blur. Then all that could be seen was a field of inky black and hot white stars. The stars seemed to rise out of the sea of pitch, luminous and burning bright.

A smoky, inconstant chorus of torchlight joined them, a field of soft light enrobing the bright pinpoints of the stars. The field of view panned downward. All who beheld it were fixed in rapt attention. This was a new scene – not a remake, a sequel or prequel – and it was reality. The stars were stars. The wooden palisades that slowly came into focus looked deadly and sharp, wooden logs formed into stakes and bound by thick hemp cord the colour of deepest emerald. Sentries bearing grim, determined expressions and identical leather harnesses stood like brutes at their elevated posts, looking out into the surrounding forest with unblinking eyes.

This was the finest, most luxurious, and easily the most *expensive* simulation any of them had ever seen. Even those without imagination could almost smell the money.

A murmuring babble grew in the ears of all who looked on, rising to a general clamour as the cameras shot down to disperse amongst the seats of the arena. The privileged patrons incorporated themselves in the front stands of this wooden arena, already populated with the actors who would be playing before them as well as countless others viewing from the sky above.

Gregory Nottingham was watching with his dozen or so attendants from a special corporate box directly opposite the wooden stage; the arena was Lyndon's territory and he graciously allowed him to soak up the limelight.

There was a hooded executioner standing tall on a crude wooden platform. He was a giant of a man, fully six and a half feet in height, with enormous shoulders and a thick, bull-like neck. His chest was a mat of black fur over a wall of banded muscles, ripping and standing out in sharp relief against the flickering fingers of the torchlight. The axe was wrought from heavy black iron, pounded flat on an anvil on a primitive forge. The blade was rough and eccentrically shaped. His large ape-like hands gripped the shaft of the long axe, wringing the neck in barely concealed excitement. His chest rose and fell like a great ocean of flesh.

There were two other men standing on the platform with him.

One was Lyndon Blackmarsh, a tall and muscular man nearly the size of the executioner – his trademark wing of hair slicing across his brow in dramatic fashion. He was a former gladiator himself; a champion of the arena. He was stripped to his waist revealing a sculpted physique despite his advancing years.

The other man was stooped and thin, hooded fully in

a patchwork leather peasant garment, stumbling about the platform drunkenly. The comic relief, apparently.

Blackmarsh extended his right hand out into the night hair, backed by the fluttering columns of torches laid out in steppes on three sides of the pavilion. The light played over his body, making him look deeply tanned and feral. His voice was rich and masculine, and boomed out over the crowd despite the lack of any apparent microphone.

"Esteemed countrymen, thank you for joining us here in the Arena of Truth for this evening's festivities. A few technicalities to dispense of before we begin: serving men and women are available at your beck and call – you'll note them flanking the aisles and near the washrooms in each section. They can account for your every need. Private lounges are available to watch the proceedings for a small fee and can be purchased at any time." At this point, the hooded fool bumped into Blackmarsh, who pushed the stumbling figure onto the floor of the platform. The audience laughed appreciatively, then quieted down to let the ex-gladiator continue the inaugural speech.

"And so it is with greatest pleasure that I welcome you all, the meek and the mighty alike, to join me in celebrating this spectacle of combat, determination, and honour that we will see before us this very night!"

The crowd roared their appreciation. Rows of busty women in loose gauze dresses and thickly-built men stripped to their waists raised their perfect voices in unison and pumped their fists into the night air. The torches continued to burn silently, as did the stars above.

Blackmarsh paused now, as if in deep reflection. The moon shone in his eyes. The roar of the crowd continued while he paced. This was the selection process – while Blackmarsh paced and stalked along the length of the flat wooden platform, his staffers were busy selecting suitable matches from within the available prisoner base and the rank and file of the *Gladiators* roster.

As if on cue, Blackmarsh stopped abruptly midstride as he approached the corner of the crude wooden stage and planted his feet. The crowd immediately quieted, only a few errant voices laughing or finishing private comments as Blackmarsh raised his hand, palm outward. Absolute silence.

"Brothers and sisters from all over this proud continent, reigning as strong and as unshakeable as the palm of my own hand – please welcome your first contestants!" Following this, the muscled giant clenched his fingers into a white-knuckled fist and drew it backward towards his hip as if preparing for a karateka's lunge punch. His jaw set and his lips formed in a thin line of granite alongside this martial pose; the people positively screamed to their feet.

A cacophony of primitive tones rolled forth from their throats, their chests; they were thirsty for death.

They wanted to see Blackmarsh rise up in front of them, enrobed in blood and staring forth with sightless eyes. To them he was a mockery. They were foolish and drunk by the cup of grandeur. The fool himself seemed to be quivering in exaggerated fear, huddled as far away from Blackmarsh as he could possibly be, looking like a small, motley dog trapped in a thunderstorm.

The wide gates at the far end of the arena opened inward, grotesque black iron faces moving aside with unwilling groans and the rasp of metal on metal.

"The challengers: Simon Robbins, Nicholas Krugman, and Thomas Hennings!"

A wave of boos immediately.

A thin and weak looking man was flanked by two slightly overweight men with pasty complexions and poor muscle tone. When the carnival trade of professional wrestling had still been in favour, these hapless victims would have been poor jobbers, sentenced to take their lumps and lie down for the three count.

These prisoners, in this new age, would be expected to put up the appearance of a fair fight until they had suffered enough injury – tonight's event was a special edition of the show featuring more than simple bloodsport. The promise of fights to the death.

The ragged group of victims huddled together as they walked down the short path leading to the center of the arena. Guards were posted at the gates and at sparse intervals around the periphery to ensure that all went smoothly. The audience hailed down jeers and catcalls on them, some hurling projectiles (conveniently available for purchase from the concessions menu) with as much force as they could muster. A few objects struck glancing blows, causing minor scrapes and bruises.

One stone slashed open the cheek of the tall, thin man – Mr. Robbins – drawing first blood. The man who threw the stone found himself a hero, with his reputation score soaring and his bank account filled with small donations from thousands. His dark face was split in a wide, obnoxious grin. He raised his arms above his head in a sign of victory, accepting the laurels and the favour that showered down upon him.

Even Blackmarsh took a moment to salute the man, nodding slightly with a crooked smile at his position in the stands, two fingers held over his breast.

"—and here's your Gladiator for this evening's first combat to the death! The Spear-Slayer, Magnus Baldurs-son!"

Magnus was the champion of the program, a hulking titan of a man that stood only a few inches over six feet tall and yet had the physique of a god of war. His musculature seemed as if it was carved from okra granite, his veins standing out over his thighs and biceps. Long strands of blond hair curled down about his face and shoulders, complemented by a broad fu-manchu moustache that trailed down his jaw and neck in large swaths.

The guards bowed respectfully and laid down their arms as he strode down the short path to the arena. Clutched in his hand, longer than he was tall, Magnus held the Spear of Destiny, covered in the blood of his previous victims. It had never been washed clean, and was baptized in the gore of at least a hundred men over the course of the past four or five years.

His face was haughty with the confidence of a man who stands as a god, a man who has never known defeat or humiliation.

The people loved him, they showered him with their affections. Many women in the crowd bared their breasts and their thighs to him; he had a reputation both inside and outside of the arena, as fierce and prolific a lover as a killer.

Sex and death were never safer than in these dream worlds. Fantasy made flesh.

A fact of which Maya Williams was intimately aware as she witnessed Ray kissing his new girlfriend passionately in the upper gallery. Her own seats were directly opposite, far removed from the action though still affording a view. Last year when she had made her annual pilgrimage to the games, her seat had been near ringside – so close, in fact, that she had been hit with a streak of blood from a mortal axe wound inflicted nearby.

The taste of iron had splashed across her tongue and

stung her eyes before she blinked and spat them clean. She still had a taste for it, even if she didn't admit it. A craving, a hunger, immoral and dreadful in some way. Her sanity kept her from delight. She told herself it would not be a delight but that, a deeper part of herself knew, was also a lie. That voice had bubbled up recently, a memory entombed and now splitting through the cracks.

Her status had slipped appreciably over the course of the past few weeks while Ray's had grown. Her age was beginning to show – despite the constant cosmetic treatments and pharmaceutical aides – and now the advance of technology offered near immortality in cosmetic terms to younger men and women at the height of their physical form.

While everyone could be beautiful here in the Arena, or in the digital corridors spanning the new internet – life went on in the corporeal world, regardless of what transpired in the illusory hallways of digital life.

Maya was feeling very old, as if even the ache of her not-so-young joints was beginning to seep into the perfect genetics of the body she inhabited here.

Digital upgrades were affordable and easily bought. Time was the only commodity that escaped the human marketplace, regardless of its immense ambition and tireless thirst for more worshipers. Jealousy, by contrast, was its best and most readily available fuel.

She had that in spades, and could feel it burning deep inside of her chest. Instinctively she looked to her right, where Ray used to be. Her new blonde boytoy wasn't nearly as smart, even if he had a better body; he didn't know how to use it. He was lazy and langourous, not driven and intense as Ray had been. Ray had a way of looking at a woman – she could see his cunning eyes and devilish expression from here – now he was stroking this other woman suggestively – that made her feel powerful and desirable.

He was smart enough to realize that, on some base level, men and women were closer to animals than to gods – appealing to these baser desires with as much skill and enthusiasm as possible had made Ray a rare and interesting man in an increasingly boring existential day-to-day.

Her new boyfriend merely paid lip service, performing his sexual duties on her without any real passion or kink – she would lie there staring, relying on her vision of her beautiful young body to drive her climax home. It was routine, almost clinical. A physical relief at intervals. Adequate.

"Oh, what fun!" her boyfriend yelped. His base, unsophisticated nature was being greatly aroused by the promised bloodshed. Maya felt a little less attracted to him, remaining silent and keeping her thoughts focused.

"Why are you being so mean to me, baby? You never pay any attention to me except for when we're alone," he whined.

"That's not true, Elias. You always make me smile." Maya pulled her best impression of what a smile might look like and failed miserably. For a defense attorney, she was a horrible liar outside of the courtroom when the stakes were this low. She didn't particularly care for Elias and if he left, he left.

"Who's that man over there?" He cut to the chase. Maybe her boyfriend was smarter than she gave him credit for.

"Nobody important. I think I recognize him from my firm. Maybe in the accounting office."

"Okay. It's just that I noticed you paying a bit of attention to him, that's all."

Once again, she hadn't heard him. Maya's attention was focused on the newly minted couple. The blonde boy toy began to feel a rush of panic that he quickly subdued. He would keep fucking Maya for a while, but the switch had been flipped and other plans began to form. Follow the money.

"Excuse me, Ms. Williams. I have to log out for a few minutes for a bio break. The show isn't starting for a few minutes, right?" Elias' voice was like a buzzing in her ear, seeming almost an ocean away.

She nodded absently.

"Yeah, I think maybe in around fifteen, twenty minutes."

He placed a small, warm hand on her forearm and then was gone, his seat not empty but occupied by a thin, ambiguous wisp of white smoke that acted as a placeholder in his absence.

Maya once again peered across the small courtyard into the stands and saw Ray excuse himself as well, heading down the stairs toward the interstitial promenade that connected the galleries.

Maya rose and adjusted her robes about her shoulders, casually making her own way to the end of the aisle and down the stairs towards the mezzanine. As she was nearing the large portal that led into the mezzanine level, Maya could hear the swell of drums building as music was pumped into the arena via invisible speakers placed around the periphery of the small fort.

She disappeared through the crude wooden doorframe as Blackmarsh once again began to speak to the crowd.

"–and now, we must introduce our guest of honour for this evening's proceedings. An enemy to all. Ladies and gentlemen, I give you the last living moments of Khalil Madi; traitor to his fellow man and murderer of the lowest degree!"

The volume of his last statements was raised to a boom that washed over the crowd like a wave that hammered into their chests. The air became charged and thick, excitement was palpable and radiating warmly beneath the calm, cold starlight. A mob roar bore down like an aural stampede. The gates swung wide again.

His head was bowed low and he was dressed only in a ragged, soiled loincloth. His barrel-chest and flat, rounded stomach were covered in dried blood; his long curly hair matted with the same. Deep black bruises stood out like great countries all over his skin. His beard was mottled and patchy, parts of it having been torn loose; by himself or by lawful correction it was unclear.

Boos rained down on the prisoner as heavy as stones, amplified to a fever pitch by programmers on the live feed. He didn't even flinch, nor raise his face to meet the stares of his tormentors. He was not led by anyone, but merely walked down the path toward the raised wooden platform. Surrounding the stage was a moat-like pit, where the actual games would be taking place.

Khalil approached the platform and raised his gaze, letting his hair fall free from his face. His eyes were expressionless, like a dead man walking. If he heard the hate of the crowd tumbling down about him, he did not show it.

As he approached the steps, Magnus Baldursson made a quick move; he struck Khalil a solid slap across the face that sent him spinning to the ground. The crowd growled their appreciation and donations flowed like water into his online war chest – they showed him the depth of their love.

Khalil lay still for quite some time and seconds slipped by. The crowd quieted slightly as some began to wonder if he was dead; had the mighty blow of the arena champion done the work of the executioner for him?

He groaned and his eyes fluttered. He coughed and spat, a loose thread of saliva trailing across the dirt.

Magnus moved theatrically in a menacing fashion, pressing toward the prone figure with a swagger. Khalil propped himself up onto his elbows, leaving his ribs exposed. Magnus whipped his head around toward the tall figure of Blackmarsh, standing on the corner of the platform. The host was looking down on the events with barely concealed amusement. It was clear that the champion was asking for the honour of executing the prisoner on the spot, to taste the blood of the traitor. The crowd sang their assent, a thousand perfect voices.

Blackmarsh pursed his lips sympathetically and placed his hands in a defensive gesture, palms outward. Not yet. But soon; just have patience.

Magnus spit thick saliva onto Khalil's back and turned on his heel, striding away and raising his arms to the cheers of the crowd. The attention was by now squarely on the glistening champion.

The patchwork fool ceased his antics and hobbled over to the stairs. The fool reached under Khalil's armpits and brought him to his feet, placing a gentle yet firm hand on his back to lead him up onto the squat wooden dais.

As the fool led Khalil before the executioner's block, he stuck his leg out in front of his prisoner, sweeping Khalil's legs out from underneath, causing him to fall heavily to the wooden planks. A cheap roar of appreciation from the stands. They could all hear him groan softly as he hit the boards; he was mic'd and amplified. Blackmarsh strode gallantly over from the corner of the platform and gripped Khalil by the hair, hauling him to his knees roughly. Khalil gasped for breath.

The fool sat with his skinny legs dangling over the edge of the platform, making rude gestures at the crowd. Blackmarsh nodded to the executioner, who stepped forward with a length of rope and began to bind Khalil's hands behind his back. As he was doing so, Blackmarsh gave one last leering smile before turning on his heel and strutting majestically to the front of the stage once more.

He abruptly threw his arms up into the air and brought them crashing down to the sound of cymbals.

"Begin!"

Almost immediately the ranks of guards closed around the champion and his three captives like an iron ring, their faces grim. The men seemed as if they would refuse to fight. A few guards loosed their arms and tossed short swords onto the sand by their feet. Magnus, the champion of the people, had lifted from the earth a long, wicked blade that curved backwards slightly towards the tip, as a scimitar or more closely, a Turkish kilij. The Spear of Destiny had been planted in the soft, sandy soil behind him. Magnus would not sully the spear initially. The crowd liked a little variety in their kills. It was part of his gimmick.

He was advancing, slowly, ponderously towards the three men who had taken on the cast of ghosts.

"Fight, you goddamn cowards!" Magnus roared, swinging the blade menacingly and slicing the upper arm of one of the men, the shortest and roundest. The crowd screamed at the condemned. The three men looked at one another with horrified expressions.

Tall Robbins and Krugman bent low to snatch up the short blades; with a high pitched squeal the already wounded Hennings broke towards the perimeter of guards. There was a flash of naked steel in the starlight. There was silence, and then two dull thumps as Hennings and his head both struck the earth, his head rolling into the peat lining the stands while his body jerked forward and fell between two of the silent guards. One of those, barely concealing his excitement, leaned forward to wipe the blood from his blade on the back of the corpse. Credits flowed into his account as he straightened up and sheathed his sword, returning to formation.

"You'll die like dogs or you'll die like men. From now

until the time I wish to end your life. That's all there is," Magnus growled from between bearded lips. His eyes were those of a lion – a predator stalking prey without fear. The reverse was mirrored in the twin sets of eyes of his victims. Khalil looked on from his position on the wooden stage without moving.

Krugman had had enough talk. On squat, shaking legs he advanced toward the giant, rushing forward with his blade at the ready. A feral grin spread across the face of the golden haired barbarian as he left his own blade slung low.

"Die!" Krugman hissed, attempting a clumsy stab at the champion's exposed ribs. Magnus, faster than a striking snake, turned his wrists and hips to swing the great sword upward – severing the prisoner's hands and sending them spinning into the air. Krugman barely had time to open his mouth in horror as he gazed downward at his own mutilated arms while Magnus reversed direction at the height of his swing, bringing the kilaj downward at an angled cut. The blade bit deep through the shoulders and collarbone and well into the chest cavity, bursting Krugman's lungs and driving him to his knees. The dying man croaked for air, his eyes bulging clear from their sockets, his tongue turning purple and black. He collapsed on his stomach and continued to rattle.

The crowd provided a rude lullaby as he expired, promising hell.

"Go to hell!"

"Yeah, Magnus! Owned him!"

"Die, ya sick freak!"

In a contact cage, not unlike Khalil's, nearly two thousand miles away – Nicholas Krugman died.

The torches seemed to dim slightly with a stirring wind that swept over the palisade walls of the wooden fort. A few disinterested souls looked about, searching fruitlessly for the source of the wind and seeing only the cold light of the stars above.

During the immense confusion during the kill, the fool slipped on a plank and slammed bodily into Khalil, knocking him forward. A few audience members caught the gag and laughed for a moment, but by and large it was a moment that quickly passed by.

No one saw the fool slip a knife into Khalil's hands.

No one saw the faint hint of a smile that crept onto his face.

Feigning discomfort and fatigue, Khalil leaned backward to obscure his work at freeing himself. The slaughter continued.

Robbins was the last man standing, and had chosen to die like a man, despite having seen how that had gone over for his shorter colleague. Admirable, and the crowd abstained from their jeers for a moment in a brief gesture of respect – a respect that was fleeting and soon forgotten in a span of seconds.

Magnus had left the kilij blade where it had struck, still protruding from Krugman's corpse near the center of the makeshift ring. He had snatched his great spear from the soil and held it with two iron hands, wielding it with confidence and grace. The moustache on the upper lip of the champion trembled as he snarled at his prey — urging him to come forward and make it quick.

Robbins held the short sword in a firm hand, showing some degree of practice — he'd obviously played a few sword and sorcery sims in his time. This time would not be a simple game — the pain would be real and death would be permanent. Magnus rushed forward with a short cry and drove his spearpoint forward, seeking to skewer his lanky opponent through the stomach. Robbins parried the blow as much as he needed to — the spear point brushed a few inches by his ribcage. He aimed a tentative punch at the champion's head with his free hand.

His fist caught Magnus across the mouth, a grazing blow that staggered the huge man but did not cause him to drop his guard altogether. Magnus laughed theatrically, licking his lips clean of blood.

"I've been hit harder by your whore of a mother, boy," he growled.

"Save your words, asshole. Why don't you come a little closer?" Robbins' already thin voice broke, lending a pathetic note to the transparently hopeless bravado.

Magnus spit, a gob of saliva and blood that landed and stretched across the dark sand at the prisoner's feet.

Again Magnus rushed forward with a thrust of the spear, and again Robbins parried the blow with his short sword. This time his block was not quite good enough, and the ragged tip of the spear caught up against his ribs, tearing into his flesh before slipping free. The spear had once again drawn blood, adding a new coat of paint. The sight of blood drove the crowd into a fury, like a pent up explosion erupting from a cannon. The wound was deep but not mortal. Robbins gasped in pain, grit his teeth, and regained his stance.

"Not long now, eh? Pathetic slob. You would embarass your father, if you even knew his name."

As Magnus and Robbins fought, Khalil crouched unnoticed on a corner of the stage. If the audience had been watching, they might have been able to see the last of his bonds falling to the ground – but all eyes were on Magnus now.

The arena champion rushed in a third time, and once again Robbins moved to parry – this time a little weakly – but was brought up surprised by a feint; Magnus stopped his thrust midway and instead whirled the long end of the spear around like a quarterstaff. The full weight of the end of the massive spear caught the lanky Robbins aside his head, knocking him to the ground.

The champion raised his arms in exultation and the

crowd reinforced him, their unending chorus of voices bringing his spirit to the heavens. He took three long running steps and then leapt into the air, gripping the Spear of Destiny with white-knuckled intensity as he arced downwards upon his prey. Robbins managed to shake his head clear for one final, horrified look as the hulking warrior descended upon him, point first.

The speartip plunged downward indiscriminately, puncturing the ribs of the prisoner, driving through his heart and lungs. Robbins rattled and gasped, wrapping his own dirty hands around the protruding shaft of the spear for just a moment before falling dead at the feet of the arena champion. A jet of blood burst forth from his chest cavity and lapped against the bare leg and thigh of the victor. Magnus wrenched the spear free and held it aloft in both hands, still dripping; the blood ran down his hands and arms before falling free to the soil below. Magnus roared, lifting his voice as high and as far as it would go, a barbarian's scream that was amplified to the point of being godlike. The crowd joined him.

Blackmarsh offered a lopsided smile, allowing the victory cheer to continue for a long moment before raising his own arms. As if a curtain had been yanked across the crimson stage, the crowd settled immediately, and Magnus turned his own attention to the raised platform.

"Excellent! A truly amazing display of physical prowess and the execution of justice! Here, tonight, in this most public of forums! You, the people, witnessing the power and the glory of this nation, in which you all share a hand! Please, give yourself the applause you deserve!"

And they did. The wooden walls of the small fortress seemed to resonate, the dark green hemp bindings failing to hold them absolutely fast. Now, the highlight of the evening. Before the games proper, the soil of the nation demanded a final sacrifice – this time in front of eyes of those assembled. Lawyers, doctors, engineers, businessmen, policymakers, escorts, idle husbands and wives all demanded the blood of the wicked in front of them, the debt of his offense against their beliefs and the morals of the nation at large.

Blackmarsh spread his arms wide in a grand gesture, as if casting a spell over his audience.

"I give you the final death of the most egregious and remorseless traitor that Central has ever seen! The death of Khalil Madi!" he stretched the name out to last, savouring the taste in his mouth. The crowd joined him, speaking the name of the convicted in a thousand timbres. Then all was silent. These were grave proceedings and demanded restraint until the deed had been done. Even the wolves that had been baying from time to time around the perimeter of the fort seemed to quieten, either in answer to the crowd or in anticipation of the meat that would follow the games.

The executioner, his hairy belly heaving and protruding, moved a few steps toward the condemned, clapping a chubby hand atop Khalil's shoulder.

"It's time. Any words?" the executioner's voice was slightly muffled by his hood, low and deep and sure. Khalil moved his head to the side in a negative gesture. The executioner pushed down on Khalil's shoulder's now, pushing him down and across the thick wooden chopping block. Blood and bone had become part of the patina of the wood. The executioner hefted his axe, taking a moment to look sidelong at Blackmarsh for the final word. With a barely perceptible nod, Blackmarsh indicated his assent to complete the order; there was an audible intake of breath from the crowd as the executioner raised his axe aloft into the night sky.

Khalil uncoiled, striking. He dropped the ropes from his hands and rolled to the side, viewers saw that he had something shiny in his hand as he stood. The axe fell heavily into the wooden block with a heavy thud, burying it a half foot deep. Khalil sprang forward as the executioner struggled to free the blade.

Khalil was free. And he was holding a knife.

Khalil dipped low, under the arms of the gorbellied man, sinking his weapon deep into the soft and exposed stomach. He tore the knife violently upward, then twisted it free with a pull to the left. In less than five seconds, everything had changed substantially; the crowd remained silent in complete shock, now beginning to buzz and babble as a brook disturbed.

"Shut him down! Shut him down! Pull the plug!" Blackmarsh screamed, jumping from the ledge of the platform and running for the relative safety of the crowd. Khalil tossed his head about, eyes blazing wildly, scanning for new targets.

Nottingham stood with his hands gripping the rail of his Corp box, his attendants screaming in fear before fading out from the net. The fool had disappeared, his motley robe nowhere in sight. Only the bodies of the three slain men, the shuddering body of the executioner in his death throes, and Magnus stood remaining on the arena floor.

No words were exchanged, for Khalil was already sprinting towards the edge of the platform, taking a flying leap from the edge to descend upon the blonde-haired champion.

Magnus held the spear at the ready, held high and aimed straight for Khalil's chest as he dropped from the air. It was almost as if time slowed down for the two men, each heartbeat felt deep within their chests. Magnus standing, moustache bristling, feet wide apart, covered in the blood of his victims, his legendary spear aimed at the breast of a most unexpected enemy.

A maddened Khalil, his long black hair tangled and matted with filth, his ill-fit and stained clothing pressed flat against his chest and thighs as the air pressed against him.

He held a long knife clutched tightly to his side in his right hand.

Khalil made a deft move with the long knife as he fell upon the spearpoint, using the flat of the blade to turn the tip of his opponent's weapon aside, the blade sliding down the shaft. There was a slight rasping sound, as steel grating against steel. A few stray sparks flew briefly from the haft of the spear, but it was over in the blink of an eye.

The prisoner saw a look of animal fear on the face of the champion, hidden deep behind his moustache and his cold blue eyes. The knife came down in a flash, biting deep through Magnus' throat and lodging at last deep in his collarbone. The hulk of a man who stood as champion immediately grabbed at his throat, blood spurting through his thick, iron fingers that grew weaker by the second. His eyes protruded pink, red, and black. He coughed and wretched, pink froth bubbled up from the terrible wound in his neck. All the while, the condemned man watched his dying opponent with undisguised disgust, his lip curled to reveal teeth. A ring of footmen slowly closed in around him, their faces alike in their fear and rage. The murmuring of the crowd burst forth like a flood through a dam.

"Feel your death as I felt it. Own it like a man or be extinguished as if you'd never lived," Khalil said to the golden-haired gladiator, by now hunched completely over and spilling his vitals onto his own lap.

Whether or not the murderer-gladiator heard Khalil, or give a shit about his words, was unclear. He merely groaned and gurgled a brief while more, and then his death rattle was heard. The last rushing of air from his lungs.

He laughed. He threw his head back and laughed as if possessed. He laughed like a madman. A wave of nauseating confusion swept throughout the crowd and fear overtook rage on the faces of the jackals closing in about the prisoner as a ring of iron. Doubt and dread uncertainty began to taint the theatre of the evening's events, twin specters which began to pry at the hearts of those in attendance – their safety no longer a guarantee. Many had already disappeared entirely, flickering out like inconstant constellations, leaving large gaps in the bench seating.

Khalil's laughter was cut short, a muted note.

21. ADRIFT WITHOUT AN ANCHOR

Maya woke up to a bare bed; her companion had obviously fled the scene as soon as things had begun to go awry. Elias had left a few of his belongings behind in his haste – his toothpaste still graced the top of the porcelain sink basin and a pair of his underwear was still bunched up on the carpet next to the bed in a little black ball. She didn't really care one way or another. Her mind was spinning out of control.

"How the fuck is this possible!?" she snarled in a rage, shattering a nearby lamp into the wall with a blow from the back of her hand. "How *the fuck* did it come to this!?"

She got up and stalked out of the bedroom and into the combination open concept living area that was the centerpiece of the condo. Overlooking the harbour below, enshrouded today in a dark, smokey fog, the condo had been her first gift to herself upon achieving the promotion to Four.

A recently-deleted e-mail notification told her, how-ever, that the condo was being re-assigned following her "relocation" to one of the more provincial neighbour-hoods in Three – worse lodgings than the ones she had held before her initial promotion for legal facilitation.

The smoke from the torches and the simulated peat and sand of the arena still seemed to linger in her senses, drawing her mind back to the conversation she'd just had with Ray.

Nothing really mattered to her anymore. She felt her world crumbling away before her; the once-powerful at-torney was subject to a new and terrifying sensation of powerlessness. Nothing she could do would bring her station back – nothing would let her stay in her beautiful condo. Hot shame flushed her cheeks.

No amount of hard work or perseverance would win the affections of Ray again – her star was fading and her career was on a downward spiral to fuck knows where.

She wasn't getting any younger. For a woman, espe-cially for a woman as beautiful and as conscious of it as she was, this was a dark and persistent thought. It darted in and out of her mind at odd intervals, dominating her lately.

Maya walked over to her dark cherrywood credenza and snatched up the bottle of cognac. She poured herself a tall glass sans ice and drank at least half of it without pausing. The fiery liquid burned its way down her throat and she was barely able to stifle a cough. She lifted the back of her hand to her lips, feeling hot wetness against her skin.

Her stomach began to twist into knots and she felt as if there was an rusted metal fist gripping at her intestines. They felt sour and diseased. The superficial warmth of the alcohol began to spread to her limbs, offering some small degree of comfort. Her anger continued to seethe beneath the surface, and she still felt like lashing out, striking something, anything.

She worked at her temple with one hand, using the other to take another long drink from the glass, nearly emptying it. She could feel the anger drain from her over the course of the next two minutes, the alcohol swimming in her bloodstream and warming the cold knot in her guts.

She kept thinking back to the events of the previous few hours, replaying them over and over again in her mind, trying to glean any information that might help halt her free fall. She found none, but the unstoppable thoughts – like a freight train running through her mind on the same circular route – had no intentions of stopping.

She remembered quite clearly her time in immersion; some people found it difficult to recall the events that had transpired while induced. She had left Elias – yes, that was his name! – and walked down the thick wooden steps down into the consumer level.

Inside, the ambiance was equally primitive in aesthetic, the thick green cords of hemp criss-crossing the ceiling like bunting. A number of kiosks lined the inner promenade, resembling tiki bars, each with its own beautiful booth girl and array of objects for purchase – both real and virtual.

The booth nearest her as she'd entered the mezzanine was offering avatar upgrades – for a hefty sum, one could outfit oneself with a wreath of ivy and a gold-embroidered robe in any number of colours, styles, and fabrics. There was not much of a crowd milling about on the promenade due to the historic nature of today's events in the arena – the show hadn't been this well publicized or hyped for years.

She saw him standing next to the upgrades kiosk on the far side of the walk, engaged in light conversation with the saleswoman, flirting just a little bit in order to leverage the price. A bright wreathe of beautiful flowers appeared above the sales girl's head, the bright and tiny florets the colour of spun gold. Gold, green, and the bright red of her long hair seemed to coalesce to form an image of classical beauty, and Maya felt her stomach tighten and constrict. The source of her sickness. She had to approach Ray; he hadn't seen her yet. She felt like she was on fire, sweating, despite the cool, crisp chill of the simulated night air.

She drew up next to the kiosk, paying only cursory attention to the second salesgirl who attempted to draw her into polite conversation, looking pointedly at Ray. He noticed her presence without betraying even a hint of emotion or surprise. A small smile touched his lips.

"Oh, hello there, Maya. Good to see you this evening." His voice was soft and held no malice, despite the uncomfortable history between them.

"And you, Ray. I haven't seen you for a while." She had kept her voice firm, despite being a wreck on the inside. He knew. He only smiled in response, waiting for her inevitable question.

"You think we could get together sometime this weekend?" The last ditch effort. Maya knew the answer before the words had even passed his lips.

"Well, no, Maya. You see..." his voice grew hesitant, distant. Maya already knew, of course, about the other woman. "There's someone else. It just wasn't clicking between you and I. We just aren't that compatible. I mean, you're a really nice girl–"

"But I'm not what you're looking for. And not a girl. A woman. A girl might suit you better." Childish, but Maya had to admit it felt good. A little devil inside of her smiled.

"No." The truth, but not for the reasons he was offering.

"It's because I'm damaged goods. I've been demoted;

I'm losing the condo. My net worth is less than yours, now, and that simply won't do, now, will it?" She couldn't contain her bile any longer, the bitterness rising hot and sour in her throat and on her tongue. Straight to the point.

It was obvious he didn't expect her to be so forward and brutally honest.

"No, no, Maya. Never! Please! Nothing so superficial."

It was. He was a good liar but only on his own terms. Honesty was not his preferred mode of discourse.

"It is. I'm through with lying. I've lost the game, I wasn't able to dodge enough bullets or lie as convicingly as some people." She knew she was beginning to ramble. She could remember Ray looking at her like she had two heads or like she was on chems.

As she remembered it in her mind, her shame grew. The heat inside of her burned white, and seemed to rise to scorch even her skin. She could feel herself sweating again.

She would always remember the hard glint that came forward in Ray's eyes as she accused him, rising like steel from beneath an implacable sea of calculated calm.

"I don't lie to anyone. You aren't my type. You are older than I prefer and you can't keep up in more than a few ways. You are a nice enough woman, very intelligent, but I feel I can do better." The verbal blows came raining down now that the pretense of geniality had been discarded in favour of baser emotion. In one fell swoop he belittled his former lover, reduced her to an object removed from his life – aging, pale, and sickly looking even here, in her prime incarnation.

Anger overrode all else, and Maya almost exploded, her words coming fast and hot.

"You lie to everyone, including yourself. Everyone in this society lies to themselves to some degree. You lied to me in order to gain prestige and status and a shot at climbing into bed not only with me, but with my superiors. I'm through lying. The truth hurts, and we both avoid it. I don't have the fucking luxury anymore."

"Look, Maya – you don't sound so good. If you keep talking like that–"

"I'll be down there sharing the stage with that poor bastard. I know. Odds are that's where I'll end up in any case. Ever since I took on this case my life has been taken out of my hands. You just went prospecting on a gold mine run dry and moved on to the next claim. You saved me a lot of time and effort; I wouldn't take your sorry ass back if you begged me. No hard feelings."

Her first lie, as transparent as a ghost. Dripping with venom.

"Take care of yourself, Maya. I have to get going." With one final, lopsided smile he touched her on the shoulder, the last time his fingers would touch her skin, and brushed past her. She felt the softness of his body intimately for that one brief moment before he broke free and left her forever.

She finished her drink and quickly poured another. By now her head was light and her heart was heavier still. She'd mentally replayed that scene a dozen times since she'd disconnected.

She had heard reports from all over of the disastrous outcome of the execution. Apparently her client had broken free, slaying not only the executioner but also the champion before being unplugged. At this rate, Maya would be lucky to keep her lodgings in Three; more than likely she would find himself living in the tenement apartments of Two or perhaps even banished to the city itself. Or she would simply disappear without a trace – it had happened to other hapless colleagues of hers and she had simply repressed it from memory over the course of the past few decades. Fear stole over her and blanketed her.

In the few moments, when she was being honest with herself, employing her intelligence and her critical faculty as well as she could while drunk, she knew she had to disappear. She could do it herself in her own fashion or she could wait for the black bag squad.

She was a stain on the flag, a reminder of an insubordination so offensive and intolerable that it must be scrubbed violently from the national memory and the history books for fear of others drawing inspiration or pity from the example of Khalil Madi.

Either way she felt very old, and the years seemed to have gone by without her remembering much of them. Her life was depleted. Details of cases she had facilitated, her record of public service, the bullet points on her resume – those things, she could remember. Cruelty marketed as success up until the very end. The rest was just a blur that seemed like it had happened to someone else. Existential vertigo.

Maya shuffled over to her desk, feeling sore and bruised and tired. Even the liquor seemed now to be weighing on her about the neck. Regardless, she palmed another drink as she sank down into her thick leather chaise. She fumbled through a pile of rubbish and loose papers on the desk, finally finding her package of menthol cigarettes. A nasty habit she'd picked up over the course of the past few years. Maya was now smoking at least a package a day – a long stone's throw from her original quota of two smokes a day.

She tapped one out of the box and rolled it idly between thumb and forefinger, simply staring at the intricate detailing of the desktop, trying desperately to derail her obsessive train of thought. A latent neuroticism common to her intelligence was rising, screaming, from her subconscious. That was her dime-store self-diagnosis, psychosomatic stabbing in the dark of a hypochondriac on the edge of what her crowd called sanity.

She placed the cigarette in her mouth and found the lighter nestled in her pants pocket, bringing it to face and lighting up. The smoke tasted good and the nicotine made her head feel a bit lighter, the mild euphoria from the first good drag bringing the first real smile of the day to her lips. She held the smoking dart out at hands length and splayed her fingers, admiring the way the cigarette crooked between them, resting between her knuckles. All the good things in life are deadly, she mused – the deadlier the more attractive the prospect.

"Are we all born with a death wish? Or is it just me?"

She hadn't meant to say it out loud, but there it was, anyway – the words fell like lead objects onto the soft carpet and were quickly swept away. There had been no one present to even consider the question, and Maya had already been putting the same questions to herself. It felt better to say it out loud. There wasn't much of a pause; it was really one question born of alienation and increasing self-doubt – the seeds of madness in both senses of the term.

Her hands became steady for the first time that day. Whether it was the naming of her fears which steadied her shattered nerves or the fact that the alcohol and pills she'd been taking had finally kicked in, Maya couldn't really be sure. She felt good for the first time in a long time and that was all that mattered, basically. The fear had fled from her, and she puffed contentedly at the filter of her cigarette, reaching her free hand back into the top drawer of the desk.

The gun she pulled loose from within was a real beauty. A Colt Anaconda with a beautiful wooden hand-grip. Steel so bright that it could blind, even after being laid to sleep in a drawer for many years. Kept loaded and forgotten about for nearly a decade.

She turned it over in her hand, keeping a firm grip, testing its weight and remembering how it felt to hold death in the palm of her hand. It felt powerful.

A vibration in the bones of her forearm told Maya that she'd received an email tagged as urgent; she felt that it could wait a few minutes while she collected her thoughts and enjoyed the soothing feeling of the drink. Maya sat in her chair for a very long time pondering her last dilemma – the question of the gun.

22. GLASS PRISON

He'd been here for a day or two, now, he thought. It was hard to tell the passage of time without the benefit of a tablet computer, a chrono, or a view of the sky. His sub-dermal had been deactivated, dead in his flesh. It was even harder when he spent most of his time trying to figure out who and what he was. The dead console under the skin of his forearm was of no assistance.

He knew he was a dark skinned man of young to middle years. He knew he had a thick black beard and hair the same. He couldn't tell if he was handsome or ugly, though his fingers could feel enough scars mapping the skin of his body to assume he was the latter. He knew that he had committed a heinous crime for which he was now being punished. He knew that he had killed men.

He knew that it had felt good. He did not know if that should make him afraid.

He was naked and unashamed. There were a few

others like him, suspended here in glass bell jars with glass bottoms, subject to a horizon that looks like what he imagined of hell. From below, a sea of inky black that moved like some sort of mirage between deep ruby and jet, slowly turning in a gradient fashion as one looked further downward. The figures in the distance ranged in shade from a pale white to the darkest black, a rainbow of human bondage. They were too far away to tell any sort of detail beyond the basic cast of their skin. Two white figures seem to pace their glass cages endlessly, often making him feel anxious. A black figure on the very edge of perception seemed to fade from his memory more often than not. He couldn't decide whether to believe in this far-flung figure or to call it a figment.

On thing they all had in common, excepting the two pacing ghosts – they all slumped low in their glass jars, almost blending into the horizon.

From time to time a thick black cylinder rose from the depths below and stared, coldly observing. It was without a face, a simple absence or abscess. He sensed that there were people contained within it, though he had nothing more an uncanny intuition that this was the case. It could very well be a God looking out upon his sparse realm of creation. He felt nothing but contempt for this strange wall, and when it raised its great eye upon him, he refused to grant it audience.

He turned his back to it and sat upon the ground,

resting his face and his eyes between his knees, wrapping his muscular arms about his shins until it removed itself from his presence.

Sometimes strange sentences intruded his thoughts, and faces of people whom he only vaguely remembered. A strange, multicoloured jacket. A moustached face and a fierce mind. A bespectacled barman with a sharp tongue and a heavy pouring hand. A beautiful face and a warm heart. A worried face and a warm embrace. All of these archetypes came to him in visions throughout the languid flow of time in this place – they would come to visit him for hours and he would enjoy their vague and unsatisfying company. They were his inventions, he thought to himself. He could not remember in the true sense. He could not recall with any clarity. He invented them so as to prevent himself from going mad, he thought. Or perhaps he was, already, and this was all inside of him. Then he felt the pains of his body and reconsidered.

When he slept, which was not often, it was of no comfort. He dreamed of his own death; in his hours of unrest he would always conjure visions of torture, and burning injustice, flaccid impotence. In his restless sleep he was always subject to a world over which he had no say, no control, no impetus. He was pelted by the stones of a crowd of mocking children. He was awake for his own autopsy.

In his dreams, he was a victim.

He often woke nauseous, and sometimes had to retch on the floor as a result. His anxiety grew with each minute that his eyes closed, and so the burning horizon and the bottomless expanse became his only source of comfort. A choice between two visions of hell. Eyes open was the only way to endure.

He would invent games to play with himself, within the confines of his own mind. He would imagine great scenarios of escape and realized that he did not know what he would do with this *freedom*. During the first few days he'd tried desperately to figure out the details of his past before it became apparent that none were forthcoming.

The only thing that he knew was that he was a prisoner, a madman, or both.

That was enough for him to decide upon a singular certainty; he held contempt for that great dark cylinder which rose above him, watched him as he struggled with sleep. He could tell that he had been drugged and that he had been abused. There was, at least, an enemy.

He dreaded the three times per day that the chamber would fill with a light gray gas and force him to sleep. Upon waking, a small tray of food and water was always present. He was unsure how they managed to enter his cell – he could see only the faintest signs of any sort of door or portal present in the glass.

The only thing he could remember with any degree of clarity were his actions on that wooden platform. He felt as if he'd been born only hours before that act. His first real memory was of being dragged like an animal into a nightmare that was not of his own creation. He was afraid and powerless. He saw other men like himself being tortured and murdered for sport in front of his very eyes. Fate had seen it proper to intervene and offer him a weapon – where it had come from he did not know. All he knew is that to a man in his position, even a simple knife can seem like the brightest star in the sky.

Anger had been his first memory. He'd killed the butchers, blood for blood. It was the one thing he comforted himself with under the burning, relentless gaze of the horizon and that damnable dark cylinder.

Who is watching me?

He had the constant feeling that was being scrutinized intensely. He needed to know who it was.

Something was changing now. He could feel a thick vibration penetrating his glass prison as the world around him tilted slightly and shifted. The translucent tether tying his cage to the sky began swinging to and fro. He looked upward and saw a new addition being lowered into purgatory.

From beneath, he could already tell that the new visitor was female. Her soft white skin was pressed flat against the bottom of the glass carriage as the tether lowered her like some sort of ornament into their strange menagerie. It appeared she was to be his new neighbour – her jar had been placed much more closely to him than the others.

As she drew even with his own cage he took the time to scrutinize her from beneath heavy-lidded eyes. A long sweep of beautiful blonde hair rushed across her forehead and shoulders, lighter than when he had last seen her, or maybe a trick of the extreme light. He *knew* he had seen her before.

She wore *that* pair of thick-rimmed eyeglasses – the only article of clothing she was wearing whatsoever. Though lust was nothing but a bed of dying ashes in his heart, he immediately thought of her beauty. She was small and slight of frame with pert breasts and short, slightly muscular legs. Her stomach was soft but flat, and her eyes glittered with natural intelligence, traced with a heavy note of barely contained fear. They also betrayed immediate recognition as she looked back at him, her eyebrows shooting upward with alarm.

She shot to her feet and squinted as if she could not be sure of the truth of what she was seeing. She attempted to speak to him with a questioning look on her face. Two syllables inflected as a question. He shook his head and tapped his ears with a forefinger to indicate that he could not hear her. She mouthed the word again, very slowly.

Khalil? That was it.

Khalil was him. His *name*. Along with it came a rush of quick associations. Snippets of memory pasted together hastily with tape and run through the projector of his mind's eye.

His parents, long gone. His childhood dormitory and the dark room where the whips bit him for hours. Too many nights spent drunk and stoned to count, usually laughing with friends who faded in and out of memory like ghosts walking in and out of his life. Only a few people really seemed to be present in each scene.

He remembered very little, but he knew his fate. He did remember her, at the last. He remembered her beating the odds and putting the sharks in their place; a tiny little mouse of a woman with a beautiful body and an eccentric smile. She was here, now, calling his name.

If Amina noticed this transformation, she gave no sign. Instead she simply continued knocking at the walls of her glass cell, trying to mouth words to him in some sort of slow motion conversation.

"Are you okay?" Her lips formed the words slowly so that he would find it easier to interpret.

He simply nodded his head, slightly. He gave a very small shrug to indicate that he was not really that sure of his answer. As he did so, a few more thoughts swam to the surface. He remembered the panicked violence of the police raid, a metal fire escape, a darkened alleyway.

He also remembered the sick doppelganger that had visited him during his executions. Here she was, made flesh, made real. He knew that had been a false memory; it did not resonate with him as did those that felt *true*. Despite his resolution, he couldn't deny feelings of intimidation and fear. Involuntarily, he still saw those images of her when he closed his eyes.

She had been continuing to "speak" to him, but he had been too engrossed in his own line of thinking to have been paying attention. He lifted his gaze and met her deep blue eyes, wet and red-rimmed.

"What happened?"

She had obviously expected the question, and thought for a moment before using her hands in tandem with her mouth to sign the events to him. Her fingers galloped quickly along the top of her palm and dropped down below. *She'd taken the fire escape downwards, as quickly as possible, and run down the alley*. Her fingers stopped, and she dropped the fingertips down on her knuckles, lifting them up and down as if tiredly heaving. *She'd taken a rest somewhere, and looked around.* Tentatively walking her fingertips along, she indicated that she'd then made her way home by walking the back streets. She laid her hand down on its side, as if resting on a bed. Then, using her body, Amina kicked hard at the air and extended her arms with hands intertwined, index fingers extended as if the barrel of a gun. *They'd abducted her in her home the very same night.*

At this point, her face crumpled and a bright blush came across her expression. Her lips quivered and she sank down to the floor as if overwhelmed by the recall of the events.

Of course, they'd raped her.

It was generally standard procedure whenever the commanding officer wasn't overly vigilant nor particularly concerned about the act in the least. Fringe benefits was the joke amongst those on the right side of the blue code.

Khalil felt sick to him stomach, but held it in check. He gritted his teeth and slammed a thick palm against the glass. His cage shook lightly on its tether, like a dancing spider.

23. LIKE A HURRICANE

The night had passed in Pixels, but it hadn't ever, really. Only about half of the patrons had gone home in the first place. Many had slept on the floor or slumped over the tables. Elliott had grabbed a few minutes of shut-eye in the back room and trusted his customers to go easy on the free drinks in the interim. Shawn hadn't left his spot since the beginning of the broadcast, save for ten minutes of extreme and almost mad exultation when Khalil had shrugged off his bonds and slain the executioner and the champion in a near blink of an eye. He felt some deep vindication that seemed to have cast his darker thoughts aside, even if temporarily.

Now, a morose mood in the room prevailed – a weight in the air that clung like an iron grip holding down a snarling, snapping dog. The majority of those who had stayed had been up all night, smoking and drinking and talking about revolution. Most people had known Khalil quite well since he'd first showed up in the neighbourhood following his escape from the Damocles camp. He was well liked by nearly everyone that knew him for his generosity, honesty, and loyalty to his friends. It turns out he had chosen wisely, for his many friends as well as others had been inspired by his actions.

Old man Josef had stayed in the bar all night, silent except for the sound of his fingers slapping against the sides of the electronic pinball machine. He had listened with an interested ear to all that was said in jest or in boast over the course of the evening. He had overheard the various threats of death to the CEOs, and the board members of Central. These threats themselves were not new, but the madness and urgency reflected in the tone was. He had strained to hear conspiratorial whispers shared across the worn bartop, snatched pieces of sentences that all pointed to death on the streets, urban guerrilla warfare with the weapons they had and those they could quickly improvise. These threats were not idle, nor were they solely the province of drunk men and junkies, although these sorts of men were amongst those willing and able enough.

Who knows, Josef thought to himself, maybe those wretches can make a stand and end their suffering at the same time – there was a time in his life when that would have been considered faintly noble. There was a time, he could remember, when men stood tall and didn't take any horse-shit from suit-wearing dandies who strolled by the work site or through the factory. Now you did what you were told by the men wearing the suit and the mask and if you didn't like it you were afforded the freedom to die.

To old Josef's ears, hearing these shouts and whispers from a few handfuls of men lifted his heart and made his breath catch in his chest. He stayed all night with no intentions of leaving – not because he had no place to go but because he felt at home, at ease. The calm before the storm.

There were a few groans as men who had drank far too much dealt with vicious hangovers; the smell of stale spilled beer and cigarettes clung to every surface in the basement bar. The music had been lowered to a dull murmur, though the arcade cabinets still sang their electronic chorus. A few diehard gamers had taken their frustration out on any number of the various games, passing the time. As the afternoon began to fade back into the early hours of the evening, patrons once again began filling Pixels as well as The Wreckage two stories above. There was to be a benefit show tonight, with the proceeds from the door going to support local community shelters for the homeless – Khalil had been homeless for quite some time after his escape and had availed himself of shelter services on frequent occasion – and to propel public anger forward into the media and into the eye of the authorities.

The crowd in general appeared hardened, their faces grim and almost serious, a far cry from the usually ener-

getic and excitable crowd that frequented the establishments. A few men of various size and description bellied
up to the bar to have a short conversation with Elliott.
They would fortify their spirits with rum and beer and
bold conversation.

He often asked Josef to watch the bar – simply meaning to make sure that none of the notorious drunks got
his hands on liquor with the five-finger discount – and
retired with his guests for a few minutes to discuss something in private in his back room. This happened at least
a half dozen times over the course of the evening and every time that anyone questioned the barman about it, he
would give them a blank stare and tell them that he had no
idea what they were going on about.

The opening band was just starting to play at the
Wreck, the sound of the amplifiers penetrating the coffee shop and trickling slightly down below into the barcade. By now the place was packed throughout, everyone
watching the band, the games, or the vidscreens, hoping
for the latest news.

While the opening band was playing their first song,
Shawn picked himself up and walked up to the bar, stretching muscles that had grown stiff and kinked for lack of
comfort or rest. He leaned on his elbows and scratched at
his growing beard. His dark brown eyes didn't rise from
the countertop. With his left hand he ran an idle finger
along the marks etched into the heavily lacquered surface.

"Rum and coke, man."

Elliott nodded and produced a thick rocks glass, scooping ice into it from a nearby bucket. He poured the rum in with a heavy hand – likely a double – and topped it off with a splash of cola. He set it down next to Shawn's hand and then set to wiping the counter free of the ashes, bits of paper, and other debris that had accumulated over the past few hours.

"What do you think they're going to do to him?" the drummer asked the bartender.

"I don't know man. I honestly don't. Just a few days ago he was right there. Where you are. He was real. They already took him away. They don't need to kill him, really. Not his body. They'll just do it again until he learns his lesson. If we let them."

"He never will *learn his lesson*. They could kill him a thousand times in a thousand ways. They might get him to say the words but they'll never make a man like that *believe* it. I won't watch it happen once."

Shawn sounded like a man with a lethal purpose. Perhaps the figurative gun he'd been holding to his own head over the course of the past few days had reversed its orientation.

"A bold thing to say, Shawn. What about Heba?" Elliott knew despite the impolitic nature of the question, it had to be asked.

"She knows how I feel. Doesn't matter. She doesn't talk

about it much. I don't think she wants to risk it. Hard to say with her. I need to be a part of it. He's my friend. He's right." Now Shawn's hands were animated, palms tilted open as if pleading for someone to understand his personal position. Elliott merely raised an eyebrow and continued scanning for loose crumbs or stains on the wood veneer.

"And?"

"And the fact is that I understand my responsibility to her. But I also understand my responsibility to my friend. You know as well as I do that we can't let this happen to us; we can't sit here and drink and drug ourselves to death. You know – a slow death. The type of death that takes a man by degrees, like thumbscrews or being pinioned to the rack. Just stretch us all thinner and thinner – thin us out until we're dead or too weak to fight back anyways. Khalil stood up for what he believed in, he stood true to himself and true to us. They killed him again and again. We don't even know where he is, or if he's alive, though I agree that we can assume that he is – if only for political gain. Who's next? Me? You? The old man, Festif? How about Heba? She's been recorded and noted at several protests that have taken place over the past two years. What about Clinton and Trevor down on the harbourfront, you know, the dockworkers? Those guys come in here and get liquored up and shoot their mouths off crazier than a cat shitting razor blades. People hear that kind of thing. Maybe it's safer here but it's not really safe anywhere."

Elliott smiled for the first time in a long time.

"What are you going to do about it?"

Shawn honestly did not know, but he leaned over the counter until he was face to face with the tall, lanky bartender.

"Whatever I can. If opportunity knocks–" he drew his thumb across his neck casually, turning his head aside. Once again, Elliott smiled, this time as widely as Shawn had ever seen him.

"We'll talk, Shawn. Don't worry about it. Stick around. There's a lot of buzz going around right now and I'm sure you'll get what you want before the week is out. If I were you, I would tell Heba to find a safehouse and go as far underground as she can. Things are going to get very, very nasty in short order. Can't you feel it?"

As if on cue, Heba strode down the stairs. She was wearing a three-quarter length leather jacket which revealed the glint of steel when it parted a certain way. She'd made her decision, apparently. She saw Shawn and Elliott conversing and made a beeline toward them.

"Hey there beautiful." Shawn greeted her, smiling. She returned his smile.

"You know better than to get too fresh with me when I'm carrying, baby." her grin deepened. Elliott backed away and raised his hands in mock protest.

"Please, don't hurt me!" the barman joked along.

"So you're serious?" Shawn immediately jumped the elephant in the room.

"As serious as you are." Heba offered back, her eyes flat and opaque, and that settled the matter.

Over the course of their conversation, Pixels had filled to capacity and beyond, and Elliott was having trouble keeping up with all the orders on his own account. The benefit concert had entered full swing and the thick blast-beats penetrated both walls; there was no louder show on Earth in this moment.

As if remembering some small detail, Heba tugged at Shawn's shirtsleeve, beckoning with her hand to come down and listen next to her lips.

"Besides, didn't you get the email?"

Taking a stack of credits from the counter and turning to deposit them in his independent storage unit, Elliott felt a quick vibration in his forearm that indicated a new IM. He tapped at his arm and read the message, keeping his wrist tight to his chest to ensure relative privacy.

To: (pixelsarcade@freehost.biz) The Staff of The Wreckage, Pixels, and even Mario's Coffee [just for having the ill-fortune of sharing in the same address, unfortunately...]

CC: 86 private recipients.

From: (anon@anon.net) Anon.

Text Body: Greetings to all of you. I have spent a little time in each of your establishments over the course of my life, and I've always appreciated your respective atmospheres. I do apologize, however, as I do not have time to spend on lavish pleasantries or to discuss your individual merits.

You don't really need to know who I am, although I am sure many of you will guess, at least some of you correctly. Suffice it to say that I am a friend in a time of great peril for all of you.

In the past five years, there have been over two hundred food riots in the North American Union. Global shortages have meant that we are fed at subsistence levels in the cities proper, though in some areas there is widespread starvation – particularly in landlocked communities with poor soil. In each instance where a food riot has been sparked, nearly all identifiable participants have been summarily convicted, imprisoned, and often executed in the name of rehabilitation. It is well known that Central brooks no peace with dissenters, peaceful or otherwise.

We have all seen what has happened to Khalil Madi. Most of you don't even know the man. I did. Most of you don't even need to have known him to understand what he represents to us. I don't have to tell you all that he's the first one among us to have proven that we still yet live, despite being ground underfoot with the passing of the years. In communities like our own, Khalil has become a legend. For many ringdwellers, he is the harbinger of their doom. Suffice it to say that I feel I speak for all of us when I say that sympathy for ringdwellers is in short supply at best.

However, I'm not writing this letter to all of you to simply reinforce the importance of Khalil's deeds and his sacrifice, but rather to inform you of the repercussions which we must expect due to his actions and, in turn, our own reactions.

It is well known to Central that the city cores are burning with support for Khalil and affiliated subversive activity; they are not stupid nor are they lacking in the infrastructure necessary to infiltrate subversive communities. At least a few of you who I've trusted to receive this message will report it back to your commanding officers in the correctional division; though I have been extremely careful in my selection I know a few of you are double agents and traitors to your fellow man.

For those of you, I simply hold pity. Your days are numbered at this point, and death is coming for you just as it has haunted us for these past few decades. Cry for your masters, for your way of life is about to change drastically. We're used to it. You are not.

For those of you who remain faithful to your communities, your families, and your friends, I give you a warning. You have been targeted for immediate arrest and en masse processing. You will be violently arrested, processed, and Freed as a collective according to the attached document, detailing Central's newest push to re-establish a conservative baseline of control over city populations. I have also attached documents from Central Conglomerate and their Board of Directors indicating the time and date of these synchronized sweeps. You will note that they begin less than two hours from the transmission of this message.

I urge you to fight, or at the very least to flee – though fleeing will do nothing but prolong the time it takes to find you and to press you into service. There is rarely any true and honest cause for bloodshed. This is one of those times. If you resist – and I assure you that many of you will resist, I have seen into your hearts as I lived among you – you will not be alone. Khalil was alone; look what he was able to accomplish. He is one man. We are many.

Anger against our oppressor is fundamentally liberating. Empathy towards our brothers and sisters is fundamentally subversive. It's time to employ both as best we can.

Distribute this message freely to those closest to you. As soon as this message was sent, the content began to be compromised. Most correctional strike teams will be aware that there is the potential for armed resistance, though they may not be expecting such a broad scope. That all depends on you.

Good luck. Watch out for yourself, and others.

Signed,
Anonymous

3 ATTACHED FILES [**Download**]

Elliott immediately clicked off the message after reading it and downloaded the attachments. He whirled around to face the crowded bar. Many of the more astute – and more sober – patrons had kept a watch on him as he read the message; it had already become clear that Elliott had been coordinating something larger than simple bartending over the course of the past twenty-four hours.

Many looked to him for some semblance of guidance and leadership, eager to do something.

They were about to get their chance.

All eyes stayed on him except for a few who were deeply immersed in games and couldn't break concentration until after they'd lost a life. He pulled on the deep wooden handle and poured himself a dark glass of stout until the mocha coloured foam ran frothy over the lip of the glass and slid down over his fingers. Tilting the glass to his mouth, he took a deep drink, savouring the dark ashy taste of the stout. He then slammed the bottom of the glass down on the bar and licked his lips clean, leaning forward.

"Well, I'm just going to be honest with you. Looks like there's going to be violence, and a lot of it in the coming days. Those of you who wish to leave should do so now. If you got a family to take care of, there's no shame in leaving. If it's just you, your life is better spent staying here if you are able; you'll likely have a better shot at survival." Only a dozen men and a handful of women took the opportunity to leave. Some apologized profusely and offered vocal excuses, some simply took their leave silently and quickly. The vast majority had stayed, perhaps some out of morbid curiosity.

"To the rest of you, I'll be distributing an email that I just received. Though it is from an anonymous source, it comes from the same proxy that has been keeping in touch with me at other times – always with a great degree of accuracy. I trust it, and in turn you might trust me."

Rumbles of assent already poured forth. Elliott was a local fixture; even if you didn't particularly care for his style, you respected his honesty and integrity. He tapped at his implant and held it up in the air, the soft blue display emanating colour through the thin layer of skin. It was unlocked and open for anyone in the bar to receive for sixty seconds. Roars of surprise and a few loud rolls of laughter tinged with disbelief came forth from the crowd as they read on. A half dozen runners immediately sprinted upstairs spread the word and share the email; others spread the news to various Usenet, the new web, and liveblogging feeds. It was too close to the time of operation for there to be any change in the responses of either party.

"Good. I see a lot of hungry faces out there. Who here has shot a gun before?"

About half of the crowd raised their hands.

"How many of you are willing to use a gun to kill?" Only a few hands dropped. Very good.

"Just one moment. Those of you who kept your hands in the air, come up to the bar here. If you're really drunk, let me know. It's important." He retired into the back room and came back grasping two large surplus duffel bags. He placed them, one at a time, on the countertop. He looked at the faces pressed in against him at the bar, many of them eager to see what was inside the bags, most of them sober or close enough to it.

He unzipped the first duffel bag and reached inside, pulling out guns of various size and description. Most were in rough shape but still worked well.

"Beretta, I think. Anyone good with a handgun?" A hand reached forward to snatch the gun from his hand. He pulled a sawed-off shotgun from the bag next. Old Josef called out to him from the far side of the bar, not raising his eyes from the pinball machine.

"Yeah, I'll take that one. Can't miss with a sonofabitch like that."

The crowd laughed, the tension easing for a moment, everyone back to their old humours. Most of the customers had known Josef for years and his support meant a lot to them. If there was enthusiasm for the cause before, now there was an outright clamour to be armed.

Hands and fists came thrusting over the countertop, hungry for a hunk of steel to hold and load and to make their mark with. With the weapon came a sense of power – a distinctly new feeling for many. Pistols, shotguns, short rifles, and a select few automatics were handed out in short order. A plan was hatched. Leaders were chosen. Only a select few, perhaps a quarter of those assembled, would stay here. Those who stayed knew the odds; they were much more fatal odds than those who left to start up their own groups in different neighbourhoods – at least in immediate terms.

Twenty minutes remained on clock by the time that all the hardware had been distributed and goodbyes had been said over one last drink on the house for everyone. The men that would stay, Elliott amongst them, took their positions.

The internet was aflame with arguments and debate. An enormous segment of the population was rallying behind Khalil; the more they learned about him and his true self the more quickly word spread about his exploits.

The initial, uncut surveillance video that had been leaked was now in complete circulation not only amongst the far-flung and cobwebbed Usenet groups but now even being leaked on proxied blogs and cloudsharing hubs.

It was clear that Central had lied. Many people refused to care. Many people lied to themselves and shrilly called the tape a forgery, refusing to budge from their patriotic stance no matter what the intellectual and moral consequence.

The remainder – a great many people living in the decrepit city cores across the Union and even a large number of ringdwellers – now questioned the legitimacy of their Government and how far their lives and liberties had fallen.

For the first instance in a great while, open subversive attitude was being displayed in public, en masse.

For most people, it was like waking up from a sickly slumber.

24. EXECUTIVE DECISIONS

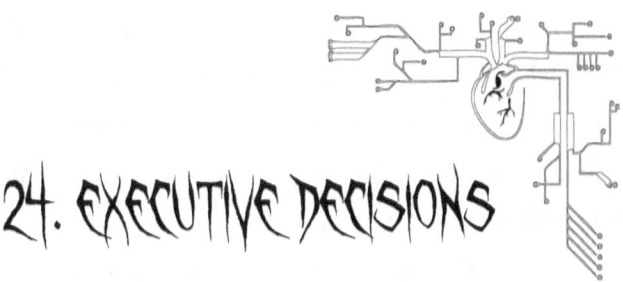

Things were bad, and were about to get much worse. The four board members and the president sat in silence for a few moments to allow the computer to finish delivering its report.

The five men sat in an enormous room, open concept taken to the utmost extreme. Curiousities from across the world, priceless works of art, historical artifacts purchased or procured from museum collections and libraries were all displayed in neat, even rows, filling the expanse of the room. The walls were flat, business gray.

The table itself was grand and rectangular in shape, no member of the board sitting any closer than twelve feet to another. Each of the men seated at the table owned over two hundred companies and five hundred "competing" brands within those networked corporate entities or "persons." In reality the wealth simply flowed upward, like a fountain, and washed over these magnates and their courtiers and courtesans like a river of gold. Collusion was the dark secret of capitalism and de facto monopoly was the first amongst the commandments – a lesson all these cunning disciples of the market had learned very, very well.

A high definition, multifaceted videosphere project-ed all of the pertinent information to each of those pres-ent. Mr. McCarthy, Vice President Communications. Mr. Allan, Vice President Finance. Mr. Tamer, looking very uncomfortable and dabbing sweat from his swar-thy complexion with an embroidered handkerchief – VP Exterior.

Notably fidgeting and as white as a sheet – Mr. Leger, Vice President Interior. The President did not use his name and was simply referred to by position, as his name was inconsequential and his office was everything. He wore a VISAGE at all times for various pertinent rea-sons. The robotic voice continued the executive briefing, doing its best impersonation of the sultry tones of a hu-man female, dictating from script.

"Since the failure of the rehabilitative act on Khalil Madi, social unrest has reached an all-time peak. Pro-ductivity amongst the administrative and consumerist rings is down, Union wide, by thirty percent. Worse, consumption of luxury items and domestically manufac-tured electronics is down by fifty percent. Demand for what are now widely perceived as crisis goods – medi-

cines, drugs, and food – outpaces our capacity to provide supply. This is resulting in extreme price gouging
by sales actuaries, further depressing the ring economy. Rings in six cities of the MEU are reporting labour
unionization and immediate strike action of essential
services – physicians in two cases, transport and ship-
ping workers in the other four. Negotiations are ongoing but seem unlikely as grassroots labour unions are
demanding comprehensive, universal health care and a
wage increase that would cut into our annual ten-per-
cent growth projections."

"Pause," the President said, his voice deep and low
and entirely synthesized. "Mr. Allan," he began, waving a
ringed hand toward the VP Financial. "What is your plan
to get this economy back on the rails and these labour
unions dissolved? We have very little time."

Mr. Allan fidgeted slightly, showing signs of discomfort despite the luxury of his bespoke suit. "President,
there is very little we can do at this point that does not
include the threat of direct violence. We have already offered the strike officials a wage increase of two percent
over four years – a generous offer given their domestic
economic positions. They insulted our offer and instead
went on a relentless recruiting drive. The transport driv-
ers union in the southwest Union, to clarify – what used
to be largely the state of California – is outright refusing
to work in any capacity unless we meet every single one

of their demands." Having delivered his report, Mr. Allen steepled his soft, manicured fingers and hid his expression behind them.

The President waved his hand broadly across the tabletop in an expansive, languid gesture. "So we use violence, then. We don't pay corrections officers to sit in the break room and eat donuts. A lot of those gentlemen truly enjoy their line of work and the action associated with it. Let's give it to them. Are the strikers actually foolish enough to walk picket lines?"

Mr. Allan nodded. "They've been on the picket line on Two in Pacifica East now for almost a week. After the events of the past couple of days, they've firmed up on their position. Couldn't have picked a worse time. We're working on nearly a dozen other major strike actions as it is, and enforcement is already being pushed well beyond expected capacity."

Allan hesitated, as if afraid to continue. He bit his lip. A childish expression and one that betrayed his nervousness at breaking bad news.

"... then there's the matter of public opinion. Both polling as well as surveillance report that the core residents are in a state of near mutiny. In some cities we are seeing active opposition. In some cities, we are even seeing *ringdwellers* expressing discontent."

He let the last sink in. Even though government was no longer beholden to democracy, but rather capital, it still required a few accomplices to keep things moving smoothly.

"Well then, we'll break the picket by force. Arrest as many as possible to make the other unions think twice about organizing in the first place, let alone walking pickets and making demands of us."

"Yes, sir. I'll call the shareholders and the board of Southwest Corrections immediately following this meeting."

"Good. Next order of business."

The computer continued in soft feminine tones, without hesitation.

"Next on the agenda is the contingent issue of the prisoner himself. Over the time he has been unplugged and kept in isolation, he has betrayed no hint of remorse or even self-awareness until the introduction of Amina Kelly to his environs. His reactions thus far show that he does indeed possess memories of his past and that the chances of his complete rehabilitation – via imprisonment or indoctrination or, even as we have seen, execution – are so slim as to be nonexistent."

Mr. Leger leaned forward on his elbows over the table and spoke in a shaking voice with a thick French accent. He was wan and looked ill. Failure had been accumulating on his shoulders for quite some time, with an anvil being added to the burden over the course of the past week or two.

"There are – there are only two options. We could execute him – behind closed doors of course. A corporeal execution in public would have disastrous consequences in terms of public relations. That is my advice. Our other option is to continue to drug him and attempt to manipulate him through Amina Kelly – she has already been quite cooperative given the obvious alternative and my technicians tell me that she is completely pliant." He spread his hands as if to emphasize the point, before clasping one fist within another and trying to remain still.

"Mr. Leger, your advice had been adequate for the majority of your first year, although this year seems to be getting the best of your abilities." The president continued his criticism smoothly, without betraying a hint of emotion beyond some sense of dark and imminent threat to Leger.

"Executing the prisoner behind closed doors, corporeally, makes him into a martyr. We can't deal with that. We're in the business of exterminating dissidents, not ideals. Much better to have a converted spokesman; if Mr. Madi can be made to capitulate publicly we can then dispose of him with impunity. Before that point, however, he lives larger than a man. Let our beautiful assistant do the dirty work for us."

"Which means, Mr. Leger, that we're taking you off the case. You've produced total and absolute failure."

Mr. Leger looked vastly uncomfortable. All that remained were details of the sentence for such infractions, the usual nature of which he was acutely aware.

"Mr. President, please! Look at my record of service! For years I've kept things under lock and key – under my watchful eye we've made trillions and kept the peace."

A few low chuckles could be heard, though who had uttered them was impossible to say. Desperation filled the room, emanating from the outgoing VP Internal like a fetid miasma. It displeased all present.

"Remove yourself from office, Mr. Leger. You will be offered permanent retirement in a housing complex of your choice in any city, ring Three. So long as you never speak to anyone about anything of gravity, you will be spared forceful debriefing. You are quite aware, however, that it is impossible for you to escape this clause. Your implant will be monitored constantly to ensure you remain faithful to this severance. Should you remove or disable your implant intentionally or unintentionally you will be brought in for immediate debriefing. Do you understand?"

"Y-Yes! Of course, Mr. President. Thank you! Thank you!" Quickly bowing and collecting his tablet, Leger stood up from the table, nearly tripping backwards over his seat. He scrabbled to grab his tablet before turning on his heel and walking briskly towards the double doors at the far end of the room, flanked by guards on each side.

It was a long walk, perhaps a full minute in the making, and not a word was spoken until Mr. Leger had exited the room fully.

"His replacement will be appointed by you, Mr. Tamer. I *trust* you to make a better decision this time than last." A lie. The President did not trust anyone fully, only by degrees. Mr. Tamer simply did not have the nuanced cunning required to make a power play, which made him an invaluable subordinate in times such as these. Mr. Tamer merely gave a tight-lipped smile and nodded in acceptance of the task. The matter was closed.

"Your report, Mr. Tamer?"

The man looked somewhat like a bulldog, with a thick and meaty jaw just barely concealed behind a sparse and bristly salt and pepper beard. His eyes were dull and flat, intellectually incurious. He was loyal as a dog is loyal, serving without thinking. He was the best VP Exterior that the President had ever worked with, but even his abilities were being strained by current circumstance.

"Mr. President." Here, again, a tight nod. "There have been increasing reports of airspace activity by the North American socialists on the Atlantic front over the course of the past month, with two distinct incidents occurring within the space of the past week alone. In the first incursion," Mr. Tamer said, working at his tablet with thick, pudgy fingers, "we were able to deter the scouting aircraft, who communicated to us that they were merely conducting defense exercises. Following a brief period of communication, they fled the scene. You are all aware of this, I'm sure, having met with your own briefings. However, there is new information which has come to light. The footage recovered from the flight team, none of whom survived the attack. We will now review the timeline of events with the new information in place."

A video clip was shown on the videosphere in three dimensions. A squadron of North American fighter jets could be seen on the screen, the HUD of their own MEU fighter cockpit displaying the location as being one hundred kilometers within their defined national boundaries. An obvious incursion that was in no way meant to be taken as a simple training exercise.

"Fearing to inflame outright war during such an uncertain time, I ordered our forces to halt pursuit at the border and further requested a doubling of satellite scans and physical air patrols on particularly strategic areas of our ocean boundaries."

The video screen now showed the MEU jets in hot pursuit, tailing the faster but more lightly armed American scramblers back to their own territory. The voice of the pilot broke through the broadcast at times to impart strategic information to his wingmates that made little to no sense to anyone but the VP Exterior, who had been a General before taking this executive position. By the time the pursuit – or, in diplomatic terms, the escort mission – had been completed, it was dusk, the sharp and angular shapes of the enemy craft fading like black dots into the horizon. The video feed was shut down, and once again Mr. Tamer spoke to the board.

"There was, as you know, another incursion. This time with more serious results." His voice took on a militant, strained cast.

The videosphere sparked into life again. This time the colours were drastically vibrant as it was a clear, blue skied day. Almost high noon. Once again the footage was taken directly from the front capture of the lead fighter jet, the audio being piped in at a lower volume from the flight commander's headset.

This time the co-ordinates showed the flight team patrolling merely fifty kilometers from their western, Atlantic coastline, along the convergence of the European and African continents, somewhat removed from their own MEU Central Presidential Office Northeast. There was a notable gasp.

The HUD displayed a trio of fighter jets and an observation plane being escorted along, flying low as if to escape electronic detection. After the event only a few nights previous, there was no mistaking this incursion as accidental. As if speaking the thoughts of all present, Mr. Tamer continued.

"This could be no accident, especially so soon after the first detection of North American forces. As you can hear..."

The general's voice trailed off; he thumbed a slider on his tablet and the volume of the video feed increased dramatically. The pilot's voice was raised in direct command to the Europeans, informing them that they had fifteen seconds to alter course and flee the scene immediately.

The General continued. "...they were warned. Approximately ten seconds later..."

The flight commander's voice immediately crackled again, this time with a distinct note of panic, ordering his wingmates to enact evasive manoeuvres immediately as they were under missile fire. He screamed, a scream that was cut short in an instant as the screen went black.

The feed was switched to the MEU fighter bringing up the rear. At the first sign of danger, the automated camera swung downward with the approach of a surface-to-air missile. A submarine had surfaced, painted deep navy and black and blending in nearly perfectly with the ocean. A red flare and flame burst from the top of the submarine and a handful of small rockets, like darts, sprung forth and struck with pinpoint accuracy. The pilots barely had time to react before their jets were torn apart in great spouts of flame, carbon, and burning metal.

"My God!" Mr. Allan spoke for them all. There was a silence that was permitted to fill the room for a few moments before the President spoke, once again with full confidence and authority.

"The remainder were taken out by unmanned drones. Remote pilots." The General remarked in closing, almost offhanded.

The screen reflected this, as the best military hardware the MEU had to offer was destroyed again and again in front of them by a small group of tiny remote aircraft. Toys destroying larger toys and the pilots within them.

"General Tamer, it appears that we will require your services once again." At this, and the use of his honorific, Tamer seemed to puff his chest out a bit further and his eyes took on a feral shine. "I am authorizing you to use any and all force necessary to repel any further incursions into our coastal borders. You may reassign all necessary personnel to ensure that no further incursions will be tolerated."

"Yes, sir," he said, bursting with pride. "I do not believe that the North Americans pose a true threat – Since the Collapse we've had enough anti-ballistic missiles installed on both sides of the Union to counter every nuke on the planet five times over. Further, they are in a likewise unstable economic position and all intelligence reports indicate that their socialist Governments are currently hung up by democratic weakness and unable to make any decisions of note beyond minor tax issues and petty environmental concerns. Certainly they are too weak to present any real threat to our sovereignty if we act now. I can have a coastal perimeter live by the end of the month – three weeks at the most."

"Excellent, General. It gladdens me greatly to hear confidence given voice in these council chambers after such a somber week. An excellent return to usual form, to be commended. Just don't rush, don't be hasty – we do not want to appear as if we are preparing for military action until it is too late for them to realize their mistake."

Those seated around the table breathed a deep sigh of relief as the retired General nodded his assent. All of their troubles were over – they had weathered the delivery of the worst news the board has seen in a decade and only one of them had felt the wrath of their President. Their jobs were safe, their paycheques would continue to grow, and their wives would continue to do whatever pleased them. Life was good, and the temporary specter of uncertainty and pessimism ushered in by the loss of a few jets and the failure of some pissant correctional goons became small issues in their minds, once again banished from thought.

"Any further issues to be discussed amongst the board?" the President asked, shifting in his seat and getting ready to call for adjournment. He took a look around the table to ensure that none of his subordinates had anything further to add, but was interrupted by the chirping of the computer.

"Apologies for interrupting the meeting, members of the board, but there is a petitioner present who wishes to add an item to the agenda before adjournment. Ms. Maya Williams and her associate are present, requesting permission to address the members of the board on the matter of her legal counsel as provided to the prisoner."

Snorts of mildly concealed disgust and chuckles of disbelief from the VP Exterior and VP Financial, respectively. The President looked at them sharply, and they fell silent.

"Gentlemen, this could be pertinent. Williams has long been useful in facilitating offenders into rehabilitation for additional manpower and, as late, has fallen a great deal in terms of station. She's the type to come crawling back, offering anything and everything for one more shot at joining us in the upper echelons – she's *not* an incompetent. Further, and more importantly, she could have some information on Mr. Madi that could help us turn him, or at least leverage him into compliance. It is imperative that she tell us what she knows, even if we don't give her anything in return. Silence, please."

The President wheeled his chair somewhat theatrically and leaned back into the soft leather cushioning, relishing the feeling of absolute power that he held at his fingertips. He would take Williams for all of her intel and make sure that the woman was never heard from again – she was too dangerous in terms of the knowledge she possessed. Addressing the computer, he gave his assent.

"Please unlock the doors and allow her to come in. As she is unexpected, please tell her that we don't have time for the usual courtroom formalities and we'd just like to get this over with as quickly as possible. We have work to do."

"As you wish," intoned the saccharine sweet voice of the computer, unlocking the far chamber doors with a distinct click.

25. ESCAPIST ARTISTS

Like a crystal pendulum, Khalil's cage had swung back and forth and he threw his weight in time with the inertia of the swing.

Like a glass ornament, his cage had broken unevenly when he'd finally managed to strike Amina's container as she clumsily attempted the same.

A few more passes and they were both free to clamber from their cages, spotting the fragments of glass on the floor no more than ten feet below, motes of perspective as the room continued to appear endless due to a lack of line and shadow.

Both Khalil and Amina were weeping blood from cuts and scrapes.

Both were naked, clutching one another tight against the warmth of the floor, like the warmth of hardwood floors with sun streaming through the window. A strange image, Khalil thought to himself.

They were a precious few seconds of comfort.

Then there was an alarm, abrupt and growing slowly in volume. Khalil's dulled wits barely knew who he was, but he knew he was being hunted. Again.

Amina rose alongside him and led him by the hand, walking briskly, away from the broken glass of their cages, away from the other prisoners.

"What about them?" he indicated with a shrug of his shoulders.

"We don't have time."

"I know you. You are in my dreams."

"Yes. Not now. No words now." Amina had to shout over the rising klaxxon.

She led him further into the light, it seemed as if what had been ivory became an unflattering orange as more and more saturation took place. They must be closer to the lightsource. It was nearly blinding now, and Khalil had to squint and shield his eyes.

The alarm wailed continuously.

Tapping on what appeared to be an invisible wall, Amina tilted her head to the side. She tapped a bit further along the wall, between what Khalil could now see were two titanic columns of illumination, bars of bright orange. Leaning close to the wall, straining to hear over the alarm, Amina spread her fingertips and pressed a position near the leftmost column.

The light parted, a perfect rectangle of darkness

carved out like a piece from a jack-o-lantern. All of this was artificial. Khalil's mind knew this simple fact to be true.

How much of this was reality? How much a construct? How much a construct of his own consciousness?

Unanswerable questions, particularly in such a situation. Without pause, Amina once again took Khalil's hand and together they plunged through the portal of complete darkness.

The cold concrete of the floor was shocking to his senses as the pads of his feet stepped from the warmth of the light. His eyes widened and he found that he was blind. Only a small sliver of light lanced in from the previous chamber through the doorframe, revealing nothing but the plain grey of the cement.

His eyes began to adjust. Amina had already strode quickly into the room, pawing at something metallic in the darkness. The squeal of metal on metal hinges. Lockers. Khalil could make them out now. His panic abated somewhat, though it was very hard to concentrate on anything.

A red light sprang to life overhead, behind a simple metal grille.

"Over here. Your stuff." As more than simple shapes took form, Khalil admired the taut lines of her body. She was the woman in his dreams and in his nightmares.

Who was she, really?

He approached the locker beside hers.

A leather jacket and a pair of battered jeans, the bottoms frayed white and loose like treebeard. Two black boots, heavy and deeply worn.

A pure white jumpsuit. Circles of dried blood mapped out a constellation on the back of the garment. Trails of blood and mucous hung like tendrils down the front collar and chest pocket.

"They put you back in the jumpsuit while transporting you here. It was streamed."

If Khalil heard, he didn't acknowledge, picking up his clothes and quickly dressing. His boots felt chill and damp, and without a shirt, the leather jacket stuck to him, clinging to him. His nudity had not shamed him, but clothes afforded more protection.

Amina's clothes. A blazer. A beautifully patterned lining, black and white, which threatened his memory. The rest passed without scrutiny, though she gazed at him without pause, his thoughts again threatening to unravel.

"No time for this, Khalil. I'm sorry. Get ready to fight, or we both die here." she shouted at him, frowning.

The alarm had long sounded off to full volume. The door at the far end of the chamber beckoned, the sliver of light behind them calling like the safety of the womb to a newborn Khalil.

As Amina's hand reached for the doorpad, a burst of

gunfire boomed out, penetrating the door and rattling it on its hinges. Men and women cried out, some gasping, some cursing, all cut short within a span of a few seconds. There had been no return fire.

A beat, a second or two of silence. Then, slowly seeping back into his awareness, the drone of the alarm.

He took the lead, no longer content to have Amina lead him into unknown danger. Pressing the door open, Khalil saw bodies, most limbless and punched deep with holes, slumped in a messy array. Firearms and stun batons strewn across the glossy white marble of the floor, gore flecking the tiles like a work of abstract art. All wore a simple black uniform, some with vests, others without, all bearing the large CORRECTIONSCORP logo prominently on the shoulder and sleeve.

Khalil pushed the door open and exited into the hallway, remaining behind the doorway and turning left to check the other side of the hallway.

He came face to face with an android. Nearly eight feet tall on multilever and multilevel tracks, with two blazing blue eyes and an array of weapons built into the body and arms, though to call them arms at all was to stretch the resemblance. Long slivers of titanium filed to a knife edge, forearms and shoulders mounted for war.

The android made their decision in a matter of nanoseconds, far faster than any human brain could think to react, let alone a confused mind.

A pair of well-oiled miniguns came to bear.

"You are not a defined target. Reporting to control. Do not move."

Khalil knew that any report to control meant a likely death sentence from his captors – but didn't this droid just kill all of those CORRECTIONSCORP officers? Deciding that discretion would be wiser in this instance, still coiled like a spring, Khalil kept his position. Amina, he sensed, remained stock-still behind him. She'd heard.

"Khalil! Amina!" the androids voice was replaced by a familiar male voice. "This is Festif. I'm inside and in control of the intranet. Cameras, androids, all clear and under my command. You need to make it to the parkade. There's lots of *human* guards around so arm yourself. The androids can't leave the prison section, but I have one last trick up my sleeve. It might help. We're leaving in fifteen minutes."

Festif? Why the hell was he here? Khalil was dreaming, he was sure of it. And who was we?

"No time to explain, Khalil." Festif spoke through the mechanical voicebox; Amina prodded him with her fingers and slipped by him, running to the downed men and kneeling for a weapon. "Get moving. Turn right. Follow the signs. Stay safe. Remember, fifteen minutes."

Nine hundred seconds that would determine whether they lived or died, with plenty of opportunities for the latter in the interim.

Khalil turned on his heel and ran to Amina's side. She passed him a small handgun. "Belt this." He did, and then knelt down, picking at the rifles, flipping over bodies. The standard issue assault rifle seemed the most attractive option. Rifling through the pockets of the dead and coming up with four spare magazines, Khalil nodded to Amina and started running towards the end of the hallway and the swinging doors that led to freedom.

As they approached the doors, Khalil spied a map pressed neatly into the wall, illuminated simply and designed in minimalist fashion. YOU ARE HERE shone brightest neon, so close to a wheel-like annex titled HUB which projected spokes in nearly all directions, a bursting star. This building was immense.

"Here!" Amina pointed with her finger, breathless. From the far side of the hub, around a raised promenade, there was a long pathway leading to the irregular rectangle with PARKADE embossed on top in cool LED blue.

Through the door, around the wheel, along the hall, and down to the bottom. He said it outloud to himself, muttering.

The swinging doors provided only a small window, and a cursory glance from Khalil revealed no obvious officers. Pushing the doors open and creeping-crouching in a low stance to reduce their profile, both of them pressed onto the raised mezzanine-level ring, the promenade overlooking the inner lobby and annex. Here the alarm was silenced somewhat, while orders could be heard being shouted from all directions below, punctuated by the stamp of booted feet.

"You, Ramirez! Move it over here, we're taking a team into PRISON to ensure lockdown and defuse those rogue 'droids!"

Khalil found that he had very little patience to listen in, every second counting down to death. Trying to be a silent as possible, he looked for cover lining the railings of the promenade.

A few potted plants, garden boxes filled with artificial flowers, the odd glass and steel display containing corporate awards and other trinkets. Nothing that would stop a hail of bullets, but enough to obscure the pair if they got lucky. They moved quickly, staying low.

After they had leapfrogged twice, making it nearly halfway around the ring, another series of orders came from ragged throats below.

Sweep the promenade and secure the parkade! Two teams! Orange and black teams!

More gunfire and more screams, sounding thin and tinny and far away, reached Khalil's ears. Amina's fingers dug into his back; she'd heard.

This time the return gunfire was equally loud, accented by the distinct noise of a pulse, or EMP weapon. Then more gunfire, growing confident.

Khalil's instincts took over, bursting from burial. He

turned and smiled grimly from beneath his black, matted beard and through his brown eyes. A spark of himself. Amina smiled back, encouraging flame. She squeezed his hand. Khalil squeezed back.

Clutching their weapons the pair rain, legs pumping, lungs drawing deep, thrusting towards the far side of the promenade.

An eye hidden behind an armoured mask peered through the swinging doors behind them; Khalil saw him and mouthed in an instant.

"Down."

Rolling behind a somewhat larger glass and steel trophy and document display, Khalil shouldered his weapon and took a knee, bringing rifle to bear and rising up just over cover. Amina was only a second slower.

Khalil took the first shot, tightening his index finger the extra few pounds of pressure it took to discharge. On burst-fire, the rifle bucked against him, slight fingers of fire escaping from the barrel. Two of the rounds struck true, shattering the thin glass of the swinging door and driving through the eye socket and jaw of the man standing behind it.

Khalil emptied the chamber and replaced his depleted magazine with an extended mag. Ninety rounds. Amina was already pumping bursts into the largely cosmetic doors, insurance shots that surely killed and maimed. It also meant that there would be only one response.

Khalil thumbed his selector switch to fully-automatic.

The CORRECTIONSCORP officers burst through the doors in a small wave, spraying and praying that their fully automatic fire would catch their prey unawares. Khalil did not waver at this hail of death, a lightshow like candles which he would soon extinguish.

Pulling down with constant force on the trigger, his mind as focused on the kill as on the peak of orgasm, a singular driving lust, a predestined course of action. His weapon grew hot in his hand, fighting against his grip like a serpent, possessed. The metal he threw forward pierced the bodies of his enemies, a stitched line of bone, gristle, blood, and gore exploding against the railing, the walls – raining on those below.

Of the squad of twelve men that had been assigned to sweep the promenade, Khalil counted only three survivors, two of them critically injured, writing and moaning their last moments out on the business-grey carpet.

One woman, however, remained.

"Die, you motherfuckers!" she cried, popping up over cover clutching a pistol nearly as large as her hand.

A hole appeared in her mask, instantly and almost by magic, then the crack of a rifle report. Time slowed, grey matter burst from her head to stain the walnut behind. Khalil turned to see Amina, her lips a twisted line, her eyes flat and dead. She took her finger from the trigger and met Khalil's glance.

"We need to get the hell out of here."

Khalil nodded in agreement and began to run down the long hallway which adjoined to the parkade, popping out his extended magazine and replacing it with a standard. Only two mags left.

The hallway was long, narrow, and lit only by thin yellowing bars of emergency lighting. Wires and pipes lined both the ceiling and the walls.

After about thirty seconds, they neared the end of the hallway, and could see a wide set of concrete stairs leading downwards to the parkade level. Khalil stopped short, something not feeling right, and managed to get his hands up at least to block the coldcock pistol whip he'd nearly run into.

Instead, took the brunt of the strike on his forearm, and while it ached, it gave him the time he needed. Snapping his head up, he felt a man's jaw clack shut with such impact that he may have severed his tongue. A curdling scream confirmed this guess, though Khalil was already in motion, dropping with all his weight and delivering a hard elbow to his assailant's kneecap.

Amina was faring worse. She'd been struck across the face by the butt of a rifle, and while the blow was a glancing bruise, it had still spun her to the ground at the foot of the stairs. As she was trying to gain her feet, the female guard that had ambushed her kicking closed the gap and viciously kicked her in the ribs.

"Not so tough now, are you *bitch?*" the CORREC-TIONSCORP guard taunted, again kicking Amina in the gut, eliciting a sharp cry of pain.

As Khalil's first victim collapsed to the ground, barely conscious, Khalil found himself set upon by a new threat. A massive bear of a man, Khalil had only begun to comprehend what had happened when he felt arms like iron cord embrace him in a crushing grasp. Like a closed coffin depriving his lungs of air, Khalil fought with dwindling strength to free himself. He felt himself fading, and felt chill. He let his arms go slack for a moment. He could feel the chest of his attacker heaving – laughter.

Khalil remembered something from what remained of his ruined memory.

In one fluid motion, he pulled the pistol he'd secreted away beneath his belt, against his hip, turning his wrist and firing just beside his ribcage. Khalil felt pain shoot through his wrist as the gun went off, the awkward angle causing his tendons and muscles great pain as he held his grip, refusing to drop the weapon.

The larger man, eclipsing even Khalil's sturdy frame, grunted in surprise and shock. Khalil felt his opponent's grip loosen. Again, Khalil pulled the trigger; this time the strain was too great for tired muscles and the gun went spinning from his hands. Now, the bear of a man behind him let go, and Khalil fell to the ground.

The gun.

Over there, by the railing at the top of the stairs.

He made a leap for it.

He felt his calloused fingers touch steel.

He felt an enormous palm clasp shut around his ankle.

The bear-man loomed over him, his eyes bloodshot and wide, his nostrils flaring, his chest heaving. Two holes in his uniform, bulletproof-black behind.

Khalil twisted onto his side and levelled the barrel of the small pistol at his enemy. He pulled the trigger again and again, feeling the gun leap in his fist, barking.

At least one had connected. A black abscess appeared in the bear-man's throat, beneath his craggy jaw. Plumblack blood rushed forward onto his chest. He gagged and instantly released his grip on Khalil, clutching at his neck in vain.

Khalil turned, looking for Amina, fearing the worst. It would appear his fears were unfounded.

Amina sat astride the female officer, raining blows down upon an increasingly feeble defense. The woman had dropped her guard entirely, now, and Amina brought blow upon blow to her skull.

With a war cry, Amina crushed her fist into her assailant's nose with one final blow. The only sound that remained were the whimpering sniffles of the man Khalil had disabled first. Another bark, another bullet, and then it was just them.

"We're not gonna make it..." Anna gasped, wiping sweat away from her pale forehead, a lock of stray blonde hair stuck to her temple. Her Eastern Bloc accent was very prominent now, and even this tangent thrust into Khalil's consciousness. This was something he had known before.

"Into their suits. Grab their collars. Our only chance." Khalil ordered, immediately stripping down the smaller victim's CORRECTIONSCORP uniform. Without complaint, Amina followed orders.

There was the sound of gunfire and a loud hissing noise coming from the far end of the long hallway, in the annex. A grating static came alive from the belt-tablet on the massive guard Khalil had just felled.

"CODE INFIDEL. Do you read?" Nice bit of work from Festif, vague enough to confuse if the recipient wasn't in on the reference.

Khalil tapped the tablet and unclipped it from the belt of the dead man, attaching it to his own stolen suit.

"Here. At the top of the stairwell and heading down."

"We can't wait much longer, Khalil. Three minutes. I've activated the sedative gas and the ceiling sentries in the annex and wiped a lot of them out, but more squads are heading to clear with pulses. Move it."

"Yea." Khalil tapped and slid his finger across the surface of the tablet to end the conversation.

"There's a lot of blood on mine." Amina complained, zipping up her jumpsuit..

"In the dark and against the black fabric we can only hope they don't notice. Did you get her collar?"

Khalil snapped his VISAGE on, and his exterior face became that of his victim, expressionless. Amina morphed likewise. It was, Khalil noted, a bit uncanny to see that feminine face restored while the real thing lay like a collapsed, bone-grey eggshell a few metres away, still warm with freshly-fled life.

It was not time for such rumination; Khalil nodding urgently towards the stairwell. Under his breath as their feet clambered down the stairs –

Follow my lead.

Stick to the shadows.

We've got less than three minutes.

They emerged after a few moments and flights of stairs in a large, low-ceilinged parking garage. Poorly lit, with weak fluorescents strung irregularly, it was a stark contrast to the neat and uniform nature of the complex itself. Like an ancient basement, a forgotten tomb, Khalil felt he might be buried alive. He shook the feeling loose from his bones and stalked to the right, following the wall and attempting to stay within the unlit areas.

The parkade level. From the mental map that Khalil had memorized earlier, the emergency vehicles were stored on the far end, in a somewhat smaller storeroom to the right.

From there, an exterior door opened outward to a frozen expanse – and freedom.

After passing by a line of vehicles and artfully dodging the small patches of light which dotted the darkness, Khalil and Amina found themselves nearly halfway to the exit.

Then the sound of boots against concrete. Erratic, spread out. Searching.

Khalil extended his hand backwards to halt Amina. She stopped in her tracks.

"Keep looking!"

"Fan out, turn on your lights! They're not here yet. Take up positions!"

Even in the correct uniform, if they were caught skulking around on the perimeter, they would be flagged as suspicious immediately. Khalil made a decision.

Walking between a long sedan and a tall cargo truck , winding towards the central area, Khalil flicked his gunlight on and then snapped his rifle to shoulder. He could hear Amina's lighter footfalls behind him, watching his back.

They pressed at an oblique angle towards the opposite side of the parkade, behind a small file of guards that were busy sweeping towards the front of the level and taking up preliminary defensive positions behind cars and trucks, aiming at the foot of the stairwell.

A few seconds later down those stairs and, disguises or not, they would have been killed.

Making a quick and cursory show of flicking the flashlights under the gunbarrel into the windows of nearby vehicles, the pair turned again about face and started their final beeline towards the rear-right corner of the parkade level. Another thin rank of three officers, one showing Sergeant's Badge on a lit display at his breast.

His heart pounding, Khalil did not break pace. He felt his lungs shuddering and the damp feeling of cold sweat on his chest. He put his faith in Amina.

The sergeant stepped forward into their path, Khalil having dropped the angle of his flashlight to forty-five degrees. He raised an arm and flagged at the two officers. One of the men with him was paying scant attention, fixated on working the tablet in his hand; obviously a comms officer or a tech wizard.

"I can't gain fucking access! We've been locked out *from the inside!*" the comms man nearly shrieked in frustration, his thin jaws clenched.

Paying little attention, rapt attention on the oncoming due of wayward officers, the Sergeant raised his fist to signal his subordinate to shut up, tilting his head quizzically and setting foot forward.

Khalil made the decision in an instant. The Sergeant opened his mouth, a wide O beneath a finely trimmed moustache.

Khalil snapped his gun up, the flashlight square in the Sergeant's face. A quick fireburst and the Sergeant's head exploded.

Amina had apparently felt the same way, bringing her rifle to bear on the other armed C-Corp soldier, startling him flat-footed and drilling a single bullet through his temple. Both men crumpled heavily to the ground as Khalil and Amina both took the time to pump a few rounds into the tech, his hand not even halfway to his holster before he found himself opened up, staring his last instants in wide-eyed surprise.

What came next was obvious – they ran for the corner of the parkade as shouts of confusion were bawled out from the far end of the garage; the other wings which had been focused on the stairwell slowly put the clues together. It would be a matter of long seconds, perhaps a minute at the most.

The same minute they had remaining to meet with Festif and his unnamed accomplice. *We*, Khalil remembered him saying.

Khalil and Amina ducked between the vehicles and sprinted along the right-hand wall of the parkade, nearing the corner now and the reinforced door which led to the emergency vehicle hold.

The door swung outward. A man stepped through. Khalil did not recognize him.

Then, another face. Attractive, female, and familiar.

Her face caused him to pause in his tracks, his mind screaming unintelligibly.

Then the man spoke, in the voice of an old friend.

"It's me, Khalil. Festif. You have to believe me."

He had no choice, despite his constant state of confusion. He hustled inside, Amina behind him, and their rescuer – *Festif?* – shut the door and barred it. A single slab of thick steel set into concrete. Might hold another minute.

Khalil turned to take a good look at the man who spoke with the voice of his oldest and truest friend, taking in the room in his periphery as he did so. A small concrete workroom, a few recessed bays for mechanics to do their work. Within them, something mechanical, parts sticking out. A thick, segmented steel door which led to the outside; the tall and angular woman that he knew, somehow, was working the panel. The door began to open with faint protest from whirring gears.

"You are *not* Festif. He's ancient." Khalil said, flatly.

"So am I, when I want to be." and then, a familiar, genuine smile. Khalil felt his knees beginning to give way, adrenaline either crashing overtop his inner dam or receding dangerously early.

"Look man, I'm *confused*. I barely know *who* I am, or *where* I am, or *why* I'm here. Or who the fuck *you* are. I need answers."

"Soon." Amina chimed in, re-appearing at his side

wearing a thick parka. She handed Khalil one, which he immediately put on. A bit big, nothing serious. The other woman, Festif's partner. Maya. He knew that much. Something within him felt repulsed by the sight of her. He swallowed his pride. Amina was giving him a very strange look, sympathetic.

Festif nodded towards Amina, then turned to speak to Maya, turning away from the bright lights of the panel now and striding back toward them.

There was a damp looking continent on the front of her parka. She'd been wounded.

"Start up the snowmobiles. We're leaving. You're with me, Maya. You know how to drive one of these, kid. Seen you do it more than once before."

Khalil took a few paces forward and saw a pair of snowmobiles, almost completely recessed in the small man-bays of the floor. They were black as night, sleek, and expensive. There were four of them.

"What about the other two? They'll follow us."

Festif shook his head – negative – hopping astride the seat of the nearest sled. The door was halfway open now and there was enough clearance to leave.

Muted gunfire, and extremely loud bangs as dimples appeared on the reinforced metal of the door. It would be a matter of seconds before the hunting party cut through.

Maya cinched her arms around the older man on the

sled and he immediately cranked the accelerator, pulling off with a start out of the bay and into nothingness. The engine spit a high pitched whine, rattling the garage bay and then piercing the outdoor calm.

Khalil ran to the second bay and lept down onto the sled, Amina landing lighly behind him and immediately wrapping her arms tightly about his chest, clutching her hands together in a lock.

The keycard was already inserted into the slot. Khalil pressed it into lock position and the sled growled to live. Khalil felt the grip tight in his bloodied hand, pulled at it, feeling the pain in his wrist from earlier.

He held on as the snowmobile bucked forward at almost impossible speed; if he remembered riding much sled in the past he certainly hadn't owned one this powerful.

For a few seconds, all he could see was darkness and the pinpricks of the stars above, stars he never dreamed he might see again. Then the light of the moon entered his eyes and slowly, refracting the pale gossamer of a new coat of snow, Khalil made out the other sled, carving a thick trail away from the complex.

They had exited the building near the periphery of the encampment, not particularly large given it's rather secretive placement and skeleton staff. No fence surrounded the low-slung bunker buildings, and all foot patrols had been recalled at the first sign of emergency.

Nearly a minute had passed since they'd escaped the garage when Khalil heard the first explosions. A great plume of flame shot up, a crimson and rust pillar, angry.

Khalil turned once to look at it, then stared straight ahead and followed the path in front of him, snow flying like powdered sugar, the tree-line beckoning in the far distant hills.

26. TRACKS IN THE SNOW, FIRE IN THE SKY

Twin motors whined as the snowmobiles sliced through the night at full speed, high and keening engines blocking out any attempt at conversation. Khalil's middle-aged friend, the man calling himself Festif, drove one, cranking the accelerator wide open, with Maya clutching the back of his jacket in a deathgrip.

The snow was light and powdery with a thick packed foundation that had settled from previous storms – the perfect conditions for their escape. Maya had been wounded by one hasty gunfire of one of the door guards when things had gotten a little messy, though it was a flesh wound and had entered and exited her shoulder. She'd returned the favour in more lethal fashion with a bullet between the eyes of the same guard who'd wounded her.

The other figure, her "associate," had been instrumental in the success of their plans.

Festif had been quite open about his financial wealth; it wasn't his fault if no one on the streets had ever taken his credentials seriously. He had spent the past decade acquiring majority stock in a number of influencial tech and biomedical corps. These moves had allowed he and Maya to gain access to the Presidential compound with ease, and had eliminated any prospect of an alarm being raised until it was far too late.

Between his black-market decrypt and control card, custom-made by the best in the world, and Maya's own security clearance and previous record on a few cases she'd won for the Executive's political lackeys, access was the easy part.

He and Maya had killed most of the guards as soon as the security door had closed behind them with silenced automatic pistols. The executive members had scrambled to raise the alarm both domestically as well as via their implants; a simple yet powerful dampening device was enough to quell all wireless communications within a few hundred feet.

It had been quite cold and methodical – Festif took little pleasure in murder. Maya Williams had seemed to enjoy it, however. Every time she pulled the trigger she felt a little bit better. Nobody sneered at a woman with a gun in her hand.

She'd smiled while shooting the President of Central Conglomerate – in turn, the President of the entire

MEU – square between the eyes. That image had been captured on video, along with the death-bed confessions of the board members, hands behind their heads, trembling on their knees.

All of this grisly imagery had been distributed to the internet as they exited the boardroom after Festif had hacked the domestic Central intranet, keycards and security authorization in hand. A flash card inserted into a console card reader, spamming the .gov and .edu mailing lists, the new web news aggregators, and spreading from there like digital wildfire.

A billion screens and suits would be streaming his death in the MEU capital, far to the south, under the same remote and uncaring stars. Those who resented the remote and unwashed bums from the Northeast Province would be convinced of their prejudice for what little time they might enjoy it.

By then Khalil, Amina, Maya and Festif were well on their way to the relative safety of the forest. The treeline grew to meet them, sparse at first but promising to thicken with fir, spruce and pine.

Festif was not an old man most of the time, though he did enjoy employing the use of the VISAGE to construct a new identity amongst people whom he liked a great deal better than his colleagues in Four.

People trusted old men with secrets; old men were harmless physically and politically. To be elderly was to be impotent in more ways than one.

His multicoloured jacket was not the only guise he had employed.

He felt Maya's arms tighten up around his waist as the party plunged through the darkness and wove their way through the sparse beginnings of the forest.

On the second machine, Khalil sat astride, teeth grinding together as he struggled to keep the machine under control; it had been many years since he'd driven a snowmobile and his memories were slow to rise to the surface. It was like learning everything all over again, from scratch.

Khalil slowed to a more moderate pace, trailing Festif in the lead. He was struggling to recognize his saviours, to place them in his past. His mind was still a bit loose from its moorings. Everything was moving so quickly.

His thoughts rested almost solely on Amina now, and ensuring that she remained safe and sound in his care. She was the only connection he could understand in what had become an entirely surreal world.

The forest grew thicker about them, and after another fifteen minutes of winding about tree stumps and avoiding large roots, the leading snowmobile slowed to a crawl by a small rock hill in the midst of the woods. Festif cut the engine, as did Khalil as he pulled up beside him, and the world fell silent.

It was snowing very lightly, tiny flakes falling down

upon the canopy of trees above and painting the leaves with an icy brush. It was not particularly cold given their warm jackets. Festif had been well-prepared for this trip; the saddlebags attached to the snowmobiles were crammed with food, tools, and medical supplies.

The trees seemed to surround them and protect them. There was a small lean to built up against the over-hanging face of the rock, with enough room to shelter perhaps a dozen people within. Thick logs were bound together with rope and a few nails, covered by thick fronds from large ferns and evergreen branches.

Khalil turned to look at Amina. Her face remained pale and shaken; she was clearly in shock. He couldn't blame her. Things had moved very quickly over the course of the past few hours. She had come back into his life and had shed a light on who he was. He felt that passion intimately. She seemed cold to his touch, and did not raise her head, even when he gently placed his hand under her chin.

"Leave her for now, Khalil." A soft voice came from their leader and saviour.

There had been little time for explanations during their escape. The lights had been extinguished in his formless prison and he felt a vague sense of nausea as he recalled the weightless sensation he'd experienced as his prison had been lowered at a breakneck pace until it had shattered on the floor. It turns out that the horizon of his cage was an illusion, a projection of an endless expanse, a parlour trick. That had been a jarring discovery in and of itself. Khalil was certainly sharing in the shock.

The stranger was middle-aged and handsome. The voice felt familiar to Khalil, though he knew he had not seen this man before in his life. His confusion must have been written all over his dark complexion, for the man laughed lightly and clapped a hand on Khalil's shoulder.

"I understand your puzzlement, old friend. You've gone through a lot. More than you know, yourself."

The man nodded sagely, his dirty-blonde hair blowing slightly as a breeze rolled through the woods. "You knew me as Festif, an old man wearing a rather unique and colourful coat. We smoked together, drank together on occasion, and you even convinced me to come to one of your earsplitting shows once. Though, to be fair, I never did take you up on your invitation to come see your band again until it was far too late."

It came back to Khalil in a rush, like a hammer blow to the head. He could see the events that the man was referring to. He remembered long and deep conversations shared with the supposedly homeless eccentric at The Spartan, and philosophical drinking sessions at Pixels or down the street at the Blue Moon. He even remembered the one time that the old man had showed up for one of his first shows at The Wreckage.

This man who stood before him seemed like a stranger, however, his face and his voice far removed from the ones Khalil was starting to remember in bits and pieces, visions of his life as it had been. Increasingly, Khalil realized, it had not been an easy or happy existence.

Khalil took a few tentative steps forward, his boots breaking through the bottom layer of snow with a slight crunching sound, his arms wide for an embrace. The small man came forward and hugged Khalil tightly, holding him close to his breast like a brother.

Khalil knew him. He was telling the truth.

Tears sprang to the musician's eyes as the last of the locks on his memories began to spring open. He wept, and could not stop. His friend held him in silence. Maya had already busied herself unloading the snowmobiles and hauling their supplies into the shelter, despite the pain of her wound. Amina merely stood up from her seat on the machine and stared like a child out into the dark.

After he'd shed as many tears as he could bear, Khalil managed to collect himself, although his spirit was still very much in a state of tumult. Khalil asked Festif about his real name, to which Festif replied that he was born Robert Napier. Robert told Khalil that he was a spy, but that he was didn't work for anyone in particular. Robert laughed to himself and quipped that, actually, he worked for Khalil.

Khalil asked him *why?* without specifying the subject.

Robert hesitated for a moment before speaking.

"Very soon, you will understand," he said to Khalil with a certain sadness in his eyes, though this time the tears were not for his friends.

As the small man made his way towards the shelter to sit and rest, Maya came over to stand next to Khalil, placing a tentative hand on his shoulder. Khalil remembered who she was, now, and could only assume that things had changed greatly since they had last met.

"Khalil, I just want to tell you that I'm sorry. Nothing I can say to you will ever change what happened. Nothing I can do from now on can change the person I was. I fucked up. I fucked over a lot of people. I'm lucky that I get a second shot." There was no fear in her voice, now.

Maya Williams had found herself, even if her wild eyes betrayed that she was still searching for *someone*. She put her trust in a spy, a man that had seen and heard her most intimate conversations over wine and whipped creme brulee. Her desperation was palpable, she continued to radiate energy and anxiety.

Khalil, by contrast, found very little hate left in his soul.

He searched himself for the flames that burned and the sickness that rested like a ball of iron in his stomach and found neither.

"Your life is your own." Five simple words. To Maya,

a pardon and a promise. She smiled weakly at Khalil and walked away to join her accomplice under the branches and the leaves of their lean-to. They began discussing logistical issues such as pushing a few mounds of snow up around the entrance of the shelter for insulation.

Amina still stood, watching nothing in particular, as if trapped in a slow moving dream. Khalil strode forward and wrapped his arms about her, bringing her close to him and resting his head on her shoulder. He could feel the tension in her body, wound about like a spring pushed to the point of breaking.

He remembered her.

He moved his lips close to hers, finally daring to press them against hers and tasting. He felt her shudder and give way, almost as if her knees were going to buckle beneath her. She cried out softly and returned his kiss, delicately at first but then with passion, bringing her own hands up to rest flat against the back of his jacket. She was crying, now, but did not stop. Her tears were hot and salty and within them was the promise of a great love.

"Khalil... I...I'm so sorry!" she cried, shuddering with great sobs and pressing her face into the safety of his chest. He held her and tried to quiet her gently. "They told me they would kill me if I didn't talk to you, to try and get you to co-operate. I was so scared! I told them I'd do anything if they promised to let me live! I would have tried, Khalil. I would have tried to do anything to make the pain go away. You don't understand! You don't!" she continued to cry violently, her heart breaking inside of her chest.

He did understand. He understood human frailty as only someone who has been broken can. He simply held her and told her that it didn't matter anymore, and that he understood. It was not a lie, but it sounded like one to her ears, and it would until the pain faded to a duller ache. Now was not the time. Forgiveness was a gift. She had given it to him the night they first met. He would give her what she had given him and what the world never had.

She leaned in to take a kiss from him, to draw him to her into a shared future. Despite the dark voice of a demon inside, snarling spiteful, begging him to turn his cheek, Khalil did not relent. Her lips were soft and he was not afraid.

He had a future. They had a future. At least the hope of one. The demon returned to its darkened corner.

"Have a seat, Khalil. Won't need to be doing much more work, tonight. Just so long as chance favours us," Robert said, rubbing his gloved hands together. Maya sat mutely to the side, organizing materials in her backpack, searching for the first aid kit to treat her shoulder. "It should be starting any minute now," the blond-haired man said with a sad smile, looking downward at the blue-backlit display of his implant.

Approaching the coastline, hundreds of aircraft floated across the ocean, pregnant with death. Like great surgical scalpels they sliced silently through the night sky. The bombers were mostly unmanned drones with precisely programmed orders.

The fighter jets were piloted by men with grim faces and dark hearts. This was not a job to be trusted to drone jockeys. The very air lit up with the sounds of cannon fire. Bright phosphorous tracer rounds and missiles danced through the patchwork of night sky visible through forest canopy.

Flashes of fire and barely visible trails of smoke appeared next to eternal constellations. Thick pounding noises beat out like a drum as bombs struck the earth. None struck nearby, though a few seemed to be dangerously close compared to the majority that fell much farther away from their crude shelter in the midst of the woods. Robert spoke, never taking his eyes away from the fire in the sky.

"Most of those bombs will fall on the security perimeters and targeted installations in the outer concentric rings. I'm sure the shipyards and the harbour will take a beating as well, though that's pure estimation. I provided full schematics and satellite images of this particular region to the net, so I assume they've made the rounds. The arterials will be pounded until there are no roads left to speak of. The people in the city proper will have a fighting chance against the security forces, at the very least. Deprived of air support, heavy arms, and supplies, I think that the correctional and security staff will find themselves outnumbered and overwhelmed quite quickly – that is, if they don't surrender to the mobs immediately. There's no leadership; the President and the Executives are all dead and the whole world knows it. It's not just the Atlantic coast, either – there is an equally large push on the Pacific front and on the southern borders by the Asian nations. The rest of the world has been waiting to pull the plug – here it is. I just gave them the pieces they needed. This legacy comes full circle and the nation of revolutionaries once again finds its roots with blood-stained, grasping fingers. This time we hope to make it last."

Robert fell silent, as if waiting for Khalil to answer.

"There will be much death."

"There was already death. There was the waking death of you and people just like you. You lived in a cage. You were cheap labour and highly disposable. You were a commodity, not a man. You refused your bonds of your own accord. I had no part in that. I simply fostered that conviction in you, gave a safe harbour for your beliefs and for your deeper thoughts. You expressed them to me. I tried to give them voice beyond the walls of The Wreckage and the streets you called home. This is, in part, the product of our own union, as individuals, as men."

He was right. Khalil had to acknowledge that. He felt no remorse, yet neither did he feel the exultation of victory over his oppressors. There would still be a great deal of death, not all of it deserved. The faces of some of his friends came to him like ghosts from a past he still didn't feel. They were likely still alive, or least he hoped so – though Haifa may have been in a targeted area and the rest were likely fighting for their lives. He felt slightly betrayed by Festif, now Robert; a dull interior ache that told him he might never altogether recover.

He simply nodded in reply, letting silence fall again. He felt Amina move closer to him, wrapping an arm around his leg as she sat with her back against the large stone that sheltered them. The flashes and explosions in the sky intensified, drowning out the starlight for instants at a time, turning night into day. The earth shook again and again, and the smell of smoke wafted through the trees. Khalil looked to his companions as the flash from the explosives lit up their faces, unnameable grief and worry written plainly across their expressions. He rested a hand on Amina's shoulder, smiling at her and feeling some slight stirring in his chest as she smiled back at him for the first time that he could remember. He felt better, and for the first time in a long time – whole. No gaps.

The city burned like coals, the edges wreathed in flame and growing darker towards the center until, like the inside of a casket, there was nothing but impenetrable black – seething, about to burst open.

Nicholas Morine is a Nova Scotian who pretends to be a Newfoundlander when nobody is looking. He read way too many books about wizards and warriors growing up and this is the end result.

We hope you've enjoyed the story. Please help us share this story with other readers by letting us know what you thought with a review on either **amazon.com** or **goodreads.com**.

Thank you kindly,
Montag Press Collective

FACE SPIRITUAL DEATH

AL-NAMROOD

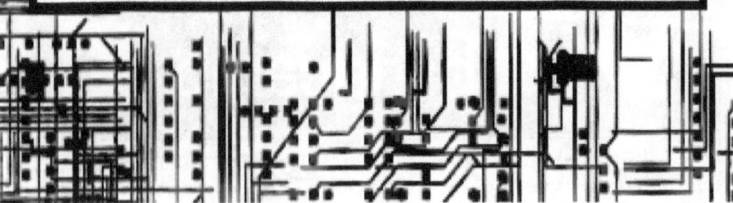

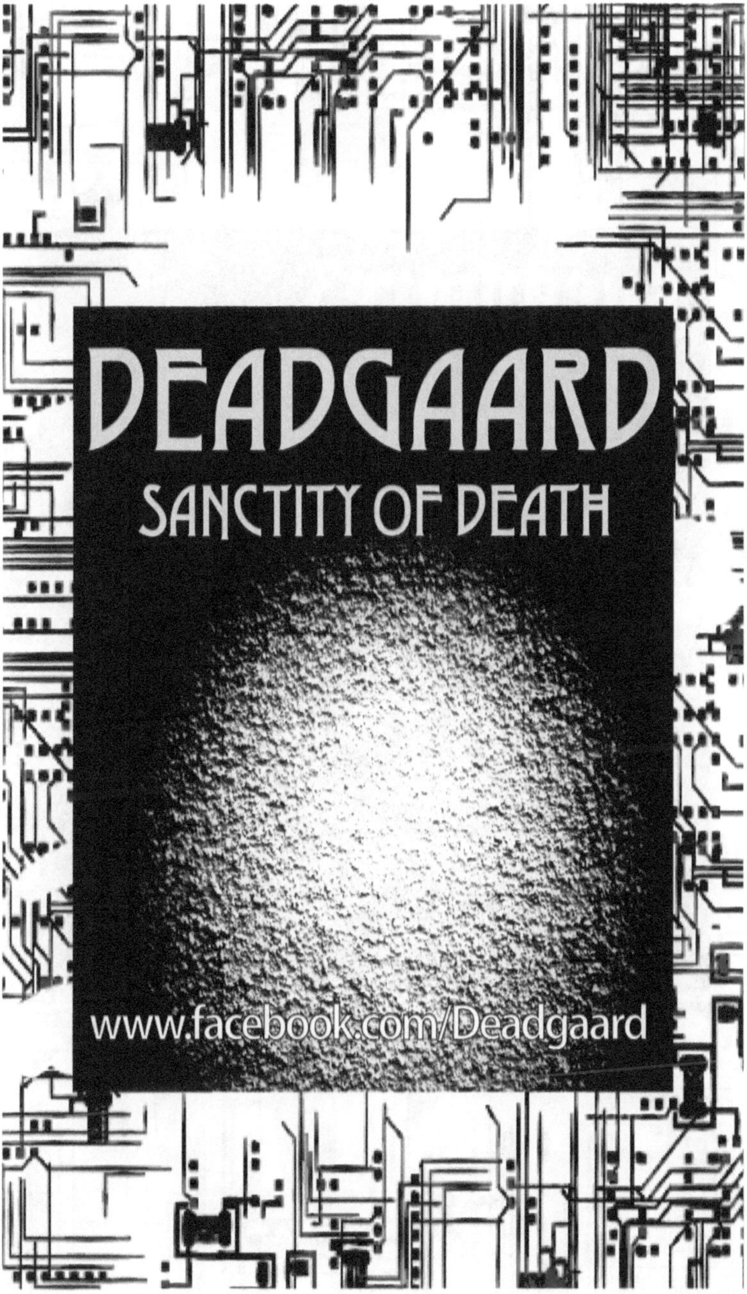
DEADGAARD
SANCTITY OF DEATH
www.facebook.com/Deadgaard

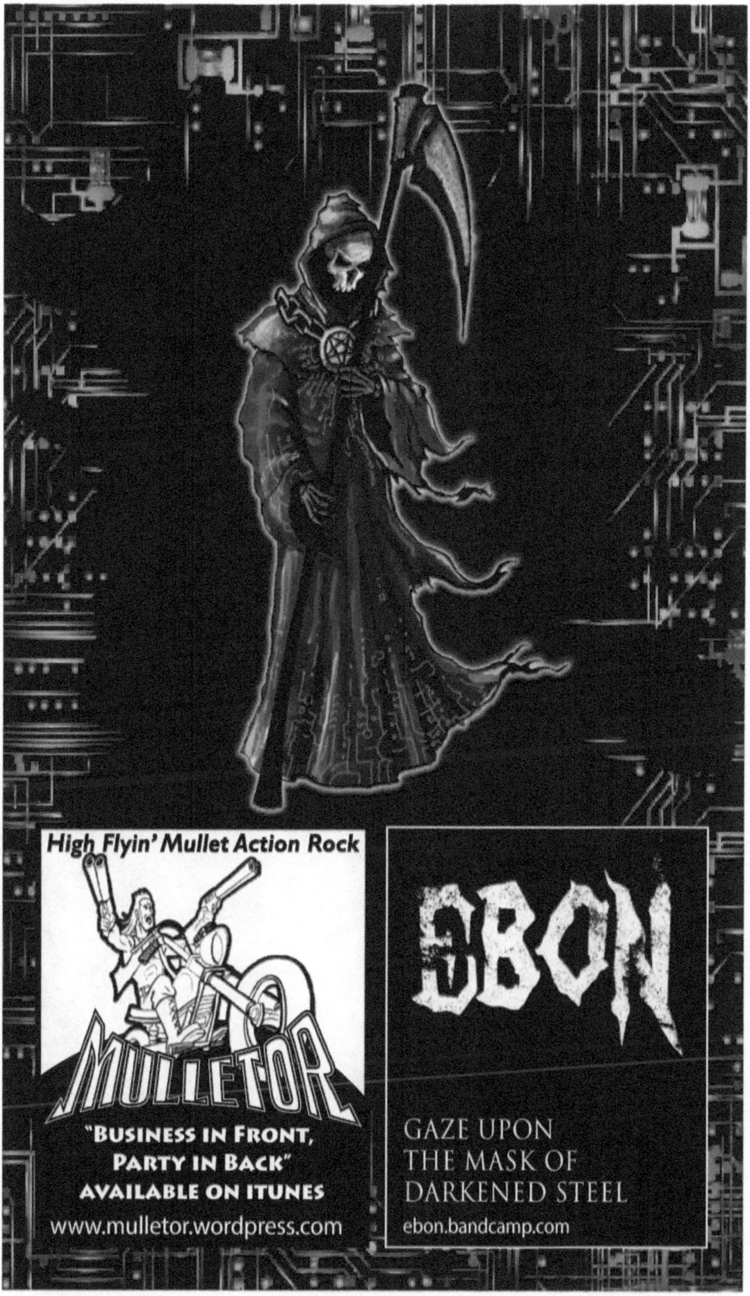
High Flyin' Mullet Action Rock
MULLETOR
"Business in Front, Party in Back"
Available on iTunes
www.mulletor.wordpress.com
EBON
GAZE UPON
THE MASK OF
DARKENED STEEL
ebon.bandcamp.com

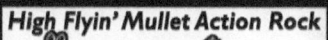

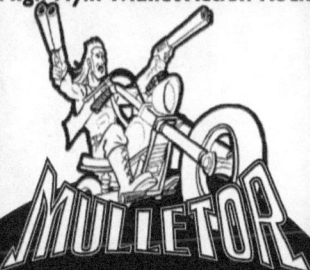

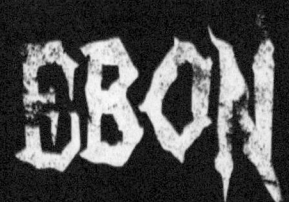

RETRO REMAINS...

GAMES, GADGETS, GIRLS

f @/GamesGadgetsGirls

🐦 @/GameGadgetGirl

GAMING

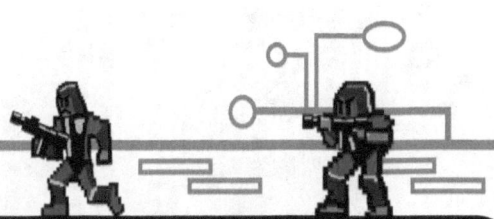

BARROOMGAMING.COM

BREWS, GAMES & REVIEWS

f /@BarroomGamer 🐦 @BarroomGamer

GRAVEYARD

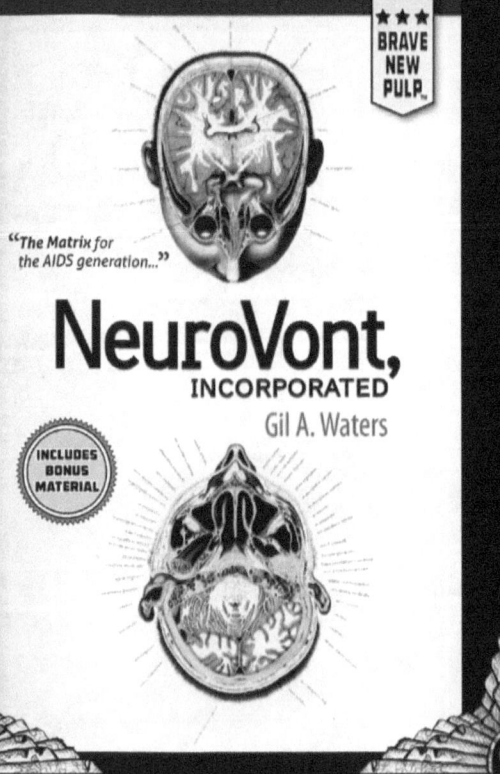

MONTAG PRESS

Purveyors of the finest in hardcore and experimental Speculative, Horror, Science and Historical Fiction, Montag Press is an underground publishing collective based in Oakland, California.